THE
BOOMER
PROTOCOLS

The Apocalypse Series

Book One

Patrick Astre

Cover and Book design by eBook Prep
www.ebookprep.com

February, 2016
ISBN: 978-1-61417-828-6

ePublishing Works!
www.epublishingworks.com

PROLOGUE

"So, am I going to die?"

Dr. Antoine LeFevre, placed his hands under his chin, fingers in a steeple position, an affectation he'd read somewhere that indicated deep thinking. He looked at his patient across the desk and saw a man who looked a bit younger than his fifty-nine years in spite of his balding head, and for the last few weeks, had taken on a somewhat stooped appearance with a tightness to his face, a slight drawing of the skin accompanied by a pallor that was a bit more than the results of a New York winter.

The patient whose name was William Bonner, looked steadily at his doctor. He had tried to put a jesting tone in his voice—a lightheartedness he didn't really feel.

"We're all going to die, William," Doctor LeFevre replied softly.

Bonner flashed back to the battery of tests he had undergone. Cat scans, Barium GI tests, several stress tests including one in which they had injected him with some sort of dye so they could watch the progress of blood though his heart, lungs and veins, even some new experimental scanner under development called an MRI. He hated the tests. It wasn't the occasional discomfort because if truth be told, there wasn't much of it. What bothered him most was the impersonal nature of it all. Sometimes he felt like an experiment, not even an interesting one. They poked, prodded, sent him through the machines, all within the time limits allotted by the insurance companies. They barely knew his name and immediately put it out of their minds before the next patient came in. Only the most perfunctory questions were answered. Anything more was deferred to his doctor. And now, Dr. LeFevre, whose fees rose substantially above Bonner's insurance allotment, was dodging the question. LeFevre was Harvard Medical and one of the best internist in the country. Bonner didn't mind paying his price, but dammit, he thought, the man should be forthright. It irritated Bonner and he failed to keep it out of his voice.

"Thanks for that wisdom, Doc. Now can you tell me what the hell is wrong with me?"

Dr. LeFevre put his hands on the desk and glanced out the window where clouds chased across the sky, driven by a cold wind sweeping out of Jamaica Bay. He turned his eyes back to Bonner as he replied.

"William, I won't lie to you. The symptoms are serious. Weight loss, general weakness and muscle pain, elevated heart rate, higher levels of blood sugar and liver enzymes, although not enough to diagnose a diabetic condition. Normally, the tests I ordered would yield results allowing me to make a diagnosis."

"So what is your diagnosis?"

Dr. LeFevre looked out the window again then returned his gaze to Bonner.

"I don't have one."

"You don't have one?"

"No William, I don't have one. The reason is that all your tests came out positive. There's no indication of a particular condition. The symptoms are there, but test results deny them."

"So what's that mean?"

"You're not going to like it, William."

"That's nothing new, I don't like any of this, so tell me what's next."

"Psychosomatic condition."

"Well, I know what psycho means. What you're telling me is that it's in my head."

"It's not as simple as that William. Sometimes life events, stress, grief, anxiety, triggers symptoms as real as the most virulent disease. The brain creates conditions in the body that we often don't understand. When all the cutting-edge medical tests science has created fail to reveal a particular condition in the face of symptoms, we have to go into that area. I know we had this conversation before. What's going on in your life, William?"

Bonner looked down at his shoes. He felt defeated, worn. At forty-nine, he thought he had arranged his life better than most baby-boomers. He'd sold his business for a substantial amount just last year. He had six months to go under his contract until the transition was completed. He had used the money to pay off his mortgage and purchase a condo in San Marco Island in Florida. His oldest stepdaughter owned a small business in Long Island, New York. His stepson, also lived there, a young professional doing well for himself. Bonner and his wife had planned to spend half the year in Long Island, and when the New York winter hit, the other half in Florida. He got along with his wife, no problems there and the old joke about retirement being twice the husband and half the income certainly didn't apply. The general plan was to sharpen his golf game and expand his charitable works, perhaps start his own foundation. No, he didn't have any life problems.

Suddenly, it came out of the depths of his psyche like a leviathan out of an ocean. The Event—but it had been so long ago, that monstrosity. Surely he was rid of it. Although it lingered in his mind, after all, it wasn't something a person could ever forget. Yet, he was sure the memory of it wasn't the cause of his health problems. It would have come around sooner. Why now, and not decades ago when he first encountered it?

April 29, 1945, he'd been a captain with the 42d US Infantry, the "Rainbow Division" and the first officer to enter the liberated Dachau Concentration Camp. All these years he'd kept the secret of what he'd discovered there, kept the secret from his own superiors and brought it back as just a handful of notes and several vials of serum. The world believed that in spite of the horrors of Dachau, medical experiments had never been conducted there. Those hellish privileges had been reserved for places like Auschwitz-Birkenau and Belzec under the demonic Dr. Mengeles, the "Angel of Death." Bonner knew better, they'd just had more time to destroy the evidence except for the precious little that he'd been able to smuggle out, enough to eventually save his then-unborn son and create Bonner Pharmaceuticals.

Of course stress from the sale of his company could have started it because certain elements had been participants in Bonner Pharmaceuticals all along. They would have known and perhaps feared the possible disclosures the sale might have brought about. One thing Bonner knew: These were the most dangerous people on earth. The sale of his company had taken three years and would be completed in six months. Bonner had worried about them at first. He had hired the best executive bodyguards in the world. Thankfully nothing had surfaced. Gradually, as time passed he believed they had accepted the sale and would not move against him. No, it wasn't anxiety. Had that been the case, it would have shown itself two or three years ago, not now. He shook his head, answering Dr. LeFevre's question slowly.

"No, doc. It simply isn't that. I've prepared for retirement very well. I have no problems or anxieties."

LeFevre stood and walked to the window. Outside his office a Cadillac sedan was parked at the curb, its tailfins like some kind of steel shark's fin. The driver stood near the car; an athletic looking man who constantly scanned his environment. LeFevre knew there was another like him right outside the door, waiting for Bonner to come out.

"Then why the bodyguards, William?"

"Like I told you once, Doc, there are interests that are against the sale of my company to Remco Genetics. It's just a precaution. Once the sale is completed, in less than six months, then I'm just a well-to-do baby boomer, retiring."

"With dangerous symptoms that the most sophisticated medical tests fail to diagnose," LeFevre added.

"Yeah, well that's your job, right? So what's the next step?"

"I want you to come to my clinic in Hampton Bay for a week. Your insurance will cover it. You just make up the difference in my fee as usual."

"What's that going to do?"

"I want to control your environment, your caloric intake, the type and amount of foods you eat. I want you on a regimen of calmative medicine and daily examinations. It's the only way we can get to the bottom of this."

"What's the alternative?"

"Without that, there's nothing more I can do. The symptoms may worsen and you might wind up in the emergency room of some hospital. Or, it may go away by itself, I just don't know at this point. My advice is to go. Let's get to the bottom of it. I'll have a room available day after tomorrow."

Bonner sighed and looked away.

"Yeah, okay, doc. Let's do it."

CHAPTER 1

Present day

The commercials started in early spring, when hints of the coming thaw popped up in the colder, Northern states and warm air from the Gulf in the East and the Pacific in the West poured over the Southern states promising warmth and rebirth. The clips appeared on all the major channels, CBS, NBC, CNN, Fox, even on local cable and major sports events.

They called the product Jeunessa, the French word Jeunesse, meaning youth, with only the last letter replaced by an A, the whole thing clearly aimed at the vast Baby-Boomer population, now in their late fifties and early sixties.

The camera pans over a housing development of various sized homes. It's a mature housing track, with full-grown trees and nice cars in well-tended driveways. No kids in the streets, but older folks walking, sitting in porches or tending gardens. Everyone looks older, tired and as the camera comes in closer, the lines of their faces and wrinkles become apparent markers of discontent with approaching old age. As the camera pans back, an empty beach is visible nearby. A voice-over begins, clear but somewhat raspy and tired.

"It's no fun to get old, don't let anyone tell you otherwise. Now that I'm finally retired, I just don't have the energy left to do what I really wanted" The camera focuses on the speaker and shifts to his wife. Her hair is gray, the lines on her face clear and dark as she slowly shakes her head.

Now the screen changes and the light changes to a golden hue, as if infused with sunbeams, bringing a glow to the entire scene. The man speaks again, but now the voice is different, vibrant, sure of itself.

"Then Jeunessa came along. We were one of the first test group and I can't begin to tell you what a difference it's made." The camera pans back and the same man is now standing on a tennis court with racket in hand. The facial lines are gone, the hair is darker, attractively tinged with gray. He's wearing a blue sport shirt and white shorts. A tennis ball flies out, the man swings at it, vitality bursting in every move, misses and laughs as an attractive middle aged woman appears from the other side of the court and puts her arm around his waist. It's the same woman from before but she appears much younger, her hair has been dyed black with blonde streaks. The lines on her face have vanished and her smile is dazzling as she looks at the camera. "I can't even describe how wonderful Jeunessa has been for us, it's like time has regressed a decade or two and just stopped"

Now the camera pans back to the man, "Look, I don't know how long we're going to live, Jeunessa makes no promise on that, but whatever time we have left, it's brought our life back."

The camera pans away, over the houses and to the nearby beach now filled with couples, walking hand in hand, jogging, playing volleyball, smiling, happy, youthful.

The scene fades away and the Remko Genetics logo comes on one side of the screen. A bottle with the name Jeunessa fills the center and to the right, the Jeunessa logo, a Peter Pan figure with a stardust-sprinkling tiny figure suggesting Tinkerbell as the voiceover concludes:

Jeunessa–Regain the years—regain your life!

As the commercials aired throughout the nation they were followed by half hour "infommercials" with scientists, many years of test results and developments, but always populated by baby-boomers who'd obviously discovered the fountain of youth, the clarion calls of vanity and sex appeal oozing out of each screen.

The tricky part is that if you screw up, you might fall under the wheels. Happened a couple of times to some hoboes who tried it with a few bottles of muscatel warming their bellies.

I'm a couple of miles from the town of Bordon Heights, right outside of Kansas. They call it that because the town is situated at the base of a series of hills. No big deal, not mountains or anything, just hills. On the other side of the track is Lockchee Creek, an offshoot of some river whose name I forget. Since the hills aren't made of rocks, the railroad decided it would be easier to cut through then build a bridge across the creek. When the trains come down and around the hill, they have to slow down to negotiate the turn. There're a few yards of flat rail bed that you can run, right beside the slowing train, grab a hold of the wagon and climb on.

It's a little past eleven at night. I figure I've got about three to five minutes, just enough to rattle some cages. That's how I want them, rattled—knowing I'm still around and messing with them. I pick up the cell phone and hit the speed dial. There's only one number there, the only call I'll make.

"Anton," the voice answers.

"You know, you really should work on your phone manners," I say. "I mean, an organization like yours? People will think you folks are inbred or something."

"Where are you?"

I laugh, always the joker that Anton Dimitri, a regular comic. "On my way to you," I reply and shut the phone down. I pitch it across the tracks into the creek. It's one of those pre-loaded cells, anonymous and untraceable. I've no doubt they have the resources to track the location of the call, but I chose it well. There's an interstate that passes nearby and a regional airport less than three miles away. Although they'll have the exact location of the call, I could have gone in a number of directions besides the train. I figure Anton will dispatch at least four teams. He'll try covering all the routes I could have taken. I'm sure Marco will be directing the effort. He'll probably run one of the teams himself. They've been trying to nail me since 1952. Especially Marco. He's missing two fingers on his right hand from the last time we met.

Daddy didn't just cure my polio back in 1950. Although he didn't know it would happen, the procedure gave me certain abilities. That's the reason why originally they wanted to study me. Capture me, poke and prod, dissect, run experiments, the whole nine yards. Over the years it's gone well beyond that.

Now they just want to kill me.

And I just want to destroy them.

I close my eyes and listen to the night. There're two people about twenty yards down the tracks. It's okay. I've run into them earlier, just a couple of travelers waiting to catch the same train. They gave me a bowl of hobo stew earlier and offered to have me travel with them. "'Preciate it," I'd replied, but I got my own schedule. Nice folks, even if they live on the edges of society, like me. They're concerned because I look about sixteen.

Actually, by last count, I'm seventy-eight. I appreciate their concerns, but traveling with me would probably get them killed.

I feel the vibrations. The train is very close. I sense a possum scurrying in the underbrush and an owl on the hunt. The moon is absent, the night is very dark under the overcast and I can smell distant mountains washed over by far away breezes.

A beam of light explodes around the bend and the locomotive comes into view. The noise level cranks up and the train passes right in front of me. I let the first few wagons pass then I run alongside. I grab the sidebar of an empty car with my left hand and swing myself into the open door. Even though my right arm and hand looks okay, there's hardly any strength there. That's the result of the polio before dad's efforts took hold.

I watch the night pass as the train enters the straightaway. It picks up speed again. I'm on my way to New York.

CHAPTER 2

A few tiny snowflakes drifted out of a sky gray as a London afternoon. Joline looked up and one landed on her glasses leaving a barely perceptible smudge. She ignored it, pushed the remote control attached to her keys and heard the car chirp as the doors locked.

Joline liked Port Washington. The town with its many Circa homes had a typical old New England feel that most locales on Long Island failed to hold. The weather—well, what the hell, it was November after all.

She felt good about meeting David. She hadn't seen her brother in over a month.

Even though they each led busy, separate lives, they'd managed to still remain close.

Probably because our love-lives sucked, Joline thought. Whatever they had going for them, a highly functional relationship gene wasn't one of them.

She walked up the gravel path leading to The Captain's Pier, the restaurant where she would meet David for lunch. The place was right on the water and one of her favorites.

Someone opened the front door and a gust of steam filled with the scent of garlic, crab-spices and cooked shellfish enveloped her. She was instantly hungry. Since she'd be having lunch with David, breakfast had been skipped.

Standing tall, almost six feet, with ash blond hair cut

short, she was attractive. She hardly thought about it, and usually wore no makeup at all. Creases were starting to show up around her eyes, what they called worry lines. She dressed plain as if she feared the femininity that nicer clothes would reveal.

The hostess led Joline to the table her brother had reserved, right at the window fronting the water's edge. Best one in the house. David was already there, a tall glass in front of him. Diet Pepsi she guessed. He stood when he saw her coming. They hugged like people who really cared about each other, no air-kisses for them.

"How you doing, David?"

"Good, you?"

"Great," Joline said. She started to sit but stood again. "Wait, I forgot something," she said.

Joline walked back to the hostess' station. A big jar occupied one corner of the counter. A picture of two kittens and a puppy adorned the face of the jar along with the name of the Port Washington Humane Society. She reached into her purse, took out a handful of coins and two singles and dropped it all in the jar before returning to the table. David grinned at her.

"What? You didn't put anything in there?"

"First thing I did when I got here," David said.

Her brother was tall as her, and lean. At age twenty-six— God, where did the years go? David had the good looks of a soap opera star. Yet there was a seriousness about him and she thought he didn't laugh nearly enough. It suited his profession as a CPA pretty well—if you wanted to follow stereotypes, that is.

Sometimes David was a mass of contradictions that she'd struggled with since he was a toddler. His good looks and athletic demeanor should have women flocking to him like moths to a porch light. Yet he had no girlfriends and his marriage hadn't lasted two years. Perhaps there was something about him that repelled the opposite sex. If so, Joline couldn't see a shred of it. He wasn't gay. She was sure she would have known.

Not that it would have bothered her, just so she'd know. What really nagged at her was that perhaps she'd missed something. That somehow she hadn't been up to the task of raising a brother six years younger than her. She thought she'd done it well. A surrogate for the father who'd suddenly left before David could walk and the mother who drowned herself in Jack Daniels until her liver curled up and died.

They ordered drinks. She'd been right. Another Diet Pepsi for David and ice tea for her. Neither of them were teetotalers but they both kept up their physical conditioning and didn't drink during the day.

"So tell me, Sis. What's going on in your world?"

She shrugged and rolled her eyes to the ceiling. Good question, she thought, wishing she really knew.

"Same old, same old," she said. "Executive Protection is doing well. We just got that contract with Pemex for their Mexico City conference. But you know that. You're our accountant."

"Yeah, but I'm concerned that your client list is too short for your expense ledger. One good dry period could tumble you over the edge."

"That why you wanted to have lunch with me today, so I could pick up the tab while I'm still able?"

She grinned at him and he didn't answer. Outside a pair of swans glided on the water and paused below their window. David lifted the pane a couple of inches and threw out some bread. The swans gobbled it and a few more came toward them.

"You better cut it out. The waitress is giving you the evil eye. Besides, those birds are so well fed it's amazing they still float."

David pushed the window closed and gave her one of his rare little smile. His teeth were white and a dimple appeared under the serious accountant's glasses.

"Yeah, you'd think," he said. "And no, that's not it."

"What's not it?"

"I'm picking up the tab and I didn't invite you to talk

about your business. I'll be over at your office on Thursday to deliver your quarterly payroll reports. We'll talk about it then."

"Sounds ominous."

"It's not."

The waitress cleared their appetizer plates and brought their main courses: Baked Halibut Alaska style for both. It was the signature dish of the restaurant.

"Actually, what I wanted to talk to you about was something I'm going to be doing, a favor of sorts for someone," David said.

"Who is it?"

"You wouldn't know him. Father Anthony. He's in my Tae Kwon Do class."

"A priest?"

"That's why he's got Father before his name."

"Don't be a smart ass. What's a priest doing taking up karate?"

"No conflict there. Lots of spiritualism associated with the martial arts disciplines."

"Yeah, I guess. Does he know you're Jewish?"

"Sure. I have a Mezuzah tattooed on my forehead."

"C'mon, David. You know what I mean."

"Not really. I mean what difference does it make? When was the last time either one of us went to temple?"

"Bat-Mitzah, Bar-Mitzah and your wedding two years ago."

"Thanks for reminding me. I'll owe you one."

She didn't reply and they were silent for a while. Religion had always been a sticking point with them. Joline always thought that her faith could fill gaps in her life. In spite of that, it seemed to be missing something, even repelled her in a sense. It angered her sometimes that she couldn't grasp her parent's faith, but then, they hadn't done such a good job of it themselves. David seemed oblivious to it. He only paid attention when Joline badgered him, and that had been during his childhood. Now he ignored it altogether—the whole thing bothered her.

"So this priest, Father Anthony asked you to help him. I guess whatever he needs, you want me to help also?"

David didn't look at her for a moment. He put his fork down and turned to her, leaning forward across the table.

"No, not right now, maybe later. The reason I wanted to tell you is that he said it might be dangerous."

"Dangerous? David, you're a CPA. An accountant for God's sake! What the hell are you going to do for a priest that could be dangerous? You're not going to go into one of those gang or drug areas, are you?"

"No, nothing like that. In fact, I can't really tell you the details. Just that since you own this executive protection service, I might need your help. I mean, probably not, but maybe, just in case."

"You know I'll always be there for you, David. Anytime. Just tell me what this is about."

He shook his head, looked out the window and opened it again. The swans were still there. He threw another piece of bread before turning his gaze back to her.

"I can't Joline. You gotta trust me on this. It's nothing illegal and probably won't amount to anything. I just wanted you to know that maybe, just maybe, I might need your help."

"David, you shouldn't even ask. You know I'll be there, okay?"

He nodded and smiled at her again, and it felt good, familiar as her childhood. A sudden gust blew through the small opening in the window. The cold air drifted in, penetrating the thin material of her blouse. She felt a shudder down her spine and goose skin formed on her arms.

Months later she would recall this moment like words from a prophet.

CHAPTER 3

Puerto Vallerta, Mexico

It slipped into the harbor just as the sun rose over the mountains, whispering in at low throttle between two giant cruise ships anchored from the previous day. It was a big yacht, one hundred and twenty five feet of sleek white fiberglass interrupted by vast expanses of smoky glass dark enough to hide the movements of those inside. Even the bridge windows reflected light as if made of the same material used for one-way mirrors.

No name painted on the stern, no numbers on the bow, and no flag adorned the short mast rising among the array of electronic communication and microwave antennas on the roof of the bridge. It seemed as if the big boat had just come out of some pristine factory, brand new and nameless.

The yacht dropped anchor a bare hundred yards from the short dock on the northeast corner of the harbor. The dock itself was a far cry from the tourist areas, neglected with pilings thick from seaweed and withered planks bleached white and gray from sun blistered seagull droppings. Several listless pelicans hung about the dock, their wings and great beaks drooping as if this decrepit piece of the harbor was their last refuge.

Three hundred meters away the harbormaster observed the yacht from the deck of his office fronting the harbor. Normally he would have visited the yacht, required them to fly their flag, identify the vessel and prepare to be boarded by a customs detail for inspection. On this morning however, the harbormaster knew no such thing would happen. The security and customs officers had no doubt been warned off, as he had been, and the warning came down from the highest levels of the federal government in Mexico City. Whoever these *cabrones* were, they held tons of influence and were not to be crossed.

A breeze stirred some cat paws around the yacht as it settled on its anchor chain. The heat rose on the breeze blowing in from the land and the harbormaster sweated even at this early hour. June in this part of Mexico brought some brutal heat and this day would be no exception.

The harbormaster watched with his binoculars as two men emerged from the aft cabin. They were dressed in nondescript clothing of light colored tropic material. They lowered the eighteen-foot dinghy with smooth, practiced movements, and only when it was secured at the side of the yacht, did the third man come out.

Now this one is interesting, the harbormaster thought. The newcomer was tall, over six and a half feet. Dressed all in white, he towered over the other two men. There was something strange about him, something that disturbed at a primitive level, like a change in air pressure, or a feral instinct. As the harbormaster watched, the man slowly turned until his eyes seemed fixed, returning the watcher's gaze. A shiver ran through the harbormaster's body in spite of the tropical heat. He lowered the binoculars, shook his head and turned away.

Standing on the aft deck of the yacht, Anton Dimitri had felt the viewer's distant eyes on him. He sensed it like a cat feeling movement in the night, and simply returned the gaze. That's all it usually took to deflect un-welcomed viewers, just the barest taste of the Power. Now he turned away and stepped into the dinghy from the swim platform molded in the yacht's rear deck. His movements were smooth and economical as he felt the strength surging in his body like the soft purr of a powerful engine. One of the men cast off the line while the other operated the controls as Anton stood, holding the console with one hand. The small boat traveled the distance to the waiting dock in a few minutes and after fastening a line to the dock, the three men walked to the end of the pier.

It was a section of the harbor where no tourist would venture. No taxis waited and roads ending there were nothing more than glorified dirt trails leading into desolate sections of the Sierra Madres. Condos and hotels didn't grace this part of Mexico mostly occupied by scorpions, a variety of vipers, and a very few, equally dangerous humans.

A four-wheel drive Ford truck with King Cab, waited there at the edge of the road. The driver wore large sunglasses hiding his eyes but failing to conceal the broad facial features of a direct Mayan heritage. He didn't say a word as the three men from the yacht approached, just got behind the wheel of the truck, started the engine and waited for the men to settle in their seats before putting the truck in gear and driving away.

El Gaucho watched the truck approach through his binoculars. He wore a tee shirt with the sleeves cut off and his arms stuck out like tree trunks. Covered with prison tattoos, one arm fully "sleeved", muscles danced under his skin with every move. They weren't smooth muscles like those built scientifically in gyms. These were rangy and tough as steel cables, taunt and ugly, the muscles of a street fighter, built from years of prison labor. Incongruously, he wore the trademark Brazilian cowboy work pants that had given him his nickname. He smiled as the truck approached and the teardrop tattoo under his left eye danced and the sun glinted off the front gold tooth with the tiny etched skull. He lowered the binocular and ran his hand along the scabbard clipped to his belt. It held the same thin curved blade that he had used to gut the *pandejo* who had knocked his tooth out a few years earlier. El Gaucho was practically a legend these days, the most feared and violent gang leader in an area that produced the worst of the worst.

El Gaucho lowered the binoculars as he heard Little Juan, his second in command come up beside him. Like his name implied, the man was short, less than five foot four, but the best man with a knife he'd ever seen. It wasn't too many years ago that heand Little Juan had ruled the worst gang in Mexico's toughest maximum-security prison.

"That the *Pandejos?*" Little Juan said.

He nodded and Juan looked at the approaching truck through his own binoculars. He spat on the ground and looked away. "They don't look like much," he said. "You'd think they'd be pissed about us taking over the product, quadrupling the price on them—send in some shooters, not two *maricon gringos*. Anyway, what'd they want with those shitty little plants anyway? You can't do nothing with'em. It ain't like we're growing coca or something."

El Gaucho didn't reply. He continued staring where the road ended at the front of the house, at the very porch where he stood. The house was a basic structure of about twelve rooms, built out of stone and cement extracted from quarries in these local mountains that produced only three basic commodities. The first was stone and sand, construction materials wrested from the mountains, shortening the wretched lives of the unfortunate laborers who had nothing else to turn to. The second was the Coca derivatives, some homegrown, most of it shipped through in the scalding, treacherous passages. It was a business rendered deadly not by the illegality or token government efforts. Those battles were fought many miles away in the north, in places like Nuevo Laredo and the border states of the US. The drug battles fought here were deadlier, with no quarter given and death the only way to vanquish an opponent. El Gaucho had been the deadliest of all with equal parts strength and cunning, until he had been hired away to protect the third product. That one was strictly home-grown, raised and harvested right in those mountains in such small amounts because it was so rare. You could barely cultivate it, and then just the slightest quantity. Neither El Gaucho nor his men, had any idea what the crop actually did and they couldn't even begin to guess who paid such huge amounts to find it, cultivate it and harvest it in such desolate, bandit-ridden terrain.

El Gaucho had guessed that if they would pay that much, why not more? It had been his experience that people always held back and if you pushed enough, there was more to be had. Once ensconced with his crew, El Gaucho had simply tripled the price, giving an ultimatum: pay or we destroy the crop.

El Gaucho looked again at the approaching truck. The driver would be no problem since he was one of his people, two men in the back and one in the wide front seat. He stared at the man in the front. Big, dressed in white, there was something familiar about him, and as he looked through the binoculars he felt a sensation of unease, a malaise he couldn't have put into words because nothing in his violent life thus far could be compared.

"The shooters ready?" El Gaucho asked.

"*Si*. Manuel and Paco are in place with the AK's, and just in case, Luis has the M-60 zeroed. You know what though? Just save the bullets, it's only three *maricons*. You let me get close and I can do them before they know what's happening. The *pandejos* ain't even carrying, like they're going to one of their business meetings, fucking *North Americanos*."

El Gaucho smiled as he thought that just might be a good idea. Little Juan was so fast with that blade you couldn't even see him move. One minute the target would be there, looking like he couldn't believe a little dude like Juan would do anything, and the next second the guy would be on his knees, both hands around his own throat, blood gushing between the fingers from slashed jugular and windpipe. El Gaucho had seen that a number of times.

"Sure, do it," he told Juan. "We don't need them alive."

CHAPTER 4

The driver of the truck felt the muscles of his arms contract as he tried to stop the tremors running through his hands while he gripped the wheel. There was no reason for such fear. The three *North Americanos*, his passengers sitting in the wide rear seat had not uttered any threat, nor had they made any moves that could be interpreted as aggressive. He glanced over at the man next to him on the front seat and saw the sweat running from his head in spite of the truck's air conditioning. No amount of cold air could suppress the sense of menace that poured out of the passengers in the back. The driver experienced the same primeval fear his ancestors felt millions of years ago, huddled around a tiny fire while hungry eyes roamed the forest around them.

The driver slowed the truck about thirty yards in front of the house, because that's what El Gaucho had told him to do. Before the truck stopped, the big gringo reached from the backseat and placed his hand on the driver's shoulder. It felt like stone claws wrapped in leather, and a wave of some sort of energy rippled through the driver's body. The gringo's hand lifted from the driver's shoulder and pointed to a spot beneath the overhang of the house right behind the hulking figure of El Gaucho and the ferret-like Little Juan.

"Stop there," the big gringo said.

It didn't matter that El Gaucho had told him to park the truck thirty yards in front, in the killing zone. Disobeying El Gaucho's orders meant certain death, but the psychic waves pouring out of the gringo spoke of primeval fears from which death by the flash of a blade or a bullet, would be an actual relief. The driver gunned the engine, and the truck surged forward until the front bumper came to rest against the pilings of the house.

The deep lines of El Gaucho's face compressed in a frown, that *cabrone* of a driver had put him at a disadvantage. The three gringos exiting the rear of the truck were out of sight of the guns. No matter, he would do the job himself with Little Juan, before cutting off the driver's *cojones*.

El Gaucho headed toward the gringos. Little Juan instinctively moved beside him, spaced about a yard apart, optimum distance for close quarter killing.

El Gaucho felt a buzzing in his head, a whirring of distant energies that increased with each step. The big gringo somehow had come closer then El Gaucho's few steps could explain. The American's body seemed to expand and the flesh of his face resolved to bone leaving a rapacious skeletal head. The white teeth elongated to fangs giving the appearance of some sort of alien vampire. El Gaucho felt the heat bearing down on him, and the very air smelled of carrion. He closed his eyes and shook his head and the gringo was now before him, just two feet away. The skeletal illusion had gone, but the gringo's pale eyes held him like a cobra before a hapless rodent. Confusion and sudden fear gripped El Gaucho, fear such as he had never experienced in the worst hellholes he had been cast into. His hand closed on the butt of the Desert Eagle .44 Magnum he carried, but he couldn't level the fearsome weapon, the weight of it dragged his hand down until the barrel pointed at the dusty ground.

Gently, in a deceptively slow movement, Anton Dimitri's hand enveloped the big Mexican's. El Gaucho's will had evaporated, gone someplace where it would never return and he was like a spectator as the Gringo raised his hand containing the Desert Eagle, and turned the weapon's business hand toward Little Juan. The smaller man stood rooted next to El Gaucho, his eyes flitting back and forth, mindless fear and helpless panic replacing any will the Mexican had ever held. A thin line of drool accompanied the barely audible whine passing over the smaller man's rotted front teeth and through his mouth. The arm hung down at his side, the wicked curved knife that had spilt the blood of so many enemies now useless in his hand.

The booming of the Desert Eagle sounded like the end of the world, and for Little Juan, it was. The magnum round passed through the fleshy part of his upper arm, blasted through his side, tearing out the aorta and lower part of the heart before leaving a baseball-size exit wound. The hydrostatic shock rippled through the Mexican as the kinetic energy of the round flung his dead body sideways.

The gun's tremendous noise snapped El Gaucho out of his stupor, but it was way too late. The gringo now held the weapon and for just the tiniest of a fraction he saw the black hole of the barrel before it exploded out another magnum round. The upper part of El Gaucho's head vaporized into a mist of bone and brain matter.

Anton Dimitri tucked the Desert Eagle into the belt of his white linen pants, took a handkerchief out of his pocket and wiped the splattering of El Gaucho's blood from his face. The two men with him stepped over the bodies of El Gaucho and Little Juan and entered the house without a word. Dimitri turned toward the truck, raised his hand, and with a lazy flick of a finger, beckoned the driver and the other man to come to him. They left the truck and came, for the surest thing they understood in their life right now, was that their only chance of survival lay in instant acquiescence to this gringo devil.

Dimitri put his sunglasses back on. He knew the effect his voice had, amplified only by the deadly menace behind the dark lenses, as if the very sight of his eyes would unleash untold carnages.

"You will round up the men with the guns surrounding this house, tell them they only have one chance to obey, and perhaps live. You will leave this offal until noon tomorrow," Dimitri said, nodding toward the bodies of El Gaucho and Little Juan. "Then take them to a canyon and dump them, to be devoured by carrion eaters."

Dimitri turned and stepped into the house. Less than ten minutes later, the men had gathered into the great room, as flies and vultures settled onto the two corpses, very visible through the front windows.

CHAPTER 5

Gustavo Diaz Ordaz International Airport
Puerto Vallarta, Mexico

The Citation XLS private jet sat on the edge of the East runway, its sleek form cast in titanium and aluminum alloys giving it the look of a steel raptor, the smooth surfaces blank except for tail numbers and the Remko Genetics logo on the rear. Boarding steps extended, Pratt & Whitney PW545C engines purring, the aircraft stood ready, waiting for its passenger.

A big four wheel drive Ford pickup rolled from the airport entrance, and stopped at the foot of the aircraft's steps. No security or customs agents had stopped the vehicle, the airport staff paying homage in their own way to the power represented by the multi-million dollar plane.

Anton Dimitri exited the truck's cab, but at first glance it wasn't quite the same man who'd left the yacht and taken care of business in the desolate and dangerous foothills of the Sierra Madres. His steps were slower, more measured as if threading on a painful surface. His normally ramrod-straight shoulders slouched a bit and he carried a white handkerchief spotted with red that he held under his nose. The pickup truck left with squealing tires and a sharp U turn, as if the devil itself would come out of the aircraft and give chase.

Anton Dimitri walked up the steps and entered the jet. Marco waited at the entrance, and stepped aside as Anton entered and sat heavily in one of the six plush seats, letting his head fall against the upper cushions of the seat.

Marco nodded at the pilot who stood at the entry to the flight deck. The pilot turned, said a few words to the co-pilot, closed the door to the cabin and took his seat at the controls. Almost immediately the jet turned, accelerated down the runway and leapt into the sky, soon reaching cruising altitude at 30,000 feet.

Marco opened a compartment, retrieved a small package and sat across from Anton. He watched outside the porthole as the aircraft left the ground, passed through some clouds and settled on its course toward the eastern seaboard of the United States. Nearly an hour elapsed before Anton opened his eyes, letting his gaze settle on Marco.

"Difficult time down there?" Marco asked.

"No more than I expected, killed two, needed the example set. The Abelia-Vie fields must be protected at all costs."

"You used the Power?"

"Of course, can't you tell from the side effects?" Anton replied, wiping another trickle of blood from his nose.

"We're going to find a cure for that, it's only a matter of time."

"We've been trying for nearly two centuries with no results, just like we've been trying to find out how Bonner's kid needs no monthly boosters and gets no side effects from using his Power, as you well know," he added, waving toward Marco's left hand that held the package with thumb and fore and middle fingers, the other two digits just tiny stumps, giving the hand a claw-like appearance.

"We'll get him yet," Marco replied.

"Even if we do there's no guaranty we'll squeeze the answers from him. Bonner took the Dachau secret to his grave if he even had it at all. The whole thing could have been an accident, a fluke of nature that we may never duplicate. Anyway, speaking of Bonner's kid Jimmy, how did it work out this time?"

"Negative–again. We know where the call came from, and I sent four teams, nothing, he could have gone any direction and no signs anywhere. I also put a team on the priest."

Anton Dimitri rolled up the sleeve of his right arm, and held it straight, palm up, on the armrest. Marco took an injector out of the package and handed it to Anton. Anton pushed the flat surface of the end of the cylinder against his bare bicep and pressed. The spring-loaded needle injected him and his head lolled against the seat rest. When he opened his eyes again, darkness ruled outside the window and a sprinkling of stars above a gibbous moon provided the only light outside of the dim cabin.

Anton Dimitri sat up, his demeanor changing to that of a person reviving from some deep sleep, laced with newly found vigor and energy. The monthly serum booster laced with a variety of drugs to offset the crushing aftereffects of using the Power, never failed to bring him back. He resumed the conversation as if no time had lapsed.

"Why the priest?"

"I don't trust him."

"Fair enough, how about the product rollout, how's that being received?"

"As well as we thought it would go. We've got about a billion and a half on the hook in major advertising campaigns and Jeunessa is all the rage right now, 26 million pre-orders as of last night."

"And the audit with the foundation?"

"Being handled, we've got a new accountant coming in. Valdemar Khan is handling that part."

"The first accountant?"

"Much too nosy for his health, we're taking care of him."

"Good. Now one more thing," Anton replied.

"What's that?"

"Get a team of mercenaries stationed on the Abelia-Vie fields in Puerto Vallerta. I don't want to have to make another visit to that shithole for at least fifty years."

CHAPTER 6

It's an accepted tenet of the accounting world that most audits do not result in murders, but at this moment David Waterman harbored doubts about that. The man blocking his path had a face the color of an angry welt, and a matching disposition.

"You dipshit pencil pusher, what the hell do you mean, lack of control? My asshole partner put you up to this didn't he? You work for him."

"I don't work for him, he hired me, but I work as an independent. We report it as we find it."

"Bullshit. He hired you—you work for him. The more crap you invent the lower the stock price and the less money I get on the buyout. Well you're not getting away with it, you little twerp."

The man standing in front of David could certainly use the adjective "little" in comparison since he topped out a solid eight inches over David's average five foot eleven. His name was Aldo "Big Al" Riggio, and he was a fifty percent owner of Riggio's Wrecking, a conglomerate of junkyards, used auto parts and recycling plants. His calluses said he's a hands-on guy, rough, abrasive, built like a fireplug and avoided like the plague by his unfortunate employees. At the moment he wore a pair of stained jeans with a company tee shirt reaching just below the waist. He was in his early forties and although his belly had started to expand a bit, he had muscular bulk that wouldn't turn to mostly fat for another decade. Tattoos on his forearms, a slightly squashed nose undoubtedly the result of a break in younger days, and faded twin scars on one cheek, told tales of a brawling raucous past.

"Gimme that fucking report," he said and grabbed the five sheets of paper from David's hand. He scanned through the first page and stopped halfway down the second. His face turned a deeper shade of red and he flung the papers away.

"You're saying I'm stealing, you little son of a bitch, that's what you're saying."

"No sir. Lack of control is not the same as stealing. You just need to implement…"

"Implement this," he replied as his right hand shot out, grasping David's tie and parts of the front of his collar, pulling him tighter.

David's left hand reached over the bigger man's grasp with a lazy, slow motion, almost a caress, and settled over the thick wrist. Big Al brought his other hand around, grasping the remaining free area of the collar of David's shirt. He closed in on David, lifting the accountant so only his toes remained on the floor. Time seemed to suspend itself in the office of Riggio's wrecking. The secretary stopped speaking on the phone, and another man at a desk halted his activities to watch, but now a curious thing happened.

Slowly, almost imperceptibly, Big Al lowered David. His right hand released the fabric of David's shirt and made a half wave in the air before coming to rest on his left forearm. The redness left his face and the angry expression fled, replaced by puzzlement and a hint of fear, as if Big Al Riggio had stepped out of the bounds of his experience.

David stepped forward, a slow measured pace, his right hand holding the big man's left wrist in a simple jiu-jitsu hold. The application of force to the nerve center at the base of the wrist remained as subtle as it was implacable.

David took another step forward and Big Al backed up an equal pace in a ballet of reversed forces until the back of Al's knees felt the edge of his chair. David moved his hand ever so slightly, and Big Al winced and fell backward to find himself sitting in his chair.

David paused for a second as if nothing had happened, just another moment at the office.

"You'll have our certified audit report by registered mail within three days," He said. He picked up his briefcase and headed toward the exit where his partner, Martha waited.

"Shit, I thought I was going to have to call 911," she said as she fell in step with him. "That big bastard looked like he was going eat you for breakfast."

"He was actually easy to handle Marty. He's big, used to intimidating people with his size and strength."

"Yeah, well he's sure been doing a good job with me. Every time I look at him I get scared, but you made it look easy. Guess that martial art stuff works."

"Yeah I guess. Anyway, we've got to finish the report and mail it in three days, that's what I told him I would do."

"Should be no problem, but how we going to get paid? I don't think we're his favorite people right now."

"We'll get paid," David replied. "We can put a legal hold or some other lien against the stock. His partner's the one who hired us, he wants to buy him out, that's why he wanted the audit, to get a valuation. He'll pay."

CHAPTER 7

I should get a dog, David thought as he opened the door to his condo in nearby Smithtown, Long Island. Twenty minutes from his office, ten from his combination gym/dojo, and eighty miles from the heart of Manhattan, the apartment was about as well located as possible. He lived alone these days, and sometimes when he opened the door the silence was like something alive, ready to devour him. But even as the idea popped up as it had so many times before, he knew it would never happen. You grew to love a dog, and when you loved anything or anyone, especially anyone, the agony caused when it was taken from you could drive you to the edge of madness. He threw the briefcase on the sofa, pulled off his tie and went into the bedroom.

David stripped to his underwear, put on biking shorts and tank top, grabbed a backpack all ready filled from this morning and left the condo. He ran down the three flights of steps, opened the garage with the remote and jumped on his twenty four-speed mountain bike. He took Smithtown Boulevard to 347, turned right and pedaled full tilt. He didn't slow down for lights, just looked right and left, dodged, zigged or zagged accordingly, and made the trip in less than twenty minutes, not a record, but respectable nevertheless. He locked his bike to a railing and walked in the building. The sign on the door read: Kim Lo, Taek Won Do, Jiu-Jitsu, Oriental Health Sciences. David stepped in, walked into the locker room with his bag and started changing into his martial arts *Gi.*

The locker room didn't have any lockers, just large shelves on the wall and benches on the floor with a nearby shower room. Another man was all ready there, just about ready to step out, and he greeted David.

"Hey, my favorite accountant. How you doing? Ready for a good workout?"

"Yeah Anthony, I could use one," David replied as he cinched the belt on his Gi and walked out to the mats.

They worked well together with the easy familiarity of old friends who had done this many times. First a half hour of stretching and *Kata* exercises, the stylized movements of attacks and defense, a staged ballet of practiced motions that could instantly turn into deadly maneuvers. Next, came a *Kumite*, mock battles where simulated blows halted fractions of an inch from their intended targets. After a half hour the *Sensei* ended the session, and Anthony headed for the locker room and showers while David went to the heavy bag.

He started with a series of kicks followed by a variety of punches. The blows resounded throughout the now empty gym, the dull thump of knuckles and feet pounding the heavy bag, threatening to blow it right off the stand. Sweat flew from David's body as the exertion increased. Each blow was a therapy by itself, the only thing capable of driving away the stress. Finally he stopped, exhausted, perhaps tired enough to sleep the night.

As David turned he saw Anthony watching him. He had been so preoccupied he hadn't seen the man coming out of the locker room. Anthony had showered and changed into his street clothes, black pants, black shirt with the Roman collar and black sport jacket.

"How are you David?" Father Anthony asked softly.

"Good as I'll ever be I guess."

The priest hesitated a moment and made to step away,

but turned again, "I know I said it before David, but if ever you want to talk, you know my door is always open."

"Thanks father, maybe one day, well, I'll keep it in mind."

Father Anthony nodded, smiled and said, "I have a client for you. He needs an audit for a charity he runs. His name is Valdemar Khan. Call him."

"Thanks, Father Anthony," David said, slipping the paper the priest handed him into his pocket, "Always could use the work these days."

"You're welcome, David. Just be careful, okay. He can be a little, well…peculiar."

"I'm used to peculiar," David replied, grinning.

"This may be a bit beyond peculiar, but I think you can handle it. Any problems there, call me, okay?"

"Yeah, sure, thanks again."

CHAPTER 8

Eleven o'clock at night, thought Father Anthony as he approached the rectory building on the side of St Marks' church where he lived. At one time the big bells in the church tower would have sounded the hour. Next thing he knew, a recording took over, sending out clear notes over Boses speakers. Just a few years ago the whole thing had stopped except for Sundays, in deference to Smithtown's newly passed noise ordinances.

As he pulled into the parking lot, he saw the big, late model Cadillac parked near the rectory entrance. The light remained on in the building since the housekeeper didn't usually turn in until Father Anthony himself was settled for the night. The other priest in the parish was pushing eighty and usually fast asleep by nine.

Anthony locked his car, a six year-old Toyota Corolla—so much for the vaunted wealth of the Catholic Church. He stepped into the rectory where Mrs. Dowling waited to ambush him.

"You should be more watchful of the hour Father. You told me you would be here for dinner at six, and here it is past eleven. You don't phone or anything," she said, her words tumbling over one another and her stern features glanced toward his office.

"I told you, Mrs. Dowling. This is one of my gym nights

and you shouldn't expect me on time for dinner. A sandwich in the fridge would have been just fine."

She made a noise somewhere between disapproval and annoyance. Back in her days priests didn't go to gyms, nor were they late for dinner. He wondered what she would have thought if she knew he held a second-degree black belt from an oriental martial art discipline. Priests definitely didn't do that in her days.

"I couldn't get rid of him. He insisted on waiting till you got back, says he knows you. I should have called the police," she continued, nodding with her chin toward the office door.

"That's okay, we're here to do God's work Mrs. Dowling."

Clearly God hadn't run that past her as she made another noise and left, muttering, toward her apartment.

Anthony stepped in the office and stopped as the visitor rose from the couch. Unfurled would be more like it since the visitor topped out at least four inches above the priest's own six foot height. There was something familiar about the visitor that tugged at Anthony's memory. Sharp angles dominated the lower part of the face below heavy brows, giving an impression of restrained cruelty like a sadistic Neanderthal. He wore an expensive suit, tight enough to discern the movement of heavy muscles beneath the jacket. He appeared to be in his early forties with thinning hair that only added to the heavy-browed effect. When he spoke, the man's voice was well modulated, almost studied, as if its owner had worked at belying his appearance, and the slight Brooklyn accent that managed to float on his words.

"Father Anthony, it's me Guy, from the neighborhood, remember?"

Now Anthony remembered who the visitor was: Guido "Guy the rope" Spataforo, a Captain in the remains of the old Genovese family, a "made man," and chief enforcer whose nickname referred to his legendary proficiency with that ancient Sicilian weapon: the garrote.

"Course I remember you Guy. How can I forget anyone

from the neighborhood? How you been?"

"Good, but I guess you would know that. You've been doing okay, I saw you on Channel Two a few weeks back."

"The karate priest thing?" Anthony asked. It had been part of a continuing series on the church and they had zeroed in on Smithtown and St Marks. There had been the usual problems on flagging attendance, budgetary woes, wayward priests, but his martial arts pursuits seemed to have grabbed the attention. Of course they had omitted all mentions of the philosophical and downright pacifist aspects of the sport in order to focus on the "karate priest." Well, they had ratings to worry about he supposed.

"Yeah, that's the one. I saw you and I thought, there's a guy from the old days, someone I can talk to."

"So you drove right over. Should have called. I might have been away. You could have missed me. At the very least I could have offered you dinner."

Guy smiled and Anthony thought it might be the kind of smile a predator would have. He wondered how many people had seen that smile as the very last thing in their shortened lives.

"C'mon Father," Guy replied, and the name came out like "Fadda".

"You know what I do, who I am, so I made some inquiries. You don't ever leave the Parish, doing good stuff, tending the sick, helping the homeless, all that good shit, excuse me Father, stuff."

"So you knew I'd be home tonight?"

"Yeah, wasn't no big deal, didn't have anything else going on."

Anthony looked at him but didn't reply. The big man ran a hand through the remains of his hair, looked away and sat on the couch. Suddenly he looked weary, maybe a bit scared as if some terrible thing he couldn't control scooted across the theater of his imagination. Anthony pulled one of the chairs facing his desk, brought it so he faced Guy on the couch, and sat down. The big man looked down at his hands for a long moment, and when he raised his eyes,

Anthony glimpsed the turmoil within.

"I came to ask for your help father. There ain't nobody else I could talk to, I mean you've always been a stand up guy."

"I appreciate your trust Guy, I just don't know if I can help you, I guess it depends on what it is you want."

Guy looked away again as if deciding to continue. The clock on Anthony's desk chimed softly announcing the half hour. There was some shuffling outside and a soft knock at the door.

"Come in," Father Anthony said.

Mrs. Dowling stuck her head in, looked around the office and settled her gaze on the visitor.

"Staying up late are we, Mrs. Dowling?" Anthony said with a grin that told her he knew she was just curious.

"Just want to be sure everything is all right father. Can I get you some tea before I turn in?"

"No thank you Mrs. Dowling."

"All right then, good night Father."

As the door closed softly behind her, Guy leaned forward, his big forearms leaning on his knees.

"Here's what I need Father…"

CHAPTER 9

As he drove to his office, David's cell phone rang. He answered it and Martha's voice came through the car's radio speakers via Bluetooth technology.

"Hey David, it's me."

"Good morning Martha. What'd you do, forget your office keys again? That why you're calling me?"

"No, wise guy, I beat you in this morning, arrived early enough to catch an important call while you were having your first coffee."

"Which call is that? The deli breakfast menu?"

"My, my, a regular comedian this morning. Let me know when you're ready for business."

"Okay, who was it?"

"Very interesting call. A new client, mister Valdemar Khan."

"Yeah, I was kind of expecting that, he was referred to me by Father Anthony, but seriously, the name, Valdemar Khan?"

"That's his name. I think it's Irish, like yours. Anyway, Mr. Khan is CEO of a not-for-profit 501© organization called The William Brogan Foundation."

"Never heard of it."

"Neither did I. Anyway, it must be pretty successful, raking in enough to meet New York State requirements for an audited tax return."

At age twenty-seven David had been a CPA for just less than 5 years. One of his first audits had been for a non-profit organization, NFR, National Freedom Radio, so he had some experience on the subject. Not-for-profit organizations chartered or operating in New York State were required to turn in a copy of their federal tax return to the Attorney General's Office, Bureau of Charities. If the organization received more than $500,000 in public contributions, the return had to be independently audited and certified.

"Did you quote him a fee?"

"Yeah, four hundred fifty per hour with a minimum of twenty thousand."

David let out a low whistle. The rate was a full hundred dollars over their normal hourly rates and the minimum four times the usual.

"Were you wearing a mask when you quoted that?"

"To tell you the truth David, I didn't want it at first even if the guy said you'd been recommended to him. He just seems cold, difficult, a little scary, for me anyway. I got that feeling over the phone. Anyway, you decide. You'll have to handle it if you want to take it. I'm tied up with those three IRS cases plus my regular monthly accounting clients. Turn it down if you want."

"Are you nuts? I don't have much scheduled for the next six weeks, and besides, for those rates, I'd take Charles Manson as a client."

"That's why I like working with you David. You're picky about your clients. I'll tell Alicia to draw up the engagement agreement and call the guy in for the initial appointment."

At the client's request the appointment was set for the nearest available time, two that afternoon. Alicia, their secretary/receptionist came into David's office to tell him the client had arrived. David got up, left his office and walked into the reception area.

A man waited there. He wore an expensive dark suit that fit his lean frame like a second skin. He looked to be in his mid to late forties, with a creased face, Mick Jagger style. His head was bald, with just the remains of a duvet-like growth on both sides. The mouth seemed wide with thin lips above a nose hooked like an Arab desert warrior. His eyes held an unusually light brown color with a slight fold to the lids, hinting at distant Asian ancestries. The man stood, unfurled was more like it. He was very tall, at least six feet four, and angular. He reminded David of what a praying mantis might look like if it assumed human form. David stepped up to the man and held his hand out.

"Good afternoon. I'm David Waterman. Thank you for coming."

"Not at all, I appreciate your time. My name is Valdemar Khan. I am director of the William Brogan foundation."

David led Khan into his office and they sat in the two chairs facing his desk. David felt it was friendlier to sit side by side, rather than behind the desk with the client in front.

"Mr. Khan, I believe my partner informed you of our fee arrangements and you are okay with our rate?"

"That's no problem. I'm more concerned about your ability to complete this audit on time."

"Your foundation operates on a fiscal year I believe, and the filing date mentioned was September 15th?"

"That's correct."

"Why did you wait so long?"

"We didn't. We had a problem with the last accountant. He resigned unexpectedly, some sort of health problem. Now we're facing this deadline."

"Then it will be done by that time. I can begin in two days at your office."

"How many people will be along?"

"Just me, support functions will be performed separately at my office."

"Good. We value our privacy at the foundation."

David frowned and locked eyes with Khan as he spoke.

"That's a bit odd, isn't it Mr. Khan? Every charitable organization is required by law to make its books available to the public."

"Of course, we understand that. The books are kept at the Foundation's office and *are* available to the general public. However, no one has ever asked to see them. The public overall doesn't really care, so you see we don't want to push the issue by having a large crew of accountants swarming over our offices and possibly pushing the dissemination of such information. We believe a single qualified individual such as yourself can do an equally thorough job with greater discretion."

"That I can Mr. Khan. May I ask what your arrangements were in previous years?"

"We had another CPA, a single professional who did a reasonably good job, and we were satisfied, the board of directors and I. This year he became ill and begged off at the last moment."

David nodded his head and said softly, "I see." There was something vaguely disturbing about Mr. Valdemar Khan. Perhaps it was the tall, angular frame of his body, or the somewhat exotic appearance of his features. That by itself shouldn't be putting David off. This was New York, after all.

"Very well Mr. Khan, there are some things you should know, rules if you will. They will be in the letter of engagement we will both sign, but I think it would be good if I explained them verbally right now and answer any questions you may have."

"Go on."

"First as a CPA I operate under a strict code of ethics which assures you, the client, complete confidentiality. This audit will be a strict and thorough examination of your organization's financial practices. I will prepare in writing a detailed opinion of the results of this examination. What I find is exactly what I will express. Payment of my fee will not affect my independent judgment. In other words, if I find problems, I will report them. If I find illegal transactions, I am duty bound and required by law to report such things to the authorities, and I carry out this obligation. Are we clear on this Mr. Khan?"

"I would have it no other way."

"Very well then, my secretary will have drawn up the engagement letter for us to sign. The retainer is $10,000 due on signing."

"I brought a check."

They shook hands and David led Khan into the outer office.

CHAPTER 10

The offices and headquarter of the William Brogan Foundation was located at 615 Metropolitan Avenue, in Brooklyn, a stone's throw from the Brooklyn-Queens Expressway. David parked his car in the garage across the street using the pass Valdemar Khan had given him. Metropolitan Avenue rambles through a good deal of Northwest Brooklyn, in and out of good and horrible neighborhoods, and this was one of the better ones. Trendy shops and upscale restaurants lined the wide, recently renovated sidewalks, interspaced with old and well kept residential brownstones. The William Brogan Foundation occupied one such four-story building.

David walked in the front and stared at the mural taking the entire west wall of the lobby. It was hand painted, an elegant depiction of a group of people in several stages of life. It was always the same people, but each stage showed the advance of age set against a backdrop of human progress that ranged from the early use of fire to the lunar module and the space shuttle. At the ending edge of the mural, the people had aged a great deal, but they appeared to be propped up by ephemeral forms and beams of light emitting from a stylized logo.

Beneath the logo, a legend stood out, blazed into the mural with beautiful renderings of light so it appeared to glow from within.

> *"Men should live as long as the trees, and age as*
> *gracefully."*
> -Alexander Grant

"Inspiring isn't it?"

David jumped at the voice. Valdemar Khan had appeared without a trace of sound. He wore an elegant shirt made out of some sort of silk material and tan slacks with loafers— country club casual. David tried to picture the man in tee shirt and jeans, and simply couldn't.

"It's a nice idea," David replied. "The name Alexander Grant is familiar. I just can't place it right now."

"You probably remember it from some distant American history class. It's a pity the educational systems do not pay more attention to him. Alexander Grant was one of the signers of the declaration of independence and a founding father."

"I vaguely remember. He was a doctor and inventor, wasn't he?"

"Correct Mr. Waterman. Alexander Grant was a leading genius of his day. He was actually the first one to use a microscope, well before that Dutch fellow, and expand the theory that illnesses are caused by microbes we can't see. He was a pioneer in longevity and human development. Pity his genius was never recognized. Not even to this day."

"Impressive. I take it he was the inspiration for The William Brogan Foundation?"

"Oh yes. In fact, he's our reason for being. Our purpose, as so aptly written by Alexander Grant and taken up by Mister William Brogan, is imbedded into our organizational documents. And, I might add, approved by the IRS for a charitable foundation."

Khan read the inscription embossed in the mural, right below the logo:

> *The extension of human life, in wisdom, spirituality and*
> *power, is the highest endeavor possible.*

"Power?" David asked.

Khan's mouth extended slightly into a thin smile, and his eyes returned to David as he spoke.

"You must remember Mr. Waterman, the language of Alexander Grant's day. These were the men who wrote the constitution and the declaration of independence. The language was flowery with the words often conveying a meaning different from what we would give it today. In this case, power meant the vitality and abilities of people as they aged. Come, let me show you our offices."

Khan placed his hand on David's shoulder, nudging him toward the entrance. In spite of the deceptively gentle pressure, David sensed the power in Khan's long arms. A large desk flanked by computer monitors on either side, dominated the reception area. On the left lay a waiting area, furnished with comfortable leather chairs, and a small couch fronting a cherry wood coffee table. Fresh flowers rested on the table, and a magazine rack stood against the wall. Behind the reception desk a wide corridor reached thirty or so feet to the end of the building. Two doors on either side of the corridor walls marked individual offices. The entire area was painted in a soothing eggshell white. Half a dozen paintings adorned the walls, including a revolutionary war-era portrait of a man David assumed was Alexander Grant. Soft music played in the background from an "easy listening" station. A commercial for the new "Baby Boomer Youth drug" Jeunessa temporarily interrupted the music.

Khan introduced him to a dour faced woman, the secretary and receptionist. He instructed her to call Mr. Whittier and let him know the auditor was here.

Almost immediately the door of one of the offices opened, a man stepped out and walked over to Khan and David. He stopped a few feet in front of them, glanced at David, then back to Khan, pursed his lips, but didn't say anything.

The newcomer was barely five feet, the short straw beside David and the taller Khan. He had a round face, clean shaven with nondescript feature, graying hair and a thin comb-over that failed to hide his baldness. He wore eyeglasses with black plastic frames, the kind that was popular in the fifties. His brown sport jacket was opened over a plain white shirt and loosely knotted red tie. He let out a small nervous cough, but didn't say a word, waiting for Khan to speak first.

"Mr. Waterman I'd like you to meet Bennett Whittier. Bennett is our full time in-house accountant and Chief Financial Officer."

David and Bennett shook hands and exchanged "how do you do's". Khan turned to Bennett and continued, "Bennett, Mr. Waterman will be conducting an audit of our organization. You are to open all books and records to him without reservation and answer all questions he might have."

"Yes sir," Bennett replied, nodding. David noticed that the man appeared nervous. There had been a slight tremor to his limp handshake, and he seemed to constantly glance at Khan, as if requiring the man's complete approval.

"I will be going now Mr. Waterman," Khan told David. "I have several appointments and will be out of town for a few days. Bennett will see to all your needs for this audit. The secretary and Bennett both know how to reach me should you need to speak to me."

Khan turned and left the building. David heard Bennett mutter "bloody good thing," under his breath, and he suddenly realized that for whatever reason, the accountant was petrified of his boss, Valdemar Khan.

CHAPTER 11

Bennett led David down the wide hall into the last office, and opened the door for him. "You can use this office," Bennett said, "I've set up everything I think you might need, paper, pens and pencils, calculator, a computer with MS Office and printer. You can use the copier down the hall or let the receptionist do the copying for you."

The office was medium size, about twelve by eighteen with deep, plush carpet. A cherry wood desk with a leather office chair occupied the center of the room. Two more chairs stood in front of the desk with a couple of worktables against the wall and another one flanking the desk. A freestanding computer station occupied the other side, and a long window behind the desk gave a view of the alley between the buildings. The walls were as bare as the desk and worktables. This was obviously a spare office, seldom used.

"I prepared copies of the foundation's last three years tax returns." Bennett continued, "also the general ledgers for those years and the trial balances."

"What software do you use?"

"Quickbooks."

"Fine, I'm familiar with it."

"I also prepared a contributor's list and fundraisers. You'll find they are all coded to deposits. All the records are kept in the office opposite yours. We keep them locked, but I have the keys and you will have full access, of course."

"Thank you. Well then I guess I'll get started."

"Alright Mr. Waterman."

"Please, call me David."

Bennett smiled, and from what he had seen so far, David would be willing to bet there wasn't much smiling that went on in the offices of The William Brogan Foundation.

"Alright, David it is," Bennett said. "My office is next to this one. I keep a pot of coffee on all the time, so feel free whenever you like. Anything you need just holler. For lunch I usually bring my own, but there's a great deli right there on the corner. We open at nine thirty and close at four. I'll give you a key and the alarm security codes in case you want to work longer. Me, I'm out of there at four like a raped-ape."

David laughed. The remark was so ridiculous coming out of the meek accountant. A little blush came up in Bennett's pale features and he laughed with David.

"Tough working for Valdemar Khan, is it?" David asked before Bennett left.

Bennett paused, half out of the office and looked down at the ground, as if the question threw him, and he had never really gave it a thought. David would have bet he thought about it all the time.

Bennett glanced down the hall and took his time about answering, as if to make sure no one could possibly hear him.

"Noo…it's not so much as tough, as it is kind of…how shall I put it, strange? You know what I mean?"

"Yeah, I think I do. He seems a no-nonsense kind of guy, the sort of person that could actually be dangerous given the right circumstances."

Bennett pursed his lips and took a moment before answering, "Well, I've heard stories. Let's just say Mr. Khan would not be an easy man to cross. On the other hand they pay me well as you will see when you examine the payroll records. I'm good at my job and there are no problems. They have never asked me to do anything improper so the arrangement is good. I've been with them for eight years now."

"Well good for you Bennett. I guess I'll get started now."

David always devoted the first day or two reviewing financial and organizational records and talking to employees and executives of the firm. He wanted to get a feel for the organization and how it operated. Every corporation, whether charitable or for-profit, had its own culture, an atmosphere born out of the business and purposes of the company, its people and the way it operated and conducted itself as a business entity. Once he had familiarity with the company and its people, it helped him in anticipating problems and trouble spots to concentrate on.

At the end of the second day, David had a fair idea of the foundation's finances, internal controls and procedures. The one thing that never came through was the elusive "feel" of the organization. Of course something like that would never be found in the auditing bible called GAAP, Generally Accepted Accounting Principles.

After two days of reviews and observations, David noticed a few things. None of them caused any alarms by themselves, but they were enough to raise David's finely tuned senses about such things.

First there was the quietness of the office. The phone hardly seemed to ring. How could this be? The foundation received a little over fifty million dollars in annual contributions. Perhaps not the biggest amount for a large charity, but still, the phone should be ringing off the wall. The second thing that bothered David was the thin staff. One director: Valdemar Khan, one accountant/CFO: Bennett Whittier, and one secretary/receptionist. The other directors apparently never showed up. Ostensibly they met somewhere once a year to approve the foundations current efforts and future plans. David was certain that they would rubber stamp anything Khan requested, and vanish with their director's stipend.

A wealthy industrialist named William Brogan had created the foundation. He had been married many years and looked forward to a long and happy retirement when he reached his early sixties. His hopes were dashed when his wife succumbed to an illness generally brought on by advanced age. Adopting Alexander Grant's two-centuries old writings and ideas on aging, Brogan created the William Brogan Foundation, and funded it with his considerable wealth. While David read the history of the foundation within its original documents, it brought up something else that bothered him. The company had no *esprit-de-corp*, as the French would say. There were no advertisements, no pamphlets or booklets proclaiming their achievement in their chosen charitable endeavor. It seemed as though no one in the foundation cared whether it succeeded or not, yet the success of the foundation was beyond doubt. Now another question came up: How did the foundation manage to snag so much in contributions? There were no ad campaigns, no fund-raisers or celebrity promotions. Ostensibly Valdemar Khan raised all contributions. Yet, the man kept no regular office hours, and disappeared for weeks at a time.

On the third day, David began the audit of The William Brogan Foundation in earnest. He was more meticulous than usual. With all the noise in the press about corporations "cooking the books" and big accounting firms giving them a pass, the public's consciousness on the issue had been raised. Enron, WorldCom and other financial debacles causing losses to shareholders had enraged people and they demanded the blood of any accountants caught up in such illegal doings. A small CPA firm such as his own, certifying the financial facts presented to the IRS and New York State watchdogs, would be destroyed if errors were uncovered later on. David understood all this very well, especially in view of his uneasy feelings about the foundation. He would protect his small firm and career through scrupulously accurate and detailed work.

David came in at nine thirty as Bennett opened the office,

but he would stay until seven or eight, several hours after the accountant and the secretary left. Friday rolled around and the week ended. David decided he would work out of his office that Saturday, setting up audit-related work for his own secretary to do during the week.

When he came into his office that Saturday morning, his partner, Martha, was already there, at her desk.

"Well, well," she said with a grin. "Wonder boy is here. You're late. What'd you do, party last night?"

"I wish. I worked late on that Brogan Foundation audit. Been like that every night this week."

"Your social life must be even worse than mine. Oh well, at least we're getting some bodacious billings out of this. You charging them time and a half after eight hours?"

"No. Not even charging them for the overtime."

"How come? You feeling so charitable you're not even charging them? I got bills to pay you know."

"I'm not charging them the hourly fee after five because it wouldn't be fair."

"Why not? You're working for them aren't you?"

"Yeah I'm working for them, but I got a feeling there's something going on. Nothing I can put my finger on, and there's a good chance I'm wrong and just being paranoid. I'm taking a lot of extra time, being overly meticulous to protect ourselves, and I don't think it's fair or ethical to charge them for it."

She looked at him and shook her head. "You're one of a kind David, you know that? At least I don't have to worry about you stealing the cash register."

"That's cause it's empty."

"There is that," Martha replied. "By the way, your sister called. Nothing urgent, call her when you get a chance. She wants to get together with you for dinner. Probably wants to discuss your non-existent love life."

"She should talk. She's not doing any better."

"Yeah, I spoke to her for a while. It's a good thing the propagation of the human race doesn't depend on you two."

"Martha…"

"Okay, okay, none of my business, I'm going back to work. Let me know if you need any help with that foundation audit thing."

"I'll give a holler if I do. Right now I got it under control."

CHAPTER 12

David Waterman leaned back in the leather-covered chair in the office the William Brogan Foundation had set aside for his use. The light coming through the window had an almost oily sheen, devoid of warm sunrays. David looked outside where heavy rain hammered the brick sides of the building next door—a dismal afternoon on a Wednesday, his sixth day of the audit. He spun the chair back around to the desk and looked again at the compilations he had prepared. He was more convinced than ever of something strange, and possibly illegal, in the affairs of the foundation. He gathered the papers, placed them in a manila folder and stepped out of the office.

Across the hall was the office of Bennett Whittier. David knocked on the accountant's door, opened it and stepped inside when he heard "come in."

Bennett sat behind his desk, an open business checkbook and bills in front of him.

Except for those items, the surface of the desk was completely clear. No pen & pencil sets, no office utensils, and no photographs, nothing. Bennett's office was much larger than the one David used, but equally sterile. White light poured from rows of fluorescent lamps built into the ceiling. Even the wastebasket next to Bennett's desk was empty. Cleaning people came in at ten every morning;

quiet people, who did their job efficiently, with just a few Spanish words here and there. The offices of the foundation had a blank feel, as if everything was temporary and the whole operation might vanish at any moment.

"Please, sit." Bennett said, waving to a chair in front of his desk. "Can I get you coffee?"

"Uh, yeah, great."

Bennett stood and walked over to the three lateral file cabinets that occupied the bottom third of the west wall of his office. A large tray with a Mister Coffee machine and condiments stood on the far cabinet.

"Milk and sugar?"

"Just sugar and black please. I can't stand that powdered artificial creamer stuff."

"I know what you mean. We should get a refrigerator to keep real cream, just never got around to it."

Bennett poured coffee into two Styrofoam cups, handed one to David, and returned to his seat behind the desk. "So how's the audit going?" he asked.

"Good. We've received some confirmations, waiting for a couple dozen more, but everything looks good so far."

All funds disbursed from the foundation had to be accounted and verified. Cancelled checks and bills were not sufficient. Many corporations had been bilked by schemes involving payments to bogus companies set up by thieves within the organization. Recipients of funds from the foundation were verified for legitimacy by David and his secretary at his office. This was done by mail, phone, independent research, and occasionally, personal visits to the vendors and recipients.

"Good. So you'll be done soon?"

"A few days," David replied. "But I do have some concerns."

Bennett frowned, and for a moment David thought he saw a flash of fear passing through the smaller man's eyes.

"Concerns? I keep meticulous records. You know that, you've been checking my work for the last week."

"Oh it's nothing to do with you Bennett. I don't see how

your job could be done any better, and I will mention this in my report."

"Well then, what's the problem?" Bennett asked, his face relaxing under David's reassurance.

"Odd things—nothing extraordinary, just odd. I thought you might be able to clear them up for me."

"What do you mean?"

"Well, look here, the contributions," David replied as he removed a couple sheets of paper from the folder he carried, and spread them on Bennett's desk, "You don't find them odd?"

"Odd? In what way?"

"Come on Bennett, three hundred and fifty million dollars coming from twenty or so corporations and a few obviously wealthy individuals who have absolutely no reasons to give any money to this foundation? There's also substantial foreign contributions, Hu Li Enterprises, in Hong Kong, Usine De La Cellullose, in Bordeaux, France, Smythe & Sons Manufacturing, in Manchester, England, the list goes on, so I'll ask again: Why and how did these companies make such substantial contributions to this foundation?"

Bennett stood very still. There was the slightest hint of a tic in the corner of his right eye and he pursed his lips, making a small sucking noise. He looked like he wanted to be anywhere but here, facing David. Finally he answered.

"Look David, I don't really know the answer to these questions. It does seem a little strange, but it's perfectly legal. You have all the documentation and it's all declared on the foundation's reports to the IRS, every last penny."

"I know that. I'm not questioning the legality of it, or your superb bookkeeping. I'm just saying it's strange, and any strange financial transactions carry an automatic burden of suspicion, does it not?"

"Not in this case." Bennett replied with a shake of his head, "Mr. Khan has many connections and uses them to the foundation's advantage."

"I would guess so. There are no other serious fund raising

efforts, no advertising, no direct mail or phone solicitations, just Valdemar Khan and his pals."

"I suppose, but David, I can't really comment on any of this. My job is to keep the books and records. I make certain that every contribution comes from legitimate sources and is spent toward the public-good purpose that the foundation adopted and the IRS approved. That's it, that's all I do, and it's all legal."

"Good, I'm glad you're pleased with it."

"I am."

"Which brings up another odd fact: After administrative costs and fund raising costs, which appear to be just Khan's travel expenses, all the money is distributed to three organizations, just three."

"Perfectly legal David, you know that."

"Perhaps legal, but certainly odd."

"Odd? Why is that odd? Those organizations are all section 501© IRS approved non-profit organization. Their purpose is attuned to ours. Our mission is supporting organizations like that. Why would you find that odd?"

"Come on Bennett, you know very well. You support just three organizations? And two of them created and run by this one pharmaceutical company with the third one a research lab that has yet to come up with one significant accomplishment after twenty years of existence?"

"All perfectly legal and above board."

David picked up his papers, sighed and stood, "I suppose so." He said, and went back to his office. By that time he was convinced of three things: Bennett knew nothing that wasn't in his well-kept records. Khan and the William Brogan Foundation were doing something unusual and possibly illegal, and third, he had no proof of anything and could not include any of this in his audit report.

CHAPTER 13

It was one of those sneaky little things you don't feel good about, that you don't even want to admit to yourself, David thought. His watch read a little past six in the evening—over two hours since Bennett and the secretary had left with their usual clockwork precision. David had stayed, working later as usual, and now discovered he needed to access additional records. He didn't want to think about it too much, but the real reason he stayed late this night, was to dig around a little more. In other words…snoop.

He stepped out of the room and looked around. The office was deserted and quiet. The rain had increased, and the noise of water hitting the building and pavement outside was the only sound in the building. He could see through the lobby door to the plate glass main entry. No one was on the sidewalk in the downpour. The rush hour had passed, but cars continued going back and forth on Metropolitan Avenue, the noise of their engines and tires on the wet pavement occasionally punctuated by the horns of impatient drivers. The front door was locked, as David had asked when Bennett left, so he wouldn't be bothered by the unlikely event of someone visiting the foundation's office.

David stepped up to Bennett's door and turned the

knob—locked as he expected. He walked toward the reception desk and tried to open the drawers. They didn't budge, also locked.

David pushed the chair away and got on his hands and knees, looking at the little lock built into the side of the furniture. It was a big cheap desk, the kind readily available at discount office supply chains, and it was secured with a small cylinder lock. He got up and went to the filing cabinets on the side of the wall. He knew those were not locked, had accessed them repeatedly in the last few days. This time he went to the cabinet holding miscellaneous papers unrelated to the foundation's business.

He went through the files, finding various items, warranties for computers and office equipment, copies of tax records and deeds for the buildings, and finally, a file for the office furniture. Right in the file, along with warranty and service information, was a spare key for the desks. He fished it out of the file, went back to the secretary's desk and opened it.

He went through the drawers, slowly, making sure that he put everything back in its place, and found what he was looking for in the last drawer beneath boxes of staples and paper clips, a ring with an extra set of keys for the office. He went back to Bennett's door, tried all the keys until he found the one that opened it, and stepped inside.

Whenever David had needed some files or other records, he'd asked Bennett, who promptly supplied them. The accountant had never let David go through the files and records himself. There was nothing wrong with that, as long as Bennett produced everything David required, and he did so without problems. But David wanted to see what else was in those files, what other items secluded away that might explain the strange, if legal, goings on at the foundation.

He spent an hour pouring through the records with no results. Everything was in meticulous, almost fanatical order. He looked at reams of papers and files, none of which were out of the ordinary. Most were duplicates of items he'd already reviewed. He gave up, closed the last cabinet, and left Bennett's office, locking the door behind him.

He paused in the hallway, looking at the first door, the one that he had never seen opened: Valdemar Khan's office. What the hell, he thought, in for an ounce, in for a pound. He stepped up to the director's office, and tried the keys without success. The key to Khan's office was not in the set that he found in the secretary's desk. Could it be that Khan was so secretive that he trusted no one else with the key? That didn't make sense, David thought. Anything really sensitive, he would keep elsewhere. It was unlikely that there were no keys to that office around here.

He went back to Bennett's office, re-opened it, sat behind his desk, and tried to open the drawers—locked. He went back to the front desk, retrieved the furniture file, found the key to Bennett's desk and opened it, slowly.

The man has definite phobias, David thought. In the top drawer he found office supplies, aligned and set up with such military precision it would have made a Prussian general proud. Six pencils were set side to side, exactly the same length, points sharpened and aligned as if an engineer had drawn and executed blueprints for such placement. Square erasers, pens, paperclips, notepads, all displayed as if about to go on parade. He went through each drawer, careful not to disturb anything, until he found a solitary key sitting on a blank notepad in the third drawer. He picked it up, went out in the hallway and tried the key on the door of Khan's office. It opened.

Khan's office could have been a duplicate of Bennett's—same furniture, same carpet, same color. There was a faint musty odor to the place and a thin layer of dust covered the empty desk surface. David had noticed that the cleaning people never went into Khan's office. Evidently the director seldom used the office at his foundation's headquarters, and he certainly didn't want anyone in there.

He sat behind Khan's desk, careful to avoid touching the surface and leaving telltale marks in the dust. The drawers were not locked, and David carefully opened each one. They contained a banal collection of varied office items except for the last drawer, a letter size file drawer. David pulled each file and scrutinized it. More routine stuff, bills and notes, letters, schedules. He was ready to call it quits when he noticed the last brown folder in the last file. The name on the jacket explained its position as last file:Zurich/Lucerne.

David removed the file and looked inside. It contained a single sheet of paper, a computer printout.

PremiereBanque Suisse de Zurich et Lucerne
Compte: 3766BZQ9941
Client: EJpremier
Passe: Brumaire18#1750-AG

David didn't need to be fluent in French to understand what this meant. It was some kind of account in the secretive Swiss banking centers of Zurich and Lucerne, an account with computer access. David copied the information, then placed everything back exactly as he had found it. He got his laptop from the other office where he conducted the audit, hooked up to the office Wi-fi and went on line, searching for the *Banque Suisse de Zurich et Lucerne.*

He found the website almost immediately, clicked on the account section, and the security window came up.

COMPTE: ----------------
CLIENT: ----------------
PASSE: ----------------

David typed in the information he got from Khan's file. Another window came up surrounded by four large red circles with white crosses inside.

ATTENTION—ATTENTAT DE SECURITE
WARNING—SECURITY BREACH
IP ADDRESS NOT AUTHORIZED

What the hell, David thought. He wasn't exactly sure what an IP address was, nor how to get an authorized one.

He needed some serious computer savvy on this, and he knew just who to call.

He pulled his cell phone from the belt holder and hit a digit on his speed dial. It rang five times before someone picked it up.

"Speak dude."

"Kurt, its David."

"Yo dude, what's up?"

An image of Kurt on the phone flashed before his eyes. Tall and thin, bright blue eyes kind of strung out looking with long blond dreadlocks falling around his head and into his face. Kurt was at once the strangest, and one of the smartest persons David had ever met. He looked and spoke like a California surfer, but underneath the spacey-looking eyes, Kurt held an eccentric genius' passion for computers.

"I need help Kurt."

"Name it dude. You know I owe you, like big time for bailing me out with the IRS and their funky-ass tax laws. They were getting ready to shut down my surf shop. That ain't righteous dude, know what I'm saying? So what do you need? I don't guess a straight CPA like you is looking to score some bodacious weed, although, if ever you need…"

"No Kurt, it's something else."

"Dude, If it ain't weed, or surfing, then it's got to be computers, cause that's all I know, man."

"Yeah it's a serious computer problem. I need to get into a website tonight."

"Hacking, right dude, that's what you need me for, right?"

"What can I tell you, you're the best Kurt, that's what I need. Can you get down to Brooklyn right now?"

"Brooklyn? No problemo, dude. I'm in Merrick now. It's going to take me a half hour give or take. I'm cool with it. Give me directions, and hey, can you get me some chow? I was getting ready to go out."

David gave him directions then went to the deli to get dinner for both of them. It was nine thirty and the rain had finally stopped. Puddles reflected the light from windows, streetlights and passing cars. The air smelled of moist concrete and city dust washed by the rain. He got to the deli just before it closed, ordered two roast beef heroes and a large bottle of Coke, and returned to the foundation's offices to wait for Kurt.

CHAPTER 14

On board the Regal Princess–370 nautical miles from Los Angeles

The smartest thing Napper Brown had done in a long time was to get on this cruise to Hawaii. Princess Cruises called it the escape of a lifetime, and in Napper Brown's case they didn't know how accurate they were.

It'd taken him the better part of six months to screw up his courage to do it. It shouldn't have been that way. After all, it was a simple accounting job, something he'd been well trained for. It should have been as dull as watching ice melt.

But the last year boiled in such tensions that it threatened to break Napper, snap his spirit as if it was a physical thing.

Napper was single, no family to worry about. That had been a factor in his decision. While he didn't have enough facts he could actually weave together into some sort of proof that law-enforcement would accept, Napper was convinced that these people were as dangerous as a crack-fueled maniac. That was why he'd run out on the audit for the William Brogan Foundation, hell, he'd flat out run out of town!

"Cocktail, sir?"

Napper turned to face the waitress; pretty brunette with

exotic features. Her nametag read Sonja–Romania.

"Why thank you, Sonja. I believe I will. What would you recommend?"

"Our special today is a Melon-Martini. It's quite good. All the passengers rave about it."

"Sounds wonderful. I'll have one."

"Would you like me to bring it outside for you?"

"Outside?"

"Yes, sir. It's a warm night. We're just a couple of days from Honolulu. I saw you looking out and I thought you'd enjoy it."

Napper smiled. The girl was delightful. If only he was a tad younger than fifty, he might give her a whirl. He smiled at the thought.

"Yes, that sounds wonderful. I'll be outside."

A light breeze ruffled his thinning hair as he stepped out on the promenade deck. It was chillier than the waitress had said. Still he felt comfortable with his sport jacket and long sleeved shirt. The night was clear, moonless and filled with stars.

Napper looked up and took a deep breath. The scent of the ocean rode heavy in the night air and it delighted him. A rushing noise, the ship cutting through the long Pacific swells, filled his ears. The sound rose and fell, loud and pleasant.

Napper was happier than he'd been in years. He knew he'd done the right thing, even if he took a coward's way out. Maybe coward was too strong a term. Let's say it had been prudent, Napper thought. Send them a registered letter of resignation and disappear with no forwarding address. He'd had enough money to do that. It had been set up last year with Barclay's bank in Bermuda. Secretive, yet accessible when needed. He'd done nothing wrong. All his money was obtained legally, saved up through years of work as a CPA and invested conservatively. Still he acted as if it was drug-money or something. That's how much the people at the Brogan Foundation terrified him.

Except for one or two couples strolling on the deck, very

few people were out. The second seating for dinner was on and the show in the main theater was filled with those who had eaten earlier.

"Have you seen the Northern Lights?"

The waitress had returned with his drink. Her smile was nice and her pupils glinted in the dim light of the deck. Was there a note of interest in those eyes?

"Uh, no," he replied.

He took a sip of his drink—a bit sweet with a hint of something strange, almonds maybe? She smiled at him.

"Actually, I can't say I've even heard of Northern Lights. Well maybe, but it's all very vague."

"Northern Lights are a rare phenomenon. It occurs in these latitudes when atmospheric conditions are just right. A night like this is perfect for Northern Light sightings."

"Would you show me?" he said. Suddenly he was surprised at himself. Where had this boldness come from? He felt light headed, like the ship didn't exist under his feet and he floated there, above the Pacific, him and this beautiful woman. She smiled at him and he felt strange, delighted-strange.

"Sure. We like to keep our passengers happy," she said. Her smile enchanted him. Was there a hint of something else in her voice? Could this woman be actually accessible to him, Napper Brown, CPA? Could it be possible she actually might desire him?

"This is probably the best spot," she said as she walked toward the stern of the ship. They were just a few feet past the last aft door on the promenade deck. The rearmost lifeboat hung suspended above them and the wind blew a bit harder. The covered space between the end of the side and the beginning of the rear acted as a funnel. It was also darker there as the row of deck lights ended and wouldn't begin again until after the curving end of the stern was passed.

A uniformed crewman worked there, moving some heavy-looking pipes from a recessed locker marked "crew only."

Napper took another sip of his drink. He'd surprised himself. More than half the drink was gone. Strange currents ran through his body, as if he'd arrived on a kind of supernatural plane, just him and this beautiful woman. He looked down the end of the deck and saw no one about. The crewman had his back turned to them and the waitress' eyes seemed to bore through his.

The night grew suddenly chilled and the air seemed to thicken about him. He leaned on the railing without feeling the polished wood beneath his limp hands.

"Are you alright, sir?" the woman asked. Behind her the crewman rose and turned to look at them.

Napper didn't answer. He felt dizzy and leaned heavily on the rail. Something was wrong, like he'd taken a load of Valium.

The excruciating pain blinded him. It obliterated his world and crushed his consciousness. By the time the crewman drew the ice pick out of Napper's neck, he was already dead.

The woman held his body, not more than a second, perhaps two. The crewman wrapped the wire fixed to the heavy lead pipe about Napper's leg. In one swift, coordinated move they flipped his body over the side.

When he hit the water, the corpse went instantly down, pulled by the sixty pound pipe. Nothing showed in the wake of the ship from the aft video cameras.

Napper's body was on its way. It wouldn't stop until it hit bottom three and a half miles down.

CHAPTER 15

Kurt stood just inside the reception office, looking around as if he'd fallen asleep somewhere, and woken up here. He wore an old leather motorcycle jacket over a bright tie-dye tee shirt, sixties style. Dark jeans and Reebok running shoes, a colorful knit cap draped over his blond shoulder length dreadlocks, completed the outfit. Several days of light-colored growth decorated his handsome features and highlighted bright blue eyes. Although he had often said he didn't want to grow a beard, shaving was a sporadic affair for Kurt. He looked like a white, California surfer type who had gone Rastafarian. He carried a big, well-padded computer case.

"Dude, is this, like legal? SWAT teams aren't gone come around nailing our asses are they?"

"No, nothing like that," David said. "I'm doing some accounting work for these people, I'm authorized, except for the hacking that is."

"That's cool. I'm used to that."

"I'll bet you are. Come on, we'll eat while I show you what I need."

David led Kurt into the office he used and booted up his laptop. He plugged into the Wi-fi, went online and brought up the website for Banque Suisse de Zurich et Lucerne. He logged on with the access codes he got from Khans' files and the security window popped up immediately.

   ATTENTION-ATTENTAT DE SECURITE
   WARNING-SECURITY BREACH
   IP ADDRESS NOT AUTHORIZED

Kurt said, "Whoa, gnarly," leaned over and pushed the power button off on David's laptop.

"What'd you do that for?"

"Shit dude, that's some serious security on that site. IP alert and all that stuff, Swiss bank, they must have some righteous shit in there and they ain't afraid to spend money to protect it."

"So what's that mean, we can't get in there?"

"Not with just that Mickey Mouse machine of yours. They've got IP-ID protection. Their security software identifies the machine trying to log in and matches it with an authorized list. If your machine isn't on the list, it raises alarms and you don't get in, even if you got the pass codes. Not only that dude, it reads your ID, your machine, so they can find out who tried to get in. That's why I shut it off."

"You think they got it?"

"No sabe dude."

"So can you get in?"

"Not with your machine. We need one that's authorized on the system. Given time and my normal equipment, I could fuck with IP security. But not tonight with what I brought. I mean dude, I thought you were going to just screw around with normal websites, not Swiss fucking banks."

"Wait a minute. I know a machine that might be authorized."

David didn't think Bennett's computer would be on the authorized list. He was convinced the accountant to the foundation was not privy to its secrets. He also had the personality that would fanatically mind its own business. David realized that was one of the attributes Khan would look for in employees. David, however, was something else. Khan must have felt secure that whatever questionable business the foundation was engaged in, it was safely hidden away.

David led Kurt into Khan's office and pointed to the computer sitting on its console, next to his desk.

"I think that one might do it. It'll probably be password protected."

"That's cool dude, cause we don't need to actually use the machine, just its IP code."

Dave watched as Kurt took his laptop from the bag he carried. It was a large thing, black matte, with no logos or identifying marks.

"Homemade dude, you can't buy a righteous machine like that. Got the latest NovaX chip from Tashimi Industries, with two slaved Intel chips. Now watch this."

Kurt powered up the machine as he attached a USB cable to a small black box. Another cable came out of the box, and he connected it to Khan's computer.

"Okay, turn it on."

Dave pushed the on switch and the windows logo came up as the machine booted up. A security window popped up asking for user name and password.

"Now what?" David asked.

"I got it dude. We don't want to actually use this gnarly piece of shit. We just want to use its IP address, you know, like boosting someone's wallet and using their credit card."

David looked at him and frowned.

"But then you wouldn't know about shit like that, would you?" Kurt said, laughing. "While the machine booted up, mine retrieved the IP address, stored it, and sent it out to the internet server. It's just like we're actually using this guy's computer. Now let's try it."

Kurt hooked up his computer to the DSL line and typed in the Swiss bank's website. He filled in the passwords and user codes David gave him, and a welcome screen with menu appeared.

"Kurt, you are an evil genius."

"Emphasis on genius, dude."

David took the laptop and began scanning the contents

while Kurt finished his roast beef hero. About ten minutes passed, and Kurt left to use the bathroom. David's eyes hadn't moved from the computer as rows of numbers, data and other information paraded across the screen.

For the first time, as he sat in the silent room with the computer on his lap, David felt a thrill of fear course through his mind. He could scarcely believe what his eyes saw and what his training as a CPA told him happened this very moment around the globe. He felt a tremor in his hand, and in spite of the cool temperature of the room, sweat ran down his armpits. He leaned his head back, still looking at the computer, when the screen blanked out and MS logo came on. He had been disconnected from the web site. He typed it back in, tried to log on again, and a security window came up.

WARNING—SECURITY BREACH
ATTENTION—ATTENTAT DE SECURITE

And he was disconnected from the site once again.

CHAPTER 16

Daytona Beach, Florida

A scant half-mile from the southern edge of the city, a mansion stood fifty yards from the beach. People strolling on the hard packed sand facing the Atlantic could pass right in front of the big contemporary structure. They would only see the top of the signature roofline, because of the manmade dune directly in front topped with a cedar fence, barring any access. From the balcony of the house that night, Valdemar Khan enjoyed a panoramic view of the ocean as he worked. The electronic trill of a cell phone interrupted his perusing the stack of documents next to his chair. He picked up the cell phone and looked at the information window.

CALLER:BANQUE SUISSE
LOCATION: LUCERNE
SATELITE ENCRYPTION:
ACTIVE MODE

He keyed the answer button.

"Khan here."

"Monsieur Khan, this is Roland Dupont," said the caller in heavily French accented English. "I am the security director for Banque Suisse. I believe we may have had a breach attempt on your account."

"Tell me what happened."

"There were two attempts to access the accounts: one at 7:42PM and another at 9:02PM, your time. The access codes were correct, but IP address verification indicated an unauthorized entry. Naturally the security devices denied access. Twenty minutes later you logged on."

"*I* logged on?"

"Well yes Monsieur. Your codes were correct, and IP address indicated your computer, and that is authorized. You are on line with the accounts at this moment are you not?"

"No"

There was a moment's hesitation before the security director replied.

"But, then…"

"It is an intrusion. Disconnect immediately and remove my current IP address from the list. I want the IP addresses of the previous intrusion attempts."

"*Oui monsieur, immediatement.*"

Less than four minutes later Khan had the IP addresses of the two previous intrusions. They were both the same, a long series of digits, numbers and symbols. Khan hit a speed dial number on the satellite cell phone. The encryption status continued to show active as the phone was answered.

"Hello."

"Hello Wayne, Valdemar here. I need IP addresses traced immediately. We have a security breach."

"Good Lord. Give me those numbers. I will get back to you in twenty minutes."

It actually took less than fifteen minutes for the return call with the information. The laptop computer bearing the IP address in question had been purchased by mail from Dell Corporation six months ago. The buyer was David Waterman, CPA.

Khan pushed another speed dial button on the cell phone after checking the encryption status once again. The call was answered on the first ring.

"Good evening, Valdemar."

"Good evening, Anton. We have a developing security problem that will require executive action."

"Give me the details."

Khan told him.

CHAPTER 17

The attack car jumped on the road from its concealment behind a stacked log barrier. It tore up the few yards separating it from Joline's Crown Victoria, and barely missed the rear bumper. Joline turned in the back seat, watched the attack car fishtail, straighten out, and close the gap within a few feet of her own automobile. She turned her attention back to the front seat, watching her driver.

The driver, a guy named Burt, had nailed the gas and now started a back and forth weave across the road, preventing the attack car from passing the rear quarter of Joline's vehicle. If it slammed the back fender it could send the heavier Crown Vic into an unrecoverable spin. Burt managed to keep the big car ahead, *so far so good*, she thought. Now the second car burst out of a clump of bushes on the left side of the road. It was camo-green, blending with the shrubbery that normally would not hide a vehicle so well. Smaller and faster than the first attack car, it was also more effective. The second car tagged the left rear of the Crown Vic and sent it spinning, blowing up clouds of brown dust from the dirt road. Burt whipped the wheel in the direction of the turn, regained control of the car and floored the gas, aiming directly ahead of the second attack car. That's when things went terribly wrong.

The engine stalled, just died right out and the Crown Vic

lost power steering and brakes. It just stopped in the soft sand on the side of the road. Joline paused a second, then jumped out from the rear door and ran straight away from the first attack car stopped directly behind her. The driver of that car didn't bother getting out, just fired right from the left front window, four nice easy shots. The rounds caught Joline in the left shoulder, neck and stitched two more hits across her lower back—at least three killing shots.

Burt jumped from the driver's door, gun in hand, rolled on the ground and came up in a combat stance, weapon directed at the shooter from the first attack car. It was too late of course. Joline was already dead and the two men from the second attack car fired half a dozen rounds each, almost every one hitting Burt, tattooing his body with at least nine rounds, all fatal hits.

Joline got up slowly and brushed the dust from her clothes. She rubbed her neck and side where the paint ball "bullets" had hit. The velocity of the acrylic-filled thin plastic balls stung like hell when they hit. She wiped the dust from her face and pulled her hair back. Standing tall, almost six feet, with ash blond hair cut short, she was attractive. She hardly thought about it, and usually wore no makeup at all. Right now she looked pissed as she walked toward Burt. The driver's expression was somewhere between sheepish and bewildered, the dozen or so paint ball hits decorating his body from shoulder to ankle.

The driver of the second attack car intercepted her before she reached the man. "Take it easy Joline, let's talk about it first," he said.

"Hell Fred, I thought you said this guy had defensive training. His application has got to be a crock of shit. Did we background him?"

"Joline…"

She stopped a moment and looked at her partner, Fred Walters. She saw a man in his late fifties, salt and pepper hair, thinning, but still neatly combed in spite of the recent car chase. Joline always thought Fred looked like an older man making an easy transition to the later stages of life, like a new and content grandfather, which in point of fact, he was. He wore thin glasses highlighting soft brown eyes that Joline felt reflected a unique combination of strength and sincerity. Even though Joline was the founder and senior partner of Executive Services Incorporated, and Fred Walters was one of two junior partners, she always considered his advice and usually acted on it, and not simply because he was her vice president. Truth of the matter was that Fred was most often right in his recommendations. He also had the ability to calm her down when her blood started boiling—a very valuable talent for their corporation. Like most successful CEO's, Joline made her mind up quickly and changed it slowly. One of Fred's most valuable jobs was making sure that Joline made the right decisions the first time.

"Of course we did a background check on him. He went through the Treasury Department's protective driving course in 09."

"Oh nine? What is he, a twenty year man?"

"Yes, the last seven in field operations. Not protection detail, and he was never a wheelman. I thought he would be more effective, I guess we'll have to re-train him."

"Yeah, no shit. Mexico City's less than two months away now and we still don't have enough people to protect Umberto and his staff"

"So let's not waste this one Joline. He'll be okay if we play him right."

Joline sighed, "Fuck," she said softly, and immediately felt guilty. Fred was an old fashioned family man. There weren't enough like him in the world. Smartass bitch that she could be, she took a perverse childish pleasure in sending a few obscenities Fred's way. He turned away for a moment then looked back at her.

"Mexico City is the reason why we need to salvage him Joline. That's why we have this setup," he said, waving his hand to encompass the fourteen acre road training site owned by Executive Services Inc.

Joline took a deep breath, filling her lungs with the pine scented clear air of Eastern Long Island. Located a scant nine miles from Riverhead and two hours from Manhattan, the site occupied parts of a pine forest intersected with a system of dirt roads and specially placed hazards that had been sold to her for a dollar by her mother. That was before her liver gave up, destroyed by years of low shelf alcohol and prescription drugs. Joline and her partners had developed it into a field-training center. With the price of land in Eastern Long Island being what it was, some would say it was Executive Services' most valuable assets. They would be wrong.

The company's most valuable asset was their impeccable record. In nine flawless years, they had prevented numerous disasters and never allowed a client to come to harm, never. If a wealthy individual or high power CEO needed guaranteed protection in a potentially dangerous environment, Executive Services Inc. was the premier choice.

Burt walked slowly up to Joline and Fred. He shuffled a bit, kicking up small clouds of dust at his feet. Rivulets of sweat ran down his face, mingling with tiny splatters from the paint ball hits on the top of his shoulders.

"Guess I screwed that one up a bit," he said.

"A bit?" Joline said. "Christ, we could have just hired a cab and gotten the same protection."

"Wait a minute, that engine stalled, otherwise…"

"Burt," Joline cut him off, holding up a hand displaying a small remote device. "This is why your engine quit. I shut it down as an exercise. In a real situation a guy with a fifty-caliber sniper rifle will do it from a couple of hundred yards away by blowing a hole in your engine block. Maybe somebody with an RPG will destroy the entire hood section, either way your car comes to a halt. The real problem is you screwed up the three most important rules: control your vehicle, control your client, and most of all, control yourself. Didn't they teach you that in protection classes?"

Burt didn't reply and she continued.

"First screw up: You didn't activate the remote lockout that would have prevented your client, me, from just walking out of the vehicle making it so much easier for kidnapers, or in this case, three bullets. The vehicles we use are armored, three inch thick bulletproof glass, re-enforced steel and Kevlar on all doors and fenders. That vehicle is the safest place to hunker down until the cavalry comes. All you need is to buy a few minutes. Use the vehicle's firing ports, the small cowl windows on either side, and above all control yourself, don't run out to get shot like a crippled deer in hunting season."

"Look Miss Waterman, I'm sorry. I haven't done vehicle protection since, I don't know, ten years at least. Can we run this through again?"

"My guess is you've never done it. You may have taken the course but you've never actually done the work. If you want to stay with us I'm sending you to a West Virginia company called Auto-Protekt for a four-day program. When you come back we'll do another run-through, see how you do then. You game?"

"Yes."

"Okay, contact Minerva at the office, she'll set it up."

Joline drove the Crown Vic back to the weathered stucco building that served as the field training office. When she got there Johnthra was waiting for her. Her second vice president wore her usual field outfit: dark jeans, faded boots and a short sleeve gray sweatshirt. At five foot five, the top of her head barely reached Joline's nose. Even though she was heavy—you couldn't really call her fat, there was strength in her thick limbs. Many an unfortunate felon discovered that during her days as a cop in the north side of Boston. Johnthra was a Filipina with broad features and café au lait skin. How she went from Manila to Boston PD, and finally as second vice-president and minority shareholder of Executive Services Inc. was a whole other story by itself. Although anyone who knew her would never doubt it. Those dark brown eyes and plain features served as camouflage for a razor sharp intellect.

"Poor ole Burt," she told Joline. "Hope you didn't chew him up too bad."

"I'm sending him for training, he's useless this way. Who else we got for today?"

"For you, nothing. Fred and I'll handle it. You got something going on back at the office. Minerva said there's a cop there, NYPD detective, needs to speak to you, and only you."

"Tell her to take care of it and blow him off to Roger. The guy probably wants some info on a client or something."

"Nope, tried already, said it's official and personal, and it has to be you. What'd you do, waste that piece of shit ex-husband of yours?"

"If I did, the cops would never know," Joline said with a grin. "Alright, you and Fred finish testing the others. I guess I'd better get over there."

Joline put on her leather riding-jacket, picked up her helmet and headed for the door. Whenever she worked at the training site, she always rode her bike, a custom, second-hand Harley Fat Boy with teardrop tank and chrome trims. She had bought it as is. The only change she'd made was getting rid of the "ape hangers" and replacing them with comfortable stock handlebars. As she stepped out the door she heard Johnthra call her.

"Hey Jo, don't get killed on that thing. I ain't got time to do your work."

"Don't worry about me kiddo, but if I were you, I'd consider getting a bike like that. It's about time you had something growling between your legs again."

"You don't know nothing about it girl," Johnthra said returning to her paperwork. One marriage and two boyfriends later, Joline had to admit to herself, that no, maybe she didn't.

CHAPTER 18

Joline pulled the big bike into the rear parking lot of the three-story professional building. The top floor served as headquarters for Protective Services Inc. Located in suburban Hauppauge, right smack in the heart of Long Island, the office had the dual advantage of being an hour from Manhattan and ten minutes from Joline's house. She wheeled the Harley to a small shed she had installed in the corner of the parking lot to house the bike on those occasions when she might have to leave it and drive her automobile instead.

Joline used the rear entrance and the stairwell instead of the elevator. She emerged into a narrow corridor flanking the waiting room and approached the one-way glass that allowed her to observe visitors without being seen.

The man waiting for her was tall with a handsome pleasant face. She judged him to be about a bit older than her own thirty-two years. He wore a quality well-fitted suit and carried a light overcoat draped on his arm, exactly appropriate for the early April weather. He didn't look like someone's idea of a cop. Joline got the impression of someone concerned about what he had to do, maybe a tad apprehensive. Looking through the glass at the man, she felt a pang of disquiet. After all, he had identified himself as a New York Police Department detective on official business, asked to speak only to Joline and no one else.

She'd racked her brains on the way here trying to figure out what this visit was all about. In the last twelve months Protective Services had two incidents, both involved shootings and one fatality, but it was the nature of the business. They protected high profile individuals who were targets of some very nasty people. Both those cases had been settled and none had occurred within the United States. Besides, such issues were handled routinely by Fred and the company's attorneys. Her own personal life, lately dull as a convention of dentists, certainly wouldn't draw any police attention, even her ex-husband, skirt-chasing liar that he was, stayed on the right side of the law.

Joline walked out of the viewing corridor and into the hallway. She opened the door to the waiting room and stepped in as if she had just arrived.

"I'm Joline Waterman, I hear you want to speak to me?"

"Uh, yes, my name is Detective Barry Anderson, New York Police."

He handed Joline a small leather bi-fold with his picture ID on one side and badge on the other. Joline barely glanced at it. Minerva would not only have scrutinized it carefully, but double-checked by phone with NYPD before letting Joline meet with the detective.

Sometimes life is simple, and things are what they appear to be, other times we sense things beneath the surface that trigger dormant senses. A turn of the eyes, a slight edge to someone's body language. Our subconscious processes the signs and sends us signals, flashes of insight, or bursts of intuitive warning, or perhaps intuition is God talking to us after all. Whatever the case, Joline felt it, a sense of dread, and suddenly she wanted to be elsewhere, because she knew clearly that whatever was coming was going to be far from good.

Detective Anderson's clear blue eyes didn't quite fix on hers, and she could tell he also wanted to be elsewhere.

"Miss Waterman," he said, and for a moment she thought he was actually going to stammer. "I'm sorry to have to tell you, uh, that is I regret to inform you…"

"Get on with it Detective. What do you have to tell me?" For a moment she could swear that he actually blushed, and she regretted her abruptness. *Nice going Joline*, she thought. *No wonder your dating book stands between sparse and zilch.*

"It's ah, about your brother Ma'am, the receptionist confirmed you have a brother named David Waterman, lives in Smithtown, has an accounting business in Mineola."

Stillness opened like a fissure in the earth, right in front of Joline. She felt like she stood teetering on the edge of an abyss while something slithered in the darkness below. She held her breath and a corner of her mind noted the pounding of her heart. She almost felt the silent surging of blood in her veins. She heard the quiet whisper of the room's climate control unit, the distant creaks of wood from the old structure mixed with the low hum of the office equipment in the adjoining room; floating above it all, Detective Anderson's soft tones.

"I'm very sorry to have to bring you this news…"

She had a vision of David, barely six years old when their father died, holding on to her arms while their mother fell deeper into an alcoholic fog.

"There was a shooting last night at the offices of a non-profit foundation. Two men were killed. We believe one of them was your brother, David."

David at ten with the shy smile that reflected her own features; he'd depended on her. She was both older sister and surrogate mother. She protected him as fiercely as any Serengetti lioness.

"You believe? You're not sure?"

"Not one hundred percent, no. We positively identified the other body. Would you accompany me to the morgue for the ID?"

She gripped the edge of the table so hard the bones in her fingers could have cracked…David at fourteen, his first serious crush, when she realized that not even she could protect him from the mysterious workings of the heart. David...David. Gradually the detective's voice penetrated her consciousness once more.

"...appears to be a drug-related incident. Your brother may have been caught in the middle."

David...at seventeen, graduating from high school with honors and a full scholarship to the University of Maryland. She had raised him, had single-handedly convinced the courts to make her David's guardian after their mother died...David. The tiniest corner of her mind registered the detective's empathy.

"I'm the lead investigator Miss Waterman. I can assure you that if it is your brother, I will make every effort to bring to justice whoever killed him..."

The room shifted under her feet and for a moment she swayed. She felt Detective Anderson's hand on her arm, steadying her. The pit of her stomach fell away and she thought she would just pass out as the pain dug right to the bottom of her soul. Her vision blurred and she felt the wetness roll from her eyes, and she was powerless to stop it. She took a deep breath and dug her manicured nails into the palm of her hand until a bright red drop ran toward her wrist.

"I'm so, so sorry," whispered Anderson. "Would you like to sit down, can I get you a glass of water?"

She shook her head. She didn't trust herself to answer as a thought formed in her mind. Whatever the reasons, whatever the circumstances, she would speak for David as she always had, would avenge him in death as she had protected him in life.

Then she could no longer contain herself as her grief poured from the depth of her being, from the very essence that was Joline Waterman. Barry Anderson, the detective with the kind face and blue eyes held her close as she stained the front of his shirt with her tears.

CHAPTER 19

Unmistakable and unique, the stomach-wrenching smell of death haunted the air. Trying to cover it with acrid fumes of bleach and Lysol, didn't work. It was there, that horrid undercurrent of torn body parts and spilt blood. Joline had never been in a morgue, but she'd known what it would smell like, anticipated it. She felt like she struggled through a honeycomb, every passage filled with darkness and the ghosts of those passed...Like David.

They walked down a long, wide hallway. The attendant led the way. The man whistled through his teeth and the keys on his belt clinked softly. Detective Anderson walked by her side, his hand resting gently on her arm. Joline felt the tile floor under her feet, heard the little squish of her rubber soles.

The attendant stopped at a set of wide double doors. A big 4 was stenciled on each door. No names, just a number, sterile as the cold bodies stored in the drawers inside the room.

The attendant took a key from his ring and unlocked the doors. Anderson and Joline followed the man to the far side of the room. The sudden chill enveloped them, a meat-locker cold that frosted every breath out of their lungs.

Wide steel drawers filled the entire wall, only the ends protruded an inch or so. A handle adorned with numbers stuck out on each drawer. The attendant pulled out number eighty-four.

That's all that's left of David, now, Joline thought—a number, a name, and memories. Even the memories will die eventually and nothing will remain of his passage in the world.

She felt her heart thump as if it would break out of her chest. Biting her lip she made a little sucking noise as the attendant rolled the sheet back from her brother's head.

She looked down and relief flooded every molecule of her being. She'd been prepared for the finality of it all, the last heart-tearing pain. She hadn't dared to hope, and now…She felt Anderson's arm on hers and she leaned on him. She was grateful for the detective's presence, his support and obvious sympathy.

"Miss Waterman?" he said gently.

"That's not my brother. Oh, God, thank you, that's not my brother."

Joline leaned back against the wall and closed her eyes. She felt infinitely better—at least for the moment. The obvious question was unanswered. She knew as she held Detective Anderson's gaze that it was also on his mind.

Where was her brother?

CHAPTER 20

Joline looked in the mirror. *Worse than usual*, she thought. Her eyes were puffy. Her hair fell in tangles and split ends. She brushed most of it out, rubbed her face with a damp washcloth and looked again—screw it, it is what it is.

She'd had a rotten night sleep. No, that wasn't accurate, she'd had barely any sleep just fell into a kind of stupor somewhere around four in the morning to wake up a few miserable hours later. David's inexplicable disappearance filled her mind and crowded out everything else.

She looked at the sailboat clock on her kitchen counter. David had given it to her a week after they'd rented a sloop for a week last July. It read nine forty five. Anderson would be here in another fifteen minutes or so. The detective had called her last night, and asked to meet her for another interview. Did he have news about her brother? She had asked. No. Then why the hell do you want to see me? Go find my brother, goddamn it. Instead she said okay.

She put on a pot of coffee, cleared the debris of last night's meal from the counter and put away the clean stuff from the dishwasher. Anderson was five minutes late and it felt like an hour until her doorbell rang. She buzzed him up and opened the door.

Anderson stood there and they shook hands. She invited him in.

"Thank you for seeing me, Miss Waterman."

"Joline."

"Yes, Joline."

"Coffee?"

"Yes, thank you."

They sat at the kitchen table. Anderson held a small notebook open—pen ready. She sat in front of him after pouring them each a cup and placing milk and sugar on the table.

"Tell me what happened to my brother."

He sighed and looked down at the table for a moment before raising his eyes to meet hers.

"What it appears to be," he said slowly, measuring each word as if he could only say a certain few, "is that David was involved or caught in the middle of a drug deal gone wrong."

"David didn't do drugs," she said. The words exploded out of her. She locked eyes with Anderson.

"Perhaps not, Joline, but there is strong evidence of his involvement."

"Bullshit. I don't believe it. What evidence do you have?"

"We've identified the body that we originally thought was David's. The man's name is Joseph DiCarlo, street name Joey D. He's a small time hoodlum with a long rap sheet and a low-level drug dealer."

"He's got nothing to do with my brother."

"Perhaps not, Joline. However, questioning of Joey D's associates revealed a couple of things. He'd been bragging about a big drug sale he was going to make that night at this office on Metropolitan Avenue. He also said the buyers were a couple of, pardon me Joline, but these are the exact words used: Jew accountants and he was going to kick their ass and take their money."

"That's absurd. I don't know what happened, but David would never be involved in something like that."

"There's more, Joline. We found the weapon used to kill both the accountant, a man named Bennett Whittier, and Joey D. It's a .22 Caliber Beretta purchased legally in West

Virginia. The buyer was identified with a New York Driver's license number 1167328 as David Waterman. The license numbers match and so does the registration number on the gun."

She closed her eyes. A feeling of vertigo invaded her world. In just two days everything had changed, turned upside down. She opened her eyes and gripped the table. She'd see this through. David couldn't have been knowingly involved. She knew him better than anyone else in the world, better than their mother had known him, even. She held Anderson's gaze and said nothing. The detective looked down at his little notepad and continued.

"What we have right now, I mean, what we surmise from the available evidence is this: Joey D met David and Bennett at the office of the William Brogan Foundation where they were working that night. He intended to sell them a large quantity of cocaine. We found traces of it in his jacket pockets where he carried it. Something went wrong at that meeting. Perhaps he tried to rip them off. However it went down, both men were killed with David Waterman's gun. There are clear prints on the weapon. We don't have David's prints. He was never in the military nor did he ever hold a position requiring fingerprinting."

"That's absurd. Why would David leave his gun behind if he shot those two men?"

"Actually, it's not uncommon. David's not a hardened criminal. People often panic and drop their weapons after such events. When we find David and take his fingerprints, it will tell the story."

"Detective, I can tell you my brother never did that kind of thing. I raised him and I know…knew." She paused a moment. A sudden flash of pain bolted through her hand and she looked down. A tiny drop of blood rested in her palm where she'd pierced the flesh with her fingernail.

Anderson's gaze remained on hers. There was an edge to it and Joline realized he'd dig for the truth no matter where it would lead. It was his nature, his job, and the rank he'd achieved showed him to be good at it.

"I said I would tell you everything, Joline, and I meant it. There are some inconsistencies in this case that disturb me. I mean no offense when I say this, but every family member tells me the same thing when their loved one is involved in…how shall I put it…compromising positions."

"Thank you for being delicate," she said.

"Oh its more than just that. Most people can't believe the darker or stupid side of their loved ones. They couldn't possibly use, buy or sell drugs, stick up a 7-11, extort someone. But they do. All the time."

"David. Didn't. Do. Drugs." She spat each word out like something horribly bitter. "You said there were inconsistencies. Tell me."

"Nothing really striking. Taken alone they mean nothing. Add them together and it creates doubt. Toxicology reports indicate the presence of heroin and cocaine in Bennett Whittier's body. But there's no track marks on him. The autopsy results do not show damage consistent with steady drug abuse. Of course, taken by itself, that means nothing."

"The hell it doesn't," Joline said. "I don't know about this Whittier guy, but like I keep telling you. David didn't do drugs—ever."

"He could have just started. Wouldn't be the first time something like that happened. When we find him, we'll sort it out. Right now we have a fugitive warrant out on him. If you know where he is, please tell him to come in. If he's as innocent as you say, there's nothing to fear."

CHAPTER 21

I hop off the freight train about a couple of miles past Philadelphia. Interstate 95 is nearby and just a couple of miles walk to a truck stop.

I walk into the restaurant part. There're about a dozen truckers there, eating breakfast. It's just past six AM. I order a hungry man special–eggs, bacon & pancakes. I skipped dinner last night and traveling always makes me hungry anyway.

Discreetly I pull a couple of tens from the hidden pocket of my cargo pants. I usually travel with about five thousand. Now someone might wonder why I jump freight trains and hitchhike when I have that kind of cash available.

I prefer the anonymous underbelly of America. The hobo's camps, truckers—rides from unknown strangers that will never be recorded on any manifest. No one knows my name. My records have been expunged long ago. I pass through like the wind, swift and unnoticed–except for those to whom I choose to make myself known.

I finish breakfast, leave cash on the table and step outside to the parking lot. I wait and watch until a certain eighteen-wheeler comes along. Ball Van Lines, good company–Chicago to New York. The truck parks and the driver gets out. He's an older man, late fifties I guess, a baby-boomer.

He's got a western kind of face, tanned brown and wrinkled under a Vietnam veteran ball cap. He goes in the restaurant. I wait.

About a half hour goes by until the driver comes out. He's with a couple of other truckers. They pause right outside and my target lights a cigarette. The drivers talk for a few moments and split up. My man walks toward his truck, alone. I fall in step with him, put a hand on his shoulder and say "Hi."

To this day I remember the first time I used the Power. I'm not sure if I should even call it that. I don't rightly know exactly what it is. I first discovered it back in 1955 when I was ten. My father's treatment had halted the polio and the Power was the first side effect. I was in the hospital convalescing. An older, grizzled nurse, impatient with her job and unhappy with her fate, touched me.

It changed both our lives.

I don't think about the Power. It's there when I want it, vanished when no longer needed.

When I place my hand on the driver's shoulder, there's a kind of spark that flows between us. Sort of a direct communication of the soul—like plugging direct into a special link lost to humanity for millions of years. He stops and turns. Our eyes lock. Later, he'll never be able to explain exactly what happened. He'll remember he met a real nice guy, hit it right off and that's about it.

"Hey, buddy," I say. "Where you off to?"

He smiles, takes a puff of the cigarette and frowns. "Smoke bother you?" He asks.

"No," I reply. "But it bothers you."

"Don't I know it, tried to quit but the dammed things are impossible to let go."

I hold my hand out. He grasps it and we shake.

"Name's Jimmy," I say.

"Ed, Ed Murphy."

"Well Ed, try this," I say while I hold the handshake. "Next time you want to light up, think of me, Jimmy, okay? That's all you need."

He blinks, turns his head and spits out the cigarette. Now he turns back and we finally let the handshake go.

"Damn," he says softly.

Ed reaches in his shirt pocket, takes out the pack of Malboros, almost full too, crushes it and flings it away.

"Damn," he says again.

I smile and he smiles back. "Where you going, Ed?" I ask.

"Hauppauge. It's in Long Island, New York. Got a load of meat for the King Kullen supermarkets warehouse. Hey, need a ride?"

"Glad you asked, Ed. I'm going to Long Island myself. Could use a ride."

Ed Murphy smiles and says, "C'mon, it'd be my pleasure."

CHAPTER 22

Joline got to David's office before the secretary came in. David's partner, Martha, awaited her. The door was open and Joline walked in.

Martha got up from her desk and the two women hugged.

"I'm so, so sorry," Martha said softly. Her eyes were red and puffy. She wiped them with the back of her hand. "He's more than a partner, you know, like my own brother. I don't know what happened, but David didn't do anything. Do you have any information on this, Joline? You've got to tell them if you do."

"I don't know anything more than they told me, Martha. There're other people involved, something's going on and David got caught in the middle. I want to get him back and nail the fuckers who did it. Right now I want that more than anything else."

Martha looked at her, just a bit puzzled. "Yeah, you're David's sister, alright. That's what he would have done."

"Has the police stopped by yet?"

"No, but a detective called from the Bronx."

"Anderson?"

"Yeah, that's his name. I told him about that guy from Riggio's wrecking."

"What happened there?"

"This guy, one of the owners, a Mafia-type named Big Al,

and David almost came to blows. David used that martial art stuff and quieted him down."

"You think that guy set him up?"

"I don't know, Joline, I just don't know. I told that to that detective, Anderson. He took all the info and said he'd get on it."

"But you said that happened a couple of weeks ago. What was he doing now?"

Martha didn't answer right away. The phone rang.

"You want to get that?" Joline said.

"No. The office doesn't officially open for another hour. Let the machine take it."

Since it was set for after hours, the recorded greeting came on immediately followed by instructions to leave a message after the beep.

A voice came on, kind of slurred with a drawn out, phony kind of accent.

"Hey, David. It's Kurt, man. I got something new from that shit last night. You didn't return my call, man. Dial me, dude."

"Who's that?" Martha said.

"That's Kurt. I met him once. David bailed him out of some IRS problems."

"Oh yeah, the surfer. I remember."

"I'll call him," Joline said. "So you were going to tell me what David was working on currently."

"Well its nothing dangerous, that's for sure. I mean come on, we're accountants for crying out loud."

"Well something happened and David is missing. I don't give a shit what the evidence is, David didn't do what they said."

"What are they telling you?"

"Drugs, some kind of deal gone bad."

"Bullshit, that's David, my partner. I know him as well as anyone. Well maybe not like you, but still, if there was a drug problem, I'd have known."

"Like I told the cops a hundred times: David didn't do drugs. Now why aren't you telling me about what David was working on?"

Martha looked up and met Joline's eyes. She put down the pen she'd been fiddling with and answered her.

"I'm sorry, Joline. I didn't mean to be evasive. It's just…"

"What?"

"Well, it's probably nothing. David was auditing a not-for-profit foundation. When they take in a certain amount of donations, their tax return must be audited. It's the William Brogan Foundation. It's a charity that studies longevity. That's what David told me."

"So what'd he find? Somebody stealing? Maybe they'd want to keep David quiet after he found out?"

"I doubt it. I mean, he didn't mention anything. If he'd found something like that, he would have told me and we would have reported it. We've been through stuff like that before, so I'm sure it isn't that."

"Well something's bugging you about it. That's for sure, Martha."

Now Joline caught the hesitation in her voice. The woman seemed embarrassed.

"I'm an accountant, Joline. I'm trained in a certain way and it suits my personality. I don't say things unless I can back them up with facts and figures. But this…I don't know."

"Martha, my brother, your partner, is missing and accused of a double murder. That's as much a fact as you can ever get. Do you understand? More than anything I want David back and his name cleared. So tell me."

"Well, okay. The man who hired our firm for this audit, his name is Valdemar Khan. I met him. Spoke to him first. I didn't want to work for him, I told David he didn't have to take this engagement, but he wanted it. The money was very good."

"So what was the problem with this Khan guy?"

"Did you ever visit the snake house in a zoo? You see those poisonous creatures, so alien. You know they'd strike you if they could, just waiting there for someone to make a mistake and stick their hand in the tank. Those eyes, reptilian, alien. That's what this Khan guy reminded me of."

CHAPTER 23

It was late in the afternoon and Father Anthony was finishing taking confessions. There'd been a pretty long line today and the afternoon wore on. Soon it would be dark. The interior lights came on and replaced the vanishing sun's rays as they passed through the stained glass. Muted murmurings came into the confessional as the few remaining worshipers began to leave. The waxy scent of the votive candles mixed with smells of incense in a familiar blend that Father Anthony loved.

He assigned ten Hail Marys, ten Our Fathers and twenty Acts of Contrition to the next to last penitent and waited till the little curtain rustled, indicating the last confession to be taken.

"Bless me Father, for I have sinned," came the voice from the other side of the confessional. Father Anthony recognized it immediately.

"Jimmy?"

"Yes, Father. It's me."

"You came."

"You called me. I will always come. I've never failed you yet."

"Of course, but one wonders sometimes."

"You must have faith, Father."

Father Anthony chuckled. "I'd forgotten how humorous

you could be."

"Much of the trouble in the world is caused by people who take themselves too seriously."

"How true," Father Anthony replied. There was silence for a moment.

"Tell me what has happened, Father."

"A good man died, another is missing, perhaps dead also."

"Good men always die. It's the way of the world. I assume *they* had something to do with it?"

"Yes, or I wouldn't have called you."

"Who was it?"

"A man named Bennett Whittier was killed. Another is missing. His name is David Waterman."

"A parishioner?"

"No. I think he's Jewish. We worked out together. He'd mentioned he was auditing the William Brogan Foundation."

Father Anthony heard the slightest rustle, like a tensing on the other side of the confessional. He had Jimmy's attention for sure.

"What else did he say?"

"Nothing, just that. Then he stopped talking, or coming to the dojo as well. Next thing I hear, he's missing and accused of murder."

"And you think the Foundation's involved?"

"What else could it be? Their usual accountant, a man named Napper Brown, vanished. David Waterman replaces him. A week later he supposedly shoots two men in some sort of drug deal. I know David. I don't believe it."

"You've been keeping an eye on the Foundation. I warned you, Father. It is most dangerous."

"You piqued my interest so many years ago, just as I left the seminary."

"Perhaps I should not have told you so much. Do you remember me saying how dangerous these people were?"

"I remember."

"People die when they get too close to them."

"Perhaps it's time to put a stop to them, Jimmy."

Father Anthony heard a short laugh in the other side of the confessional. It was a youthful sound, the laughter of a teenager. Jimmy had not aged in all the time Father Anthony had known him.

"Father I have all I can do to keep myself alive against these people, let alone take them down."

"There is another life at stake now."

"Who?"

"David Waterman's sister, a woman named Joline. I know her. She won't let it go. Right now she's digging. It's only a matter of time."

"Tell me about it," Jimmy said.

CHAPTER 24

Joline parked her car a couple of hundred yards from the Bronx Precinct house. There weren't any spaces closer. Visitors with pull double parked on the street by the front entrance and left their cards under the windshield. If they didn't have the required juice, they got towed away.

She drove a six years old Camry, plain gray, nondescript, exactly the way she liked it. Although it blended in pretty well, she hoped all the wheels would be on when she got back. It was that kind of a neighborhood.

The precinct was three blocks away and she walked it. The air had that big city morning smell, a combination of concrete dust, asphalt and exhaust. In this area, whiffs of decay rode over it all. Papers and assorted debris flew around her feet, pushed by a brisk morning breeze. In spite of the sun, the world seemed gray to her eyes. Would she ever get to the bottom of David's disappearance? She told herself—yes, she would sort it out. But the fear remained. The palpable terror that David might already be dead, his body rotting somewhere in an unmarked grave. If that happened, a piece of her would be torn out, a chunk of her heart that would never be replaced.

She walked in the precinct and went to the front desk. It was quiet inside. The first shift must have left and very few cops were around. Stale aromas of the previous night's activities still lingered like the remains of a bad dream. Hints of vomit that heavy disinfectant couldn't quite drive away, stale tobacco, coffee and the musty smell of garbage that should have been picked up long ago.

"I have an appointment to see Detective Barry Anderson," she told the desk sergeant.

He frowned, looked down on his paper and didn't answer. She waited.

"You Joline Waterman?" he finally said.

"Yes."

"You ain't gonna see Anderson, he ain't around. You got an appointment with Dee-tective Earl Leroi."

"No I don't. I spoke to Barry Anderson. That's whom I have the appointment with."

The desk sergeant sighed with the weary attitude of bureaucrats everywhere.

"Tell it to city hall, lady. All I know is what's on this here paper. Talk to Earl or don't talk to nobody."

Joline had the sudden urge to bash this pencil-pushing toad in the head. It'd feel so good. But she knew the system as well as anyone. She'd dealt with it often in the course of her business. She sat on the rough wood bench and waited.

Less than five minutes passed and a short, balding black man came out of one of the side offices. What the man lacked in height, he made up in bulk. Joline guessed he'd once been a weight lifter and had let all that muscle turn flabby. He wore an off-color white shirt, plaid tie and a badge hung on a chain around his neck.

"Miss Waterman," he said. "I'm detective Earl Leroi."

"I have an appointment with detective Barry Anderson."

"Yes, I know. I'll be handling it."

She looked at him and he held her gaze.

"I want to see Anderson."

"Come in my office and we'll discuss it," he said.

She followed him into an office not much bigger than her walk-in closet. There was a gun-metal gray file cabinet, shelves and a narrow metal desk. Every inch of space was covered with files and stacked papers of varying sizes. A lot of it was layered with dust as if progress was not a factor in the detective's work. A computer monitor occupied a raised shelf on the desk and a keyboard protruded from the side. A screen saver of cartoon dogs wiggled up and down the monitor.

Earl took some papers from the only chair in the room and placed them on his desk on top of a stack of bulging manila files. He pulled the chair up to the desk and motioned her to sit.

"Can I get you some coffee? We keep a pot on."

"No thank you," Joline said.

Earl made his way behind the desk and sat. Joline thought he looked like a man who didn't enjoy his job at all—at least not at the moment.

"Miss Waterman, Detective Anderson is no longer in charge of your brother's case. I am."

"How come he didn't call me?"

Earl shrugged. "He doesn't have to. I'm telling you now."

"I want to speak to detective Anderson."

"Look, you see all this?" Earl said, waiving his hand around the stacked papers. "They're all missing person cases in the Bronx. Some are as old as five years. I've got'em all, me and three other guys. I have absolutely no time for bullshit. You want to talk to me, fine. You want to chase around for Barry Anderson, go ahead. Up to you."

Suddenly she knew with certainty that she'd get nowhere with this man. Something had changed. She felt betrayed, like her brother's disappearance had set in motion a series of treachery that was only now beginning to appear.

She stood, didn't say a word and walked out of the cramped office.

CHAPTER 25

Stuck in traffic on the Throgs Neck Bridge, Joline felt her blood begin to boil. Nothing moved and she heard on the radio of an accident further up on the Belt Parkway. She picked up her cell phone and hit Fred Walters' speed-dial number. He answered immediately.

"Fred, it's me."

"Joline, you okay?"

"Good as I'm going to ever be. I need some help."

"Sure. What do you want me to do?"

"Something's going on at NYPD in the Bronx, something to do with my brother's disappearance. Two days ago I spoke with a detective Barry Anderson. He was going to work the case, looked like he knew what he was doing. Now he's apparently taken off the case, replaced by a detective named Earl Leroi, and the guy doesn't seem to give a shit. I know we got contacts inside NYPD. Find out what's going on if you can. Also get me information on these two detectives, Anderson and Leroi, and get me Anderson's phone number. I need to talk to him."

"Should be doable. I'll get on it. What else?"

"I dunno, Fred. Just a feeling, but I want to carry—all the time."

There was a hesitation and she pictured Fred on the phone, worry lines creasing his forehead.

"Fred?"

"Yeah, Joline. But I'm concerned. Why don't I send one of our guys to hang with you. Jerry's free and so's Don."

"No, nothing like that. Just get me the permit so I can carry my weapon all the time. You know how to do it."

"Okay, I'll put you as a supervisor on a current protection case. I'll register you tomorrow so you can carry concealed. But don't be stupid. Tell me what's going on."

"I did. Somebody took a competent detective off my brother's case and put it on a lower level guy who's so swamped he could care less. That's all I got. Maybe it's nothing, I dunno."

"Okay, just keep me in the loop and don't play it dumb. You coming in tomorrow?"

"Yeah, I should. Talk to you then."

She disconnected and traffic began moving again. It took a half hour to get through the Throgs Neck and the Long Island Expressway wasn't much better. It was nearly noon by the time she reached her apartment.

She pulled a small notepad from her pocketbook, opened it and dialed a number.

"Surf's up," came the answer. The voice was young and she pictured a gum cracking teenage clerk.

"Kurt, please."

"He's not in. Hasn't been around the shop all day."

She dialed Kurt's house and got the recording again. After digging in her pocketbook, she found his cell phone number. David had given it to her once. If ever she needed a computer whiz, Kurt was the guy, he had said. She dialed it, the ringing went on and on, but no message. She let it ring.

Finally someone answered. The voice sounded wary, as if the owner was afraid of being bitten.

"Hello?"

"Is this Kurt?"

"Uh, yeah. Who's this?"

"Joline Waterman. You know my brother, David, the accountant. I'm looking for him. He disappeared."

Silence. She waited.

"Kurt?"

"Yeah, I'm here."

"I'm calling about my brother. You know what happened?"

"I heard. I called his office yesterday. Look, I'm not sure we should be talking." There was an edge in his voice. The man was scared, about as far from the carefree surfer as you can get.

"Why shouldn't we be talking, Kurt?"

"Look, I'm getting out of here. I got somebody to take the shop for a while, cause I'm leaving. I don't know where David is, but there's something big going on and more people are going to get killed over it. I know it. I want out of here."

"Alright, Kurt. I appreciate where you're coming from. But my brother's disappeared and he may be in danger. I'm going to find him and get to the bottom of it. You understand, Kurt? We need to talk before you go."

"No fuckin' way, man. Gimme your email and I'll send you what I know anonymously so nobody can trace it to me, okay?"

She decided to bluff it out.

"No, it's not okay, Kurt. Here's the deal: We meet and you give me all the information about what went on with you and my brother and the William Brogan Foundation. Once you do that, you're clear. You disappear into the happy surfing ground."

"Sorry, I ain't doing it."

"Fine, here's the alternative: I yank on my contacts at NYPD, including Detective Barry Anderson at Bronx homicide. They pull you in as a material witness, question the shit outta you, let the whole world know what's going on then release you to hang out and dry all by yourself. You want that Kurt?"

Silence, then finally;

"Shit, man. David once told me he had a sister who's a tough chick."

"You have no idea, Kurt."

"Okay, I mean, I feel bad about your brother. He's a righteous dude and helped me out. I tried to return the favor, that's all, and the worst part, I think that whatever happened, had everything to do with that. Shit, man, I just tried to help him, like he asked."

"That's what I'm after. I want to know what you did for him."

"We got to be careful."

"We will be. Here's what I want you to do," and she told him.

CHAPTER 26

I think after over two hundred years, it may finally come to a head. The world is changing too rapidly for things to remain the same. Natural supplies are dwindling, population is increasing exponentially and the baby boomers are aging, sucking up precious resources.

I read about a subdivision they built out in Arizona. When they prepared the land, they bulldozed a culvert that'd been sheltering several nests of rattlesnakes. Three workmen were bitten and one died. The changes and activities drove the snakes from underground—just like modern changes are driving *them* from under their rocks. Only they're far deadlier than any nest of rattlesnakes. I know, I've been up against them for better than sixty years.

I'm pretty upset over what Father Anthony told me. Something's going on, that's for sure. I've heard and seen other things also, and like weathervanes, they tell me of dangerous events yet to come.

From what I figure those things have caused financial ripples. They're excellent at covering their tracks. They like the shadows. It hides their even darker secrets. But sometimes things get too far out of hand. Like a pressure cooker with steam escaping from its sides, wisps of information get out and financial issues come to light. That's probably what happened to the first accountant, and most definitely why the second one, that David Waterman fellow disappeared.

The snakes are starting to come out and they're biting.

I got a room at Holiday Inn with internet access. I've done some research. Also I've visited the offices of the missing David Waterman, CPA. Spoke to his partner, Martha. Got some information, but not nearly enough.

Next I'm going to talk to his sister, Joline.

CHAPTER 27

Joline turned off the Long Island Expressway onto the William Floyd Parkway. She headed south, toward the ocean and Smith's Point. Ten minutes later she reached the bridge that spanned the Great South Bay, separating it from Fire Island. At that spot and for miles running on either side, the island is just a spit of sand, a barrier separating the bay from the Atlantic. It was unseasonably cold for early December. The wind blew hard, pushing errant flakes of snow from a sky like gray cottage cheese.

She crossed the bridge and entered Smith Point Park. It was practically deserted as she took the road toward the campground—also closed, wouldn't even open for another five months.

She passed the Park Police station with a solitary car parked in front, and continued for a few more yards. Driving her car off the road, she pulled onto the packed-sand shoulder. She'd stopped directly in front of a waist high concrete wall.

Joline got out of the car took the pathway that led directly behind the walk into the stone and concrete structure itself. This was the TWA 800 monument built facing the spot on the ocean where the jetliner went down over a decade ago. No one was there. Fresh flowers and a variety of talismans testified to visits by those who cared and perhaps had even lost loved ones.

Right now though, the place was deserted. That's why Joline had chosen this spot to meet Kurt. The man sounded on the edge of paranoia, she knew he'd spook easily.

She was early. The gray daylight grew dimmer and shadows blended in the murky evening. A strong northeast wind kicked up the surf and crashing waves masked all other noises save for the raucous cry of seagulls. Sand peppered her feet and legs, blown into the monument area from the beach. The air smelled clean and salty. In a few months the season would start and this place would be packed with tourists and locals.

The lights came on as night fell. She spotted a solitary set of headlamps and followed them as a car crossed the bridge. The vehicle continued on the roadway and pulled off the road, parking right behind her car.

Kurt drove an old Buick station wagon, from the eighties, Joline figured. It was big enough to hold tons of equipment plus surfboards on the carriers built onto the roof rack. She recognized Kurt when he got out of the car. She'd met him once and he hadn't changed. Dreadlocks, John Lennon glasses, flower shirt under a worn bomber jacket and light cotton pants in spite of the freezing weather. He looked like an aged California beach bum transplanted into a New York winter.

He paused and looked around. His head flitted back and forth as if to discern some hidden enemy. He saw Joline but didn't go toward her immediately. She waited.

Finally, Kurt stepped into the walkway where Joline stood.

"Hey," he said. He looked around again, turned and faced her. "Anybody follow you?" he asked.

"Yeah, Kurt, a whole army. I told them to wait till you got here."

"Not funny, man."

"Don't I know that?" she said. "Two men are murdered and my brother is missing, remember? But I'm careful, not paranoid."

He nodded and his eyes continued flickering, around, behind, out front. The man was petrified.

"Tell me what's happening, Kurt. Have you noticed anything unusual since my brother's disappearance."

"I think so. I mean, I started paying attention when I found out. There were some people I didn't recognize, like they were looking at the shop, looking for me. One of them came in, asked some questions, said he wanted to surf, but it was bullshit. I can tell. Then my phone…"

"Your phone?"

"Yeah, I mean there's a click when I pick it up now. I heard that's a telltale sign of monitoring. Shit, I don't know, man. Maybe I am paranoid, seeing things, know what I mean? What I saw with David, and then the way those guys got killed and David vanished. It's gotta be related, man. There's some heavy duty shit goin' down, I know it."

"Tell me how you got involved in this stuff with my brother."

"He asked me to help him hack into a website."

"What? My brother hacking?"

"Yeah, way outta line for him. He's the straightest dude I know. For him to get me to help him do that, he was digging up some real gnarly shit, and I think that's the reason for everything that happened."

"Do you know what it was he found?"

"Something with lots of money, big money. I got it on flash drives."

"What are you talking about, Kurt?"

"When I hacked this site, Bank of Zurich…"

"Bank of Zurich? You and David hacked into a Swiss bank? What the hell were you smoking?"

Kurt took a deep breath and drew his bomber jacket tighter. The cement wall kept out most of the wind, but it was still freezing, and getting colder as the night deepened.

"We were as straight as a couple'a Catholic monks, Joline. David thought this foundation was involved in some major illegal financial shit. He wanted to get to the bottom of it."

"Alright, tell me about what you recorded. How'd you do that anyway?"

"I got a sleeper program built into my machine. When I surf websites, it records each page. I had the program running that night and transferred it to a couple of flash drives. Everything David saw, I got on drive. Here, you might as well take it," he said, handing her a small device. "I don't understand it, you need a financial dude like David to figure it out."

Kurt paused as Joline held up her hand. Headlights flashed on the road, slowly getting brighter. A car approached at low speed. Joline leaned out and saw a Park Police SUV coming. She pulled Kurt into the shadows. The SUV came off the road and parked behind Kurt's Buick.

"S'okay, its cops. We ain't' doing nothing wrong, man," Kurt said.

Two officers got out of the car. One remained by the SUV and the other walked toward the monument.

"Hey, you, come out of there," she heard the man say.

Joline pulled Kurt deeper into the shadows toward the beach. There were only a few more feet when a spotlight created a wide pool of incandescent light that almost reached the water's edge.

She saw the officer draw his weapon. She recognized it and knew something was definitely wrong. She pulled Kurt down just in time. The officer fired two shots. The rounds hit the monument above them in a tight group. It barely missed them. Little shrapnel of blasted granite flew about them. Joline felt a stinging on her cheeks. She crouched down lower. There was nowhere to go. She wished she'd brought her own weapon, but she hadn't gotten it from Fred yet. Now she saw the other officer run to the side, covering the shooter. They hadn't called on the radio. The long barrel of the heavy caliber automatics they used, told her it was far from a traditional law enforcement weapon. These guys weren't cops.

Now the first shooter held a flashlight and the beam stabbed her and Kurt, clearly exposing them. She saw the backup man approaching and the first shooter hold the weapon toward them. The eye of the barrel fixed them and Kurt whimpered.

There was nowhere to go and in the monument's sodium light, she saw the contraction of the gunman's hand as he began to pull the trigger.

CHAPTER 28

I used one of my licenses and credit cards to get a rental car. It's good for one-shot, a throw away ID that can't be traced. I'd been following the woman, David's sister, for the better part of the day. From what Father Anthony had told me, I figured she'd be on their target list. I followed her until she reached the bridge leading over to Smith's Point. I'd be spotted then because the place was practically deserted. Since I wore a warm-up suit and jacket, the disguise was natural—jogger.

I parked the car and took the pedestrian path across the bridge, following their headlamps as they crossed and traveled on the road a hundred yards or so to the TWA 800 memorial. I decided to stop halfway there in case they decided to leave, that way I'd have time to double back to my car so I wouldn't lose them.

I saw the second car cross over, a relic of an old, big Buick wagon. I watched the car park behind the woman's car and saw the driver get out. The guy was a skinny hippy-type. He appeared nervous, glancing about him with quick, darting movements. No threats there—the woman was obviously meeting the newcomer.

I broke into a light jog, didn't want to be too far from them at this point, and that's when I saw the two police officers.

They came out of the security offices and they didn't act like park cops. Something was going down.

I started running while I kept my eyes on the two cops. They'd removed weapons from their belts, long barreled automatics, not the kind cops normally use. Holding the weapons in a classic combat stance, they headed toward the TWA 800 monument.

I tugged my little homemade weapon from its place while putting on a burst of speed. I can run quite fast when needed, faster than most athletes in fact.

It didn't take me long to reach them, but it looked like it might be too late. I couldn't see the woman, Joline, nor the guy she'd met. The wall of the memorial hid them both. The pseudo-cops however were clearly visible. The first one leveled his weapon and I heard two shots. The second guy moved in as backup. There's no time. Even now I might be too late. I set the weapon and drew on the far shooter.

My creation is both humane and powerful. It's actually a slingshot made out of composite synthetic rubber and plastic. It fires hard rubber bullets the size of a man's thumb. The whole thing folds into an inoffensive rubber ball invisible to detection devices.

My first shot hits the guy in the head. He drops his gun and falls to his knees, I hit him again and this time he's down for good. He'll wake up in an hour or two with a hell of a goose egg on his head and a monster headache.

Now I reach the monument and fire another rubber bullet at the second gunman. He's drawing a bead on Joline and the man. They're huddled down, just visible at the dark edge of the wall.

The hard rubber pellet hits the guy in the back of the head, just above the neck. He drops to his knees—they always do. Now I slam the guy in the stomach and he falls completely, retching. He drops the gun and I kick it away.

I fold my slingshot and walk a few steps to the two people huddled there.

CHAPTER 29

Joline had reached a point where she knew she was going to die. She wondered if she'd see David, be reunited in some kind of angel's white light. Time slowed down and the air thickened. Her senses picked up things normally ignored. The thin cry of a seagull out on the ocean, the rustle of windblown sand about her and the cold chill of sea brushed air. She stared into the open dark hole of the big-bore gun. The face of the man remained shrouded in darkness so Joline couldn't see his eyes when a curious thing happened.

She heard a soft thud, like someone tapping on a cantaloupe. The gunman dropped the weapon and fell to his knees. Joline scrambled back, pushing Kurt along, neither of them managing to stand.

A figure ran out of the shadows and deftly hit the man. He collapsed with a grunt and the newcomer kicked the gun out into the sand.

For a moment Joline thought she'd been affected in some way, that she was hallucinating. The guy who had saved their lives was just a kid—high school or maybe a precocious first year college freshman. He wore a simple tracksuit, jacket and running shoes. He wasn't agitated about downing a deadly, armed man. Not more than, say, a youth climbing to level two of some new video game.

Yeah, Joline thought, just a pleasant, harmless-looking kid, yet there was something about him Joline couldn't quite place her finger on. She suddenly thought that maybe she'd seen him before. The kid smiled at them.

"Hi, I'm Jimmy," he said.

"What the fuck, dude," Kurt said. He looked at the gunman down on the walk then started to backpedal toward the beach. Joline stopped him with an arm on his shoulder.

"Actually that might not be a bad idea, miss," Jimmy said. "Those are not the only two guys around. They usually send three teams at once."

"Who are you?" Joline said.

"I told you, Jimmy."

"Yeah, I got that. But who *are* you?"

"I know you've got questions, but first we need to get out of here, then I'll answer them."

"Good idea," Kurt said. He started toward the road. Jimmy stopped him with an arm on his chest.

"If you go back this way they'll pick you right up with that big wagon. You'll be in surfer's heaven before morning."

"Oh man, I don't know shit. I just helped David hack into a website. I don't even know what I got. I'll just give it to you and split, okay?"

"They'll torture you first to find out where the data is. Then they'll kill you. Either way you'll be dead. You have no choice. It's already done."

Joline said nothing but continued staring at Jimmy. A burst of wind sent a scattering of snowflakes around them. At the bridge another set of headlights appeared, slowing down at first then picking up speed.

"That's it folks. We're out of time, let's haul ass," Jimmy said.

CHAPTER 30

They ran to the beach until they were past the light from the TWA 800 monument, up close to the crashing waves. Jimmy led the way, Kurt was in the middle, pushed on by Joline. The wind howled right off the ocean, cold as arctic pack ice. Spray misted on their faces and the surf blotted out all other sounds. Up near the road they saw the headlights stop near the monument and another set of lamps indicated a second car further down. The second and third teams, like Jimmy had said.

Jimmy led them about a hundred yards or so before he headed back toward the road. At that point the road curved away and a large concrete block building stood with its own little path leading to the main road. The building had a big door on rollers. A serious-looking padlock secured the door to the concrete frame.

"Man, I'm freezing my ass off. We should just talk to these dudes. Whatta we doing here, anyway?"

"Kurt, you better stop smoking all that weed. You brain cells are fried. Just shut up and follow, okay?" Joline said.

Kurt looked at her, at least Joline thought so, she couldn't make out his features in the dark. He didn't reply and pulled out a cigarette. She slapped it out of his hand.

"Why don't you just wave at them with a flashlight?" she said.

She looked at Jimmy. He was bent over the lock, doing something she couldn't' see. She heard a metallic click. Jimmy had opened the lock somehow–must have picked it, in the dark too. Best trick she'd seen in a long time.

Jimmy slid the door back and before Joline could say anything, told them to wait there and disappeared in the dark interior.

He wasn't gone more than a few minutes when they heard the low pitch growl of a small engine and a boxy shape on wheels came out of the dark building.

"Climb on," Jimmy said.

"What the hell is that?" Kurt asked.

"It's a beach utility vehicle. An ATV. The Park Department uses it for beach patrols. It'll get us away pretty fast."

"Yeah, but where, Jimmy? This is part of Fire Island. The next bridge is in Nassau County, thirty or forty miles from here," Joline said.

"Yeah, and they'll be watching it too just like this bridge. You can bet on it. That's why we're going to find another way, now get on."

She didn't have a better idea so she told Kurt to get on and climbed on it herself.

The ATV controls were similar to a motorcycle with the throttle on the steering handle. Jimmy drove close to the water's edge and the sound of the engine disappeared in the crashing noise of the surf.

He drove for about fifteen minutes and the lights of the road and bridge slowly vanished. Even though the sky was overcast, a sort of luminescence floated from the sea so it wasn't pitch black. Lights from waterfront homes across the bay danced on the choppy water.

Jimmy veered away from the ocean side and started riding close to the bay. He slowed the ATV and scanned the beach as he drove.

"What are you looking for?" Joline asked. He didn't reply, just kept going, and looking at the dark beach on the bay side.

"Dude?" Kurt said.

Now Jimmy stopped the ATV and shut off the engine. He pointed in the darkness.

"There."

"There, what?" Joline said.

Jimmy didn't reply. He jumped from the ATV, took off his shoes in two fluid motions and stepped into the water.

"Dude, this ain't no time to go for a swim," Kurt said.

Jimmy waded a few feet into the water. It barely reached his knees. Now they couldn't see him. Joline stepped to the water's edge.

"Jimmy? You alright?"

Now his form appeared out of the darkness. Another large shape lurked behind him. When he got closer Joline saw it was a wide rowboat covered with swamp grass.

"It's a duck boat. Hunters use it and leave it moored in shallow waters in the bay rather than lug it home at night. No one steals them, well, except for tonight, but we have no choice."

"Dude, how'd you see that thing?"

"I have good eyesight."

Joline thought she'd have to talk to him about that sometime. Good vision was one thing. Perfect night vision was another—and how'd he opened that lock so fast in the dark?

They got in the boat and Jimmy pulled two sets of oars from the bottom.

"They don't use outboards. Wild ducks are too smart. They'd spot the unnatural looking motor. They just row a few yards out in the bay."

Joline and Kurt sat on the rear bench where Jimmy directed them. He handed them one oar each and took a set himself.

"At this point the bay is less than two miles wide. We should make it across fairly quick."

They rowed smoothly and the exertion warmed them. Jimmy rowed with long, powerful strokes, both pulling and guiding the clumsy duck boat. It wasn't long before Kurt started wheezing and coughing. His oar slipped out of the water several times until Joline finally took it.

"I better quit smoking, man," Kurt said.

"And doing weed," Joline replied. "You'll be a complete burnout before you hit forty."

They'd made it almost three quarters of the way across when they heard it bouncing off the water—a rhythmic thumping steadily growing louder.

"Helicopter," Jimmy said.

"Is it looking for us?" Kurt said.

"Has to be. There's no other reason for a chopper to be here tonight."

Now the machine appeared with flashing strobes reaching to the ground and searchlights piercing the night, floating bright patches on the dark waters. The chopper made a wide turn and headed toward them.

"Duck down under the weed," Joline said. "Maybe they'll think it's an abandoned duck boat."

She saw Jimmy's smile in the echoes of the reflected strobe lights from the helicopter.

"Won't work. They'll have infrared thermal imaging."

The helicopter moved directly over them. It steadied to a low hover, no more than fifty feet. The backwash from the big propellers blew away the marsh grasses disguising the boat. The noise deafened them and twin spotlights skewered them into a brilliant circle of light.

CHAPTER 31

Something horribly painful intruded into his skull, pulsing in waves of pain tuned with his heartbeat. He was in total darkness, and it took a few moments for David to realize that his eyes were closed. He needed a conscious effort to force his eyelids open as if someone had decided to Crazy-Glue them together. Once open it wasn't much better.

He was in a world of gloom and pain. He tried to sit up and a wave of nausea went through him. Retching, he fell back down. His head banged on the floor and he just lay there while starbursts of pain marched through his head.

Time passed and he lay still as things settled down. He tried again, slowly this time. Running his hand over his head, he felt crusted blood matted in his hair. His fingers passed over a goose egg topped by a gash. He remembered working in the foundation's office–last night–how long ago exactly? He couldn't tell. There'd been a commotion of some sort in the hallway outside the office. He recalled getting up from his desk, stepping out the door and that was it. Now he was here—wherever here was. He took in his surroundings, and relaxed his muscles as he sat in a lotus position.

The air had that pleasant smell you find in antique shops and very old places, the scent of aged wood and materials that have been around for hundreds of years. The room was filled with gloom, the only illumination coming from the tiny openings between the door and windows and their frames. The floor was made of oak-planks, tongue and groove, solid and perfectly aligned like plots in a graveyard, the room empty and silent.

David cleared his mind and waited.

CHAPTER 32

Bracing herself on one elbow, Joline starts to rise from the floor of the boat. Jimmy reaches out, grasps her arm and holds her back. The helicopter above them sends out a gale of wind, flattening the swamp grass covering the duck boat they're huddled in. Kurt stands, blinking in the spotlight, wild-eyed fear plastering his face. Joline sees Jimmy reaching for him, but Kurt is in the front and the distance is too great. An amplified voice booms out of the hovering machine above them. The words are unintelligible, snatched away by the chopping blades.

Kurt leans out and dives into the black water. Joline screams at him. Her voice disappears in the din. Kurt swims away from the boat. The spotlight follows him and the amplified voice of someone in the helicopter booms out again. This time she catches a few words: Stop…will fire…Kurt keeps going. With all his time in the water he's a strong swimmer.

It came down straight from the open side hatch of the machine, hidden from Joline's sight. A stream of bullets from an unseen automatic weapon boils the water around Kurt.

He flings his arms up and Joline sees his eyes open wide. Kurt's body jerks like a marionette in spasms under a crazed puppeteer. Gouts of blood erupt from his chest as he falls back and disappears beneath the darkness of the choppy bay.

Joline froze under the enormity of what had just happened. She turned to Jimmy and he grasped her hand. His fingers locked on hers and something passed from his body to hers.

Time stopped in a psychic suspension. Joline saw the whirring blades of the helicopter as if they stood still. She felt a burst of energy from Jimmy and for a flash, she understood, looked into his soul and he into hers. She'd never known this kind of sensation, didn't even understand how it could exist. It was as if their brains, their souls, everything that they were, suddenly fused for a flashing, never-forgotten moment. She felt the energy pour from him. Suddenly she understood what had to be done and the moment was broken.

They dove into the dark water as the helicopter spun back toward them. The icy shock of the water flashed through her. It would have paralyzed her flesh, but Jimmy was there. Heat poured from him, warmed her. She followed him under the water.

Visibility was less than a foot. She couldn't see her hands or Jimmy. A dull glow from above told her that the helicopter's spotlight was above them. She kicked out, Jimmy's hand still enfolding hers. Moments later the glow vanished and they came up for a gulping breath. The helicopter was just a few feet to their left. The spotlight speared down into the black water, searching. They swam away until the beam continued a wide circle and approached them once more. They dove under the water again and again.

Joline felt the eel grass at the bottom brush her face. She tasted salt water and tidal mud. Her lungs were about to burst and the frigid water threatened to take her breath away and stung her flesh until she could no longer feel her limbs. But Jimmy hung on and his energy passed to her like flowing electric currents from some psychic transformer.

The glow of the spotlight disappeared as the machine

moved on. They surfaced again and swam further on. The search circles were getting longer as the helicopter covered an ever-increasing area without seeing them. Every minute they weren't spotted brought them closer to safety–if they survived the cold.

They continued that way for what seemed an eternity. The frigid water sucked out her energy, driving out her very life force steadily, inexorably.

Joline's head popped up from the water again as the helicopter moved away. She opened her mouth and sucked in salty, cold water. She coughed and gagged.

"I can't...can't"

And Jimmy was there.

"Hang on Joline, you can do it. Feel my hand, it's warm."

And it was warm. Jimmy was like a little nuclear furnace, passing life-sustaining heat to her. But still, the water seemed to reach her very core and freeze her blood. She felt a strange warmness steal over her. It would be so easy to just surrender, let go.

"Joline, think of David, your brother," said the voice of the strange man holding her up.

David. Her brother's image suddenly floated before her eyes.

"He's being held somewhere. You're the only one who can help him, Joline."

David.

"Okay...kay...gotta hang on..." She threw her arm around him and they kept swimming.

Now Joline sensed the mud bottom beneath her feet. She really couldn't feel her limbs and her teeth chattered uncontrollably. A dim corner of her mind told her hypothermia was approaching. She knew the only thing that kept her going was Jimmy's grasp on her hand and that weird psychic energy that poured into her. She stepped a few feet further and the water only reached her waist. Her feet sank in the soft mud. She grasped a handful of marsh grass and pulled herself on the bank while Jimmy helped her.

"Atta girl, hang on, we're there now. Just hang on." He was panting, his voice wavering just a notch.

Over the bay the lights of the helicopter dimmed as the machine headed out of the area. A night breeze flowed over her soaked body bringing the tang of the ocean and mud scents of the tidal flats. They had made it to the other side. The lights of the bridge cast a pool of light whose edges barely reached them. Joline felt a warm lassitude overtake her senses and she slowly sank to her knees.

CHAPTER 33

I felt the bottom rise beneath my feet. Another couple of yards, and we reached the shore. I helped Joline onto the small sand dune marking the edge of the bay.

Her eyes were glazing and I knew I was losing her. I held her hand, put my arm around her waist and focused on her.

"C'mon, Joline. Almost there, don't give out on me now, girl."

All I needed was a few more minutes. If I collapsed, we were both lost. We staggered up the walkway parallel to the bridge. My car was parked at one of the side streets near the end of the bridge's pedestrian path.

It seemed as if it would never end, but we made it somehow. Just as we reached my rental car, two police cruisers flew by on the main road, sirens howling. In the distance I heard the approaching noises of more emergency vehicles. The real cops must have been alerted to the mayhem at the memorial.

I put Joline in the front seat, started the engine and blasted the heat. It took a while to warm up the interior.

"We need to get you out of those wet clothes," I said.

She looked at me, her mouth moved and then she understood.

"Alright, alright…help me…Jesus, I can barely move."

I got her out of the soaked clothing and wrapped her in

my jacket. I felt my own energy dissipating. We had to get somewhere safe and warm, fast. There was only one place like that I knew around here.

I looked over at her, huddled in the front seat like a drowned kitten. Her eyes were closed. I shook her.

"Joline, Joline, look at me."

She didn't answer. I grasped her head with both my hands, leaned forward until our foreheads touched. She opened her eyes, blinked. She seemed to focus on me and I knew she was back.

"Who are you?" she whispered.

"Someone who needs you alive. Stay with me. Don't fall asleep and you'll be okay."

She nodded and shivered violently. The car's blower blasted out a stream of hot air from the vents and she leaned her face into it.

"I'll hang in there. Just get us the fuck out of here."

That's when I knew she'd be okay.

I took William Floyd Parkway back to the Long Island Expressway and headed west. The heater blasted away and the temperature climbed. We desperately needed the heat, soaked it into our bodies.

It must have been two in the morning. The roads were thankfully deserted. This would have been a very bad time to run across one of the hit teams. Even explanations to disbelieving authorities would have been difficult.

Finally I pulled off the expressway and turned into a wide, empty boulevard. Following a series of side streets I found the familiar buildings; St Agnes church and the attached rectory. I parked the car close as I could get and helped Joline out of the passenger's side. She hugged my jacket around herself. Her legs were bare but dry by now. I rang the doorbell. No answer. I pounded on the door and finally heard movement inside but no lights came on.

Before I could react, the door flung open and a huge figure reached out of the darkness. I couldn't make out his face but there was no denying the glint of the big bore automatic in his hand—aimed exactly between my eyes.

CHAPTER 34

Andre Dumont Castle, Sixty-two miles from Essex, Connecticut

Valdemar Khan looked out the window of the Bell Ranger 11B helicopter that carried him. Andre Dumont castle rose out of piney woods, dotted with hills, clearly visible at this altitude. Although it was more a collection of large revolutionary-era brick buildings, linked together by perfectly tended walkways and gardens, it had been called a castle since its creator, Pierre Dumont, one of the conspirators who had created the Essex Junta in 1802, had first built it three years later.

The main building stood back into the woods, outlined by the remains of last week's snowfall. To the left of the old brick structure a maple grove flanked a helipad marked by three giant red X's on the pristine tarmac with two of the X's obscured by helicopters. Khan recognized the sleek, predatory shape of a Dassault Hirondelle. The machine was a civilian version of a European copy of the US Apache attack helicopter. Khan would bet it had quite a few surprises built into it for a "civilian" chopper. The machine belonged to Anton Dimitri, its dark predatory shape carried a sense of menace as if it would suddenly jump to life, shredding anything that dared cross its path–just like its owner would.

Khan's helicopter settled on the remaining X of the helipad. The pilot pushed some buttons and the door lifted open. Khan stepped out before the rotors settled to a stop.

The air was brisk and cold with no hint of the warming that wouldn't come for months. Foliage-bearing ornamental trees lined the walkway their branches awaiting the buds that would turn into leaves when tropical breezes came down from the south. Still it felt good and smelled clean.

Two men met Khan by the helicopter. They were oriental, wore dark jumpsuits and appeared unarmed. Khan knew better. He nodded to the men and they each returned a slight bow. They followed him a few steps behind. He knew the way.

As he walked toward the building he noticed the parking lot. Several Mercedes, an armored Bentley, a couple of Cadillac limousines with their chauffeurs inside or loitering near their vehicles. Counting the passengers of the helicopters, the Junto would be complete.

Khan reached the door and it opened before he could grasp the handle. A silent man in colonial livery stood just inside, his hand extended in a welcoming gesture.

Khan ignored him and stepped inside. More jump-suited guards stood in the great hallway. They stepped aside and bowed as he passed. He turned into a wide, marbled corridor and followed it to a massive oak door. Another livery attendant opened the door. In spite of its obvious great weight, it slid open effortlessly on machined hinges. Khan walked in.

The room was long and wide with heavy dark paneling. It looked as if it had been modeled from a governor's mansion in Colonial days. Paintings hung on the wall— famous expensive ones depicting varying stages of American history. From Winchester to Whistler, this collection would have been the envy of many museums.

The centerpiece of the room was a giant table crafted over two hundred years ago from prime New England oak. Around the table were arranged ten plush, antique chairs.

Each chair had intricate carvings on the tops of the high-backs and armrests. Each seat but one was occupied. Khan stepped in and sat in the remaining seat.

Ten men seated around the table, glancing at each other, saying nothing. Khan didn't have to look at his watch to know it was a few minutes before nine in the morning. Two ornate candelabras hung above the table. They provided no light yet the room was perfectly well lit with no visible source of illumination. The technology in the room was astounding in its scope and cutting edge, yet one would be hard pressed to find it until it manifested itself. A huge intricate grandfather clock stood in one corner of the room, complex gears turning silently within. At exactly nine o'clock a muted whirring of gears sounded and the clock sounded nine deep notes.

Like the others seated at the vast table, Khan turned his attention to the wall facing the head of the table.

A panel slid back on precision-machined hinges and darkness emerged from the opening. It wasn't so much darkness, but rather an absorption of light. A cube the approximate size of a small automobile floated toward the table. Within the cube no light escaped, as if somehow a cosmic black hole had been brought inside this room. Khan fought the urge to flinch, to retreat from this apparition. Intellectually he knew it was the product of the highest technology, a reversal of the properties of lasers, a complete blanking out of light. On a gut level, the effect was disturbing.

The darkness rolled to the edge of the head of the table and stopped. The voice that came from within was smooth, well modulated, a voice that exuded authority, the kind of command that made a listener want to follow it. Khan knew that years of psychology and reams of technology had gone into the creation of that voice.

"Welcome, gentlemen. This meeting of the Essex Junta is now in session," the voice said. "We have much to discuss. First and most important item is security. Mr. Anton Dimitri, you are the Security Chair. Please report to us on the threat to the Abelia-Vie plants in Mexico."

Anton stood. He wore opaque glasses that shielded his eyes. Standing very still his body looked poised to strike at some unseen enemy. His glance traveled through the nine Chairs until it returned to settle on the cube of darkness. His voice held a deep quality like distant thunder.

"Thank you, Mister Chairman. As you all know, the Abelia-Vie Plants can only grow in the mountain regions near Puerto Valerta. That is most unfortunate. The area is uncivilized and very dangerous. While drugs are not actually produced there, it has become a major pathway toward the US border. Scores of bandits and assorted outlaw prowl the region. We've had tight security, but one of those we hired turned on us. Took over the growing field and attempted to extort us."

"Did we pay him, Mister Dimitri?"

"Paying is not the problem. We could afford it. But if we did, we'd send a signal of weakness. We would wind up in escalating demands until another rival took over. It would turn into a spiral that would end up in the probable destruction of the field."

"That must never be allowed. You know the importance of the field."

"I do, Mister Chairman. That is why I acted personally and immediately."

"We succeeded I gather?"

"Yes we did. I killed them, a fearsome outlaw who went by the name El Gaucho and his second, Little Juan. I left their bodies as an example and placed a team of mercenaries to keep it secure. It will be a while before someone else tries it."

"A while?"

"Yes, a while. Another outlaw will come along. They always do. When the Abelia-Vie plant and its fields were discovered in 1819, the world was different. The area was a desert. The only ones interested in it were botanists and biologists. Things have changed a great deal. There's only one solution to securing the crop: Move it to a secure location. Have we made progress on this yet?"

"That would be a question for one of our Science Chairs, Botany. Progress report please."

Another man pushed his chair back and stood. He was stooped with a shock of white hair and thick granny glasses. His voice belied the somewhat eccentric appearance. It was a voice of authority, backed by certain knowledge.

"No, Mister Chairman, we have not found the answer yet. We have been searching since the serum was first created and its properties accidentally discovered in the mid-1800's. We have managed to grow the Abelia-Vie plant in our laboratories, but the serum derived from those plants doesn't work. There is something in that area, an element that has eluded us. The only effective serum comes only from those plants grown naturally in that region. Nowhere else. You may be assured we will continue our efforts. Our very survival depends upon it."

The room remained silent as the Science-Botany Chair sat down. The voice from the dark cube returned.

"It is satisfying that you have re-secured the field, Mister Dimitri. But we have other security concerns remaining, do we not?"

Khan felt Dimitri's gaze on him as he replied.

"We do Mister Chairman. They are centered upon the William Brogan Foundation and its accountants."

"Explain."

"US Federal treasury regulations require annual certified audits of the foundation because of the amounts of money…shall we say…donated to it. One accountant had been doing this satisfactorily for a number of years. Last year it was determined he had delved into areas we wished to remain confidential."

"Isn't that the job of an auditor?"

"Strictly speaking, no. When we discovered this, the man attempted to flee. From his rather clumsy attempts to cover his tracks, we surmised he carried knowledge that would have been detrimental to our efforts. I eliminated him."

"And that ended the matter?"

"I'm afraid not. Mister Khan, the Foundation Chair, found another accountant to perform this audit. Within one week we caught a cybernetic break-in from his computer into our Bank of Lucerne accounts. It was determined our transfer sheets were viewed. Once again I was forced to act. Mister Khan, perhaps you would elaborate on our rationale."

Khan stood up. He felt a vague discomfort at the situation. Somehow it appeared as if he was partly responsible–and perhaps he was. Yet for the life of him, he couldn't figure out what other options were open to him.

"Mister Chairman, we found ourselves in a quandary. If we eliminated this accountant outright, it would look suspicious and perhaps bring the IRS down upon us. It is doubtful we could stand this scrutiny. Mister Dimitri staged a shootout at night in our offices. It was made to look like a drug deal gone bad. Our in-house accountant was eliminated along with a street level drug dealer we hired. We then abducted the accountant, one David Waterman and made it appear as if he was involved and left the state with the cash and drugs."

The silence stretched. Khan held his breath and released it slowly. All eyes remained on Khan and Dimitri.

"It seems overly complicated."

"I don't see any other way out of it, Mister Chairman. As we all know the Jeunessa drug rollout is crucial to reaching our goal of a diminished population. Have you scrutinized the financials I sent you?"

"I have. The sums we must spend are massive. We will be selling the drug for a tiny fraction of its actual cost."

"That is correct, Mister Chairman. We must all remember that we are in the age of drugs, terrorism and all the resulting money laundering. Federal authorities are quite vigilant and efficient in detecting such activities. In order to obtain and distribute such vast sums we must use the Brogan Foundation. Without a favorable audit report turned in with the Foundation's tax returns, the IRS will promptly shut us down, our funding will be cut off, and the entire Jeunessa project will be terminated setting our goals back a century. "

"May we all be assured that you will use whatever methods are needed to, how shall I say? Persuade this accountant?"

"You may be certain of that, Mister Chairman."

CHAPTER 35

The BOLO-DNA, a new type of police alert went out throughout Nassau and Suffolk Counties a little past midnight. The alert flashed over all police cruiser radios and appeared over the on-board computer screens. A patrol officer doing the graveyard shift caught first sight on William Floyd parkway. The officer reported it and immediately received instructions: Follow, do not stop or apprehend, because that's what BOLO-DNA meant, Be On the Lookout-Do Not Apprehend. She followed the vehicle to route 25 where it turned and headed west. Another patrol picked up the vehicle and still a third when the subject turned onto Jayne Boulevard where St Agnes Church stood on the corner of Jayne and Smithtown Boulevard.

The vehicle parked by the rectory and two people were observed emerging from the front. A young man got out first and went around the vehicle to the passenger door. The officer frowned, the kid didn't look old enough to drive and normally he would have stopped him, asked for license and registration, especially this time of night. But he had his orders so he just observed.

The young man helped the passenger, a woman, out of the car. Even at the distance the officer could tell something was wrong. The woman barely stood, staggered and almost fell, held up by the young man who practically carried her to the door of the rectory. The office radioed in and once again was told not to interfere. The rectory door opened and the young man went in, at that point carrying the woman. A half hour went by and the officer was finally told to leave and resume normal patrol duties. He shook his head wondering what's up with all that, then put the gearshift in drive and headed back toward Route 25.

The fourth-term Suffolk County executive had been worried for all four of his terms, worried in the same manner of someone who owed a large favor to persons of questionable character—one never knew when they'd knock on the door demanding unsavory returns of favors. That had been before his landslide elections, certain political favors had been rendered along with large amounts of contributions to campaign coffers. The results had propelled him into the top spot in the county with unprecedented influence.

When the call came the county Executive roiled under a wave of relief. Such a little thing, probably not even illegal, well not much anyway. He'd passed it on to the County Police Chief who owed his appointment to the County Executive. Again no big deal, legal even, maybe not normal but nothing that would trigger investigations or scandals.

The results of the BOLO-DNA was relayed from Suffolk County PD to the Chief who relayed it to the County Executive who picked up the phone and dialed the number he'd kept for a dozen years. The call was answered by a curt "Yes?"

"It's me," the County Executive said, not even bothering to give his name.

"Results?" asked the voice on the line.

"The subjects are in the rectory of St Agnes Church at Jayne and Smithtown Boulevard. Two people, first is a young guy, a teenager, and second a woman. The woman appears injured and the kid carried her inside."

"Anyone else involved?"

"Not that the officer could tell, except of course for the people in the rectory. You know we've never had any tr…"

"We'll take it from there," the voice said, cutting him off. "Get rid of any records of this event."

"But what if there's a problem, I mean what would happen, how could I explain?"

"I said we'll take it from there, nothing will come back to you." Anton Dimitri told the County Executive as he hung up the phone.

"Got you, you little bastard," he whispered as he massaged the small nubs that were all that remained of two of his fingers. He turned his chair, facing the man standing impassively by the door and gave him his instructions.

CHAPTER 36

I stared right into that little black hole, a tunnel no bigger than a half inch across, the business end of what looked like a police special .38 that if fired would have sent the round directly between my eyes.

The face behind the man who held it looked like it had some experience in that direction. Eyes so empty they could have been in a jar on the dusty shelf of some crime museum. His face all angles, sharp and rough with a five o'clock shadow that could have carried splinters. He looked like one of Robert DiNiro's associates in the mobster movie Casino.

I know that the so-called "Immortals" the original remains of the Essex Junta dating back to 1802 have debated this point for two centuries: Is the Power mind reading? Well, yes, to a degree, but not quite what it seems. It's more like the reading of emotions, especially those imprinted on the psyche by violence. The more recent the violence, the greater the imprints made on the brain, impressions that may dim with time but never vanish.

I read much past violence in that person's mind, harsh acts glowing in the man's brain like old embers from some doused campfire, embers that projected like a dull glow from a thermal imaging device. None of it recent, thank heaven, which meant Father Anthony was probably okay, or at least this man hadn't participated in anything that might have been perpetrated against the priest.

I locked eyes with the man and felt his will slip, the confusion suddenly taking hold, locking him into a temporary paralysis. I slowly reached over and gently moved his hand away, the gun now pointing at the floor, the spot where our flesh touched hot and electric, and now I read him. No violence or animosity against the priest—Father Anthony was all right.

The man shook his head, his psyche slowly emerging from the depths where my probing had sent him. He licked his lips, a thin drool emerging from a corner of his mouth, tongue tied until he spoke, hesitant, as any confidence he had evaporated like yesterday's dreams.

"I…uh…you're…I mean. Did Guido send you?"

"No," I replied, "but it's okay, he'd want me here. Where's Father Anthony?"

"In the rectory, you…?"

"Yeah, it's okay, we'll go see him, but we need help for this lady, she's suffering from exposure. Get some blankets, an electric one if possible."

The man nodded, looked at the weapon in his hand as if seeing it for the first time. He shook his head, slipped the gun in his waistband, turned and left the room. I followed him out, half carrying-half dragging Joline. Her violent shivers had subsided, the lids of her eyes drooped, her voice slurred, all the symptoms of advanced hypothermia.

"What…warm, it's warm…" another symptom of hypothermia, the phantom sensation of warmth.

We walked through the door and I saw Father Anthony rushing toward us. He grasped Joline on her other side, walked us toward a doorway when a heavy set woman wearing a bathrobe emerged from one of the doors.

"Get Sister Anita, fast," Father Anthony shouted at her. The woman gathered her robe and rushed down the hall. "Sister Anita is an RN at St Francis, she'll know what to do," he threw over his shoulder at me.

CHAPTER 37

Even though I'd known Father Anthony and his church for the better part of half a century, it was the first time I'd been in the rectory. The room had a warm feeling to it, the kind of feeling a place gets when good things go on within its walls. Between Anthony and I we carried Joline like a big rag doll, fits of violent shivering the only signs of life from the young woman. Anthony led us to a door at the end of a long hall and opened it. It was a small guest bedroom, probably used by visiting priests. It held a single bed, night table, and a small armoire against the wall next to a window. An old fashioned radiator hissed as it sent out waves of heat. A crucifix hung above the bed and biblical scenes decorated the walls while an incense smell hovered over it all. We put Joline on the bed and covered her with blankets as Sister Anita walked in.

The nun was a large woman with skin the color of Kentucky coal, and when she spoke the musical lilt of Caribbean dialect danced in her voice. She wore a sort of colorful African shift, a bright bandanna around her hair, ivory loops hung from her earlobes and a large silver crucifix dangled from rosaries around her neck. She burst into the room as Father Anthony and I stepped aside for her while she sat by the bed and opened the large bag she'd been carrying.

Sister Anita placed her hand on Joline's forehead, caressed her cheeks and inserted an electronic thermometer in her mouth. She took a blood pressure cuff, wrapped it around Joline's bicep and took a reading, removed the thermometer from her mouth and read that also. Joline opened her eyes and started to speak, Anita placed her fingers on her mouth, "Hush," she said, "there'll be plenty of time for that later."

Sister Anita turned to Father Anthony and said, "This young woman is suffering from hypothermia and may go into shock. I don't suppose you want to tell me what happened?" The last question held the inflection of one who'd been down that road before and sure wouldn't get any answers this time. Father Anthony hesitated, opened his mouth and started to speak.

"Never mind," she said, cutting him off. "Go into the main hall closet and bring me the electric blanket, left side on the bottom. You," she continued, looking at me, "top shelf, same closet, you'll find three water bottles, fill them up with hot water, not scalding hot mind you, run the water on your wrist, when it gets too hot to keep your hand there, it will be just right."

We both looked at her a little too long I guess. She waved at us with one hand as she adjusted Joline's pillow, "Go on, git, what're you waiting for mon, the second coming?"

We both took off for our assigned tasks.

A couple of hours passed as we sat by Joline's side. Bundled under electric blankets turned on high, snuggled with hot water bottles, her core temperature rose to normal and she soon passed out of the danger zone and fell asleep. Sister Anita insisted on staying with Joline, dozing in a big easy chair we brought in for her. Anthony and I left to make coffee in the kitchen. We sat across from each other at the big rectory table. A clock ticked away in the silent room as the noise of a jet on its way to nearby MacArthur airport rumbled softly overhead. The kitchen smelled of incense and boiled cabbage, reminding me of my first few years at the Cabal's orphanage.

Father Anthony rose, went to the cupboard, took out a bottle of Makers Mark and poured a dollop in his coffee. He took a sip, smiled and said, "The Lord will understand."

"I'm sure. Now you want to tell me some of the details."

He took another sip, shrugged and nodded in the direction of Joline's room. "I recommended her brother for the audit on the Brogan Foundation."

"You told me that already, and so did she. What I don't know is, why David?"

"He's different from other accountants, he's...tougher, maybe smarter."

"Okay, so you thought he'd find out some things and relay them to you?"

"Eventually."

"How'd that work out?"

"Not very well, but it does tell us that something big is going on at the Foundation, and it affects the entire Cabal, just as I thought it might. Jimmy, there's something big going on in there and it can't be good."

I nodded. Good things and the Essex Junto Cabal were never synonymous. I started to speak, but was suddenly cut off as an explosion blew off the front door.

CHAPTER 38

They traveled in a convoy of three vehicles. Anton
Dimitri in the last vehicle, a nondescript sedan behind three
midnight-blue Hummers with five men in each. They
arrived at St Agnes and parked just one block away. They'd
already had the layout of the place emailed to them and
brought up to the onboard computers.

One Hummer went to the left side at the main entrance,
the other to the right, the rear exit, five men in each vehicle,
they quickly exited, moved to their respective positions in
fast, fluid moves.

At the front entrance, the leader placed a shaped charge
on the door, armed a fuse and stuck it dead center in the
Semtex, military-grade explosive, pulled back and waited.
Three seconds and the door exploded. Simultaneously the
rear entry team blew the lock off the door with a three-men
battering ram. The whole thing took less than five seconds
and they were in, shock and awe at its best.

They were all dressed in loose fitting sweats, black as a
moonless night, wearing utility belts, carrying stubby
machine pistols, a civilian mercenary version of a SWAT
team.

The first man charged in, ran into a teenager, must have
been the one they were warned about, Jimmy. He raised the
weapon and they screamed about getting down on the floor,

but a strange thing happened. The teenager kind of melted away and the room shimmered with heat waves, confusing the operator.

A man ran in holding a large caliber pistol, but he was clearly outclassed as one operator put a tight, three round group into his chest, dead-center body mass.

The man fell like a dropped laundry bag. Now the second man went around him, carrying a syringe and plunged it into the teenager's arm.

It didn't take genius-grade thinking to figure out that they'd tracked us, and they were good. I focused on the first one, disoriented him, but before I could move back, I felt the sting as the second plunged a needle in my arm. Some kind of narcoleptic drug, I could sense it and knew I only had seconds to react before the drug coursed through my blood stream and put my brain to sleep. I whirled and grabbed the man's arms sending him a full dosage of the Power. He blinked and slowly crumpled and sat on the floor.

Three more burst in the room from the wreckage of the front door, five more from the rear, I stepped back and felt the floor move under me, I only had precious few seconds remaining because once they had me, it was over, drugs would do the rest and I would be theirs for whatever of my life remained. I had no choice, the Scream the only thing available even if it killed me, as very well it might.

CHAPTER 39

———◆———

I'd often thought about the Scream and wished I could have a scientific team study the whole thing, but let's face it, the only ones studying it would be the Cabal, the Essex Junta and their minions, leaving me with my own theories.

I'd read the doctor's evaluations of my X-rays and CAT Scans, about that mass in the hypothalamus and extending to the cerebral cortex, what it could mean. They really didn't have a clue. It wasn't cancer, and it might be benign, but what was it exactly? No one knew, but I believed that's where the Scream came from.

Slowly melting on the floor, my limbs turning to mush, I visualized Father Anthony, Joline, Sister Anita, placed them in a protective bubble…and let loose the Scream.

The nearest thing that could be likened to the Scream is a psychic hand grenade, a veritable brain-melter. The moment it went out I felt its terrible effects in my head, like a blowtorch inside the confines of my brain. I reached on either side of my temples, held my head and sank to the floor as waves of unbearable pain stole away the remainder of my consciousness, dropping me into a bottomless well of darkness.

All ten members of the assault team simply melted down like puppets with their strings cut. Some held their heads, eyes rolling into white, tongues lolling as their brains short-circuited into a dark unconsciousness from which most would never awaken. Every living thing within a fifty-yard radius stopped functioning, most of them died from the combined effects of frayed brain tissues and strokes. Fifty to a hundred yards caused massive headaches, minor hemorrhages and what felt like the world's worst migraines, from a hundred to two hundred yards, all felt sharp pains lancing into their cerebral cortex, but I wasn't aware of it.

Like Elvis, I'd left the building.

CHAPTER 40

Father Anthony understood the power of the Scream. He had some idea of what it was, that Jimmy was the only one of the Immortals who could summon such a thing and he also knew it could very likely kill him.

He'd felt the echoes of the psychic energy wave and sensed how he, Sister Anita and Joline were somehow shielded from the disastrous effects. It was like they were held inside a diving bell as tornados and lightning raged around them, wrecking everything, but somehow keeping them safe.

The two men holding him dropped to the ground, grasping their heads as if under such pain that it would likely kill them. One looked already dead, the other blew red froth from his nostrils through shallow rapid breathing that would shortly cease.

Father Anthony stood, walked through the kitchen, stepped over a black clad body and past the corpse of Guido Spatafore's man still bleeding through a sucking chest wound. He stopped, kneeled by the fatally wounded man and knew that medically he could do nothing, but there was one service he could render: He stayed on his knees and gave him last rites. By the time he finished the man had stopped breathing.

Father Anthony rose from his knees, paused and plucked

the cell phone from the dead man's hand. He'd obviously been trying to call for help. Two more black-clad intruders lay in a tangle by the door. The men's eyes rolled in their heads so only the white showed. One lay very still while the other made feeble mewling noises punctuated by tremors. He continued on and found Jimmy curled up in a tight ball, his attackers crumpled around him. He felt the young man's pulse—okay, thank heaven—shook his head, opened one eyelid, no response.

Father Anthony picked up Jimmy in a fireman's carry and went to the next room where Joline and Sister Anita huddled behind a table. "Come on," he said, "We've got to get out of here fast," and led the way out.

CHAPTER 41

Anton Dimitri sat in the sedan one block away facing the entrance to St Agnes rectory. He'd seen the assault team blow the front door and enter, guessed that the rear team also succeeded. Ten men in all should be more than enough, except for that damned Jimmy. Last time he'd tried, it hadn't been nearly sufficient.

Enough time elapsed that the leader should have reported to Anton, but the radio remained silent. He keyed the mike on the encrypted hand-held VHF and called the team leader. A single click responded then silence followed by a buzz saw shrill that cut directly into his brain, painful enough to bow his head, drop the radio and cup both hands around his ears. But the trouble wasn't sound waves, couldn't be shut out by blocking the eardrum. A thrill of fear ran through Anton Dimitri. *It was happening again*—just like nearly fifty years ago in that brownstone in a suburb of Philadelphia.

They had cornered him then, just like today, and he'd cut loose with some sort of psychic blast wave that decimated his men, caused his bowels to liquefy and forced him to crawl away. Blinded in agony he'd reached the entrance of a dumbwaiter and placed his hand on the edge, perhaps to jump down and find refuge inside the silent tunnel.

The heavy platform had hurtled down the dumbwaiter, severing two fingers on his hand.

Even though he'd reasoned it out to himself, better to stay outside the perimeter and direct the operation, deep down Anton Dimitri knew the truth: Jimmy and his Powers terrified him.

They stumbled out the rear door of the rectory, Jimmy unconscious, head lolling back and forth, one arm around Father Anthony's shoulder the other around Sister Anita as Joline helped prop him up.

Moving down the dark street they reached the corner bordering a construction site where heavy machinery rose in the gloom like ancient leviathans and a sign illuminated by a single bulb proclaimed to all the dangers within, including prosecution for trespassers.

They paused as Anita stumbled, grabbing the sign to steady herself. Her eyes, luminous under the glow of the sign, focused on Anthony.

"Father, what's going on here? Who are those people, how come we ain't calling the cops?"

Father Anthony shook his head and failed to keep a tremor out of his voice. "The police wouldn't help, it would put us in greater danger. I'll explain it eventually, but you have to trust me for now."

"Greater danger? This don't make no sense no how. I'm a Catholic nun and a Registered Nurse, you're a priest, we're members of the clergy, how could calling the police put us in danger? Who's going to help us? "

"It's on the way," Father Anthony said, placing a hand on her shoulder as he took the cell phone he'd removed from the dead man out of his pocket.

In the glow of the screen he found the contact list, scrutinized it and pressed the one marked "G"

Guido Spatafore asked, "Chuck, what's going on?"

"Chuck is dead," Anthony replied. "I got his phone. We were raided and managed to escape. We need help now."

"Where are you?"

Anthony told him.

"Stay where you are, I'll be there in five."

CHAPTER 42

Headlights appeared down the block and devoured the distance to the edge of the construction site where Anthony, Joline, and Anita waited, holding the still unconscious Jimmy.

The vehicle was a big Cadillac Escalade. Both front doors opened and Guido jumped out the driver's door. Another man emerged from the passenger side. He held an assault rifle, walked to the front of the vehicle and waited.

It didn't take long for Guido to take in the situation. He grasped Jimmy under one arm and he and Anthony lowered him into the rear of the Escalade.

Guido drove in silence for about thirty minutes until they crossed the Queens border and reached the edge of the Belt Parkway where he parked in a silent and deserted side street. He turned and faced Anthony in the back seat. "Better tell me what happened, Father." He said.

"This I gotta hear," Joline cut in, "Everything's been completely fucked since last night and nobody seems to have a clue except him," she said, nodding toward Jimmy.

Father Anthony and Sister Anita looked at her. Anthony had one brow raised.

"Sorry," Joline said.

"Don't worry," Anita said, "I know how you feel."

"Look," Anthony said to Guido, "It's a long, long story

and I won't be able to tell you all of it, but here's the bottom line: We need a place to hide for a day or so, there are some very bad and resourceful people after us."

"Are they the ones who killed Chuck?"

Father Anthony nodded. Guido brought one fist to his mouth, bit the knuckle and mumbled a Sicilian curse.

"You know you're going to have to tell me more, Father."

"Eventually, but for now get us to a place where nobody in the world will be able to find us for a day or so."

"I'll get you to a place where nobody ever can get you," Guido replied.

He put the car in gear, drove onto the Belt Parkway and headed west.

CHAPTER 43

Guido got off the parkway and entered a maze of side streets filled with rows of houses built on concrete and wood stilts, the kind of construction used near ocean beaches where flooding is always a threat. Many homes seemed brand new and Anthony guessed it was the result of the reconstruction spree that followed super storm Sandy back in 2012. Ancient symbols seemed incongruous on the modern facades and flashes of Russian Cyrillic letters appeared on storefronts, sometimes with English beneath, mostly not.

Guido led the Escalade through a narrow alley and into the back of another house. Narrow stairs ran into a second story apartment, a solitary streetlight out front gave out a reflection that barely penetrated to the rear entrance. Glowing eyes appeared on the stairs as a cat ran down and disappeared in the dark. Distant sirens howled muffled by breaking surf that couldn't have been more than a block or two away. The scent of ocean brine filled the air.

"Where are we?" Asked Sister Anita.

"Brighton Beach, this house belongs to an old friend and business associate," replied Guido.

"I know this area," Joline said. "It's a Russian neighborhood."

"Completely," Guido said. "You might as well be in

Petersburg or Stalingrad. No one will find you here."

"But we're in Queens for heaven's sake" Anthony replied.

Guido smiled and it resembled the kind of grin a wolf might let out, all teeth and carnivorous eyes.

"Father, suppose you take care of the Lord's work, like we agreed, and I'll take care of this. You're about to enter into a safe house that belongs to what the media likes to call the Russian Mafia. We have certain business arrangements that are sacred to them as the Sacristy is to you."

"Don't blaspheme, Guy."

Guido shrugged and opened the door. "Come on Father. Let's get you all inside and we'll get a doctor for your young friend here. I guarantee your safety in this house."

CHAPTER 44

The sun rose late next morning, hidden by a cloud cover that soon blew out to sea. The bay window on the front of the apartment faced south so the sun's ray didn't penetrate the apartment directly. A cold breeze blew toward the ocean whose whitecaps could be seen over the roofs of homes fronting the beach. The neighborhood awakened with cars and delivery trucks passing on the street, their noises covered by the ever-present crashing surf.

Anthony had foraged through the tiny kitchen and came up with a Mister Coffee machine and enough supplies to put on a large pot. He stood near the window, looking out toward the ocean, occasionally turning one eye to the television, tuned to CNN, its volume nearly muted.

The upstairs apartment where they stayed was composed of the single living area, small kitchen in the back with full bath next to it, and three bedrooms surrounding it all. Jimmy had been placed on the bed in one of the rooms and Sister Anita stayed in that room, keeping an eye on her new patient, sleeping on a portable cot that Guido had brought up. Father Anthony and Joline had each taken the remaining two bedrooms.

Joline came out of her room, mumbled something and walked to the window.

"Good morning," Anthony said.

"Coffee," she replied. Definitely not a morning person, Anthony thought as he waived her toward the kitchen.

She poured herself a cup and walked back in the room, sitting in front of the television, mumbling something unintelligible.

"What?" Anthony said.

"It's a sacrilegious obscenity, Father. You don't want to hear it."

"I can always take your confession."

"I'm Jewish."

"Makes no difference to me, and I suspect not to the Lord either."

Joline rolled her eyes and mumbled something about it being too early in the morning for this.

"It's almost nine o'clock," Anthony said, and they both finished their coffee in silence, watching CNN. Joline reached for the remote and clicked through several channels, all had the same story so she returned to CNN.

Two blocks on either side of St Agnes church had been evacuated. The cameras showed bewildered people ushered out of their homes by a phalanx of letter-authorities, FBI, ATF, Sheriff's Department, County and State Police, while Hazmat-suited people from homeland security walked in and out of the church and rectory. A news blackout had been imposed so everything shown was either from early footage or taken from a distance. Even a big CDC (Center for Disease Control) motor home stood parked near the police barricades.

"I guess this is really yanking their chains," Joline said.

"Not surprising," Anthony replied. "There are at least a dozen armed military-type men who appeared to have suffered some kind of stroke simultaneously, as if they were felled by a chemical agent. I saw what happened to those guys, they're either dead or comatose, probably dead most of them. Then we have poor old Chuck, probably a known mobster, shot to death and all personnel from the rectory vanished. From their point of view there's a pretty dramatic and mysterious terrorist event going on."

Joline sighed, gulped down the last dregs of her coffee and looked at Anthony.

"So now what?" she said.

"We're getting out of here."

"I thought Guido said we'd be safe here."

"He's wrong, not with the kind of people after us, not to mention the FBI, CIA and God knows who else."

"But we didn't do anything wrong. Why don't we just walk out of here, drive to the FBI building and ask for help."

"Joline you have no idea the kind of power these people wield. We'd be dead or in their hands by nightfall. You've seen yourself what they can do. It's only because Jimmy was with us that we escaped last night."

Joline stood, stretched and yawned. "Never should have given up smoking," she said. "I need a drink or a cigarette and it's too dammed early for a drink and I already quit smoking."

"So have another cup of coffee instead."

Joline mumbled something that brought a grin to Father Anthony's face, as she returned from the kitchen with a full cup.

"Can I ask you a question?" Anthony said when she sat down.

"Sure."

"Last night when we arrived you asked Guido to loan you a laptop. He brought you one from downstairs. Did you look at the flash drive that David made?"

"How'd you know about that?"

"Jimmy told me."

"That's another thing, this guy Jimmy. What is he, an alien? He's psychic or something, knocks people out with brain waves or some kind of weird shit, never ran into anyone like him."

"Let him tell you himself when he comes out of his coma."

"What if he doesn't?"

"He will. But right now I need to know what's on that

flash drive."

Joline pulled the small device out of her pocket, looked at it and sighed. "Hard to believe David made this and vanished."

"What's on it?"

She wiped the corner of her eye where moisture rolled down her cheek. "I don't really know. It's mostly financial stuff, movement of money, lots of money, from all over the world it seems. It would take someone like David to figure it out. The only thing I sort of understood is that it has something to do with that Jeunessa youth drug and something called Targeted Vectors."

Anthony bolted upright, his features pinched, eyes wide as if a giant bat had suddenly burst through the window. "What did you say?"

"Movement of money, lots of money…"

"No, no, the other thing."

"Jeunessa and something called Targeted Vectors"

Father Anthony's face blanched, he rubbed his eyes and sat heavily. Joline saw shadows run across the priest's eyes. He looked haunted as he looked at Joline and asked, "Was there something in there about a Doctor Li Wu and Brookhaven National Lab?"

"Yeah, come to think of it. No clue what it means. You have any idea?"

"Dear God in Heaven, they wouldn't, couldn't…"

Before Joline could ask anything else, the door to one of the bedrooms opened and Anita burst into the room.

"Father, come quick, its Jimmy, he's waking up."

CHAPTER 45

Swimming in a dark whirlpool, I reached toward the only streak of light, a dusty murk, barely lighter than the surrounding storm clouds. Things spun around me, neurons firing half a century old synapses in my memory—Valdemar Khan, his militant aide Anton Dimitri, the Immortals populating the Essex Junta, a secret society going back to the time of the American Revolution whose founders were alive today, having barely aged in the last two centuries. Then there was Father Anthony, who was he really? Did I actually recall his face going back to the 1950's?

A streak of muted light, white this time, flashed across the top of my eyelids. Feeling vague sensations of pain I opened my eyes and jagged streaks tore across my consciousness as if someone rubbed ground glass inside my nervous system. I must have let out some noise because I felt gentle fingers pulling up my eyelids and saw Sister Anita's dark face, her eyes gentle and filled with concern. I held my lids open and tried to give her a smile that must have come out like a grimace.

Her voice murmured, soothing and warm as she brushed a damp rag across my forehead. "There," she said, "don't try to move, how do you feel?"

"Like the world's worst hangover," I said.

"And I bet you don't even drink." She smiled as she moved my limbs, felt the resistance as my muscles slowly responded to her skilled prodding.

I sat up, winced at another stab of pain and settled back on the cushions.

"Got anything to eat?" I asked her.

"Anything you want, let me get Father Anthony first," and she left the room.

Joline came in followed by Anthony. The priest's forehead wrinkled and shadows loomed in his eyes, I'd never seen him like that before.

"What's the matter?" I asked him.

He shook his head and replied, "Never mind me, how are you doing?"

"Fine, got a headache and starving."

I heard some pots and pans clattering in the next room, Sister Anita at work I guessed.

"Wow, you're back," Joline said. "You gave us quite a scare you know."

I was about to say, you should have seen the other guys, but I suddenly realized what actually must have happened to them.

"How did we get here, what happened, tell me," I said, and Father Anthony related everything that happened, but still, something unspoken stood between us.

"And…" I said.

"Later," he replied, turning away.

I ate scrambled eggs and drank coffee in the room facing the bay window, looking out to a clear blue sky that blended on the horizon with calm ocean water. It must have been close to eleven and the sun reflected in silver flashes from distant waves. Someone had cracked open a window allowing currents of icy salt water breezes whistling around the room, mixing with the chemical scented forced air heating system blowing through vents in the floor.

Father Anthony had just told us we were awaiting delivery of a safe, untraceable car to carry us to our next destination.

"And where would that be? And when we get there, then what?" Joline asked.

"Either way I ain't going with you," added Sister Anita. "You don't need me no more, I gotta get back to the hospital, people counting on me there."

"Out of the question, Sister, you must come with us."

"Why, Mon? What could anybody want with me?"

"Because Sister, they will catch you immediately, drug you and torture you until they get every scrap of information you have, and when they're satisfied they have everything, they will kill you."

"But I don't know nothing," she protested.

"Makes no difference, you'll be just as dead."

"Is that what's happening…?" Joline asked. Her eyes were luminous as she dabbed some moisture from her nose, her lower lip trembling slightly.

"To David?" Anthony finished her sentence. "I don't think so. David's a different case with different issues, but when we get to our destination, I'll be able to contact them safely, and bargain for David's life."

"A deal with the Devil?" I said.

"Somethin' like that."

Sister Anita muffled a sob, took a handkerchief from the folds of her garment, wiped her eyes and blew her nose. Father Anthony reached over and enfolded her in his strong arms. I leaned toward her and placed my hand on the back of her neck. Her distress was like a floundering boat in a dark storm-tossed sea.

I connected with Sister Anita and her sobs subsided. I felt her spirit calm as Father Anthony and I locked eyes over her shoulders.

"You're like a shot of floating Valium, aren't you?" I heard Joline say behind me. I'd forgotten about her for the moment.

Father Anthony walked out to the fire escape and looked over the sea of roofs to the ocean stretching out until it blended blue-on-blue with distant horizons. It was time to make the call. He felt an intense wave of distaste, but he understood the necessity.

He walked down the stairs, paused to be sure no one had noticed or followed. Reaching the street, the priest moved to the narrow alley between the houses and took a cell phone from his pocket. It was a particularly special phone. Although the priest was certainly not an expert on such things, he knew the phone would work via satellite, avoiding local cell towers—traceable to be sure, but needing much more time to trace a call, and used military encryption to boot so any conversations would be incomprehensible without the encryption key. He powered the phone via the tiny switch that completely disconnected the battery so the phone remained untraceable, and dialed the one and only speed dial number. The phone rang only once.

"Getting bold calling me, aren't you?"

"Not nearly enough, Valdemar."

"Maybe you're encouraged by your narrow escape, Anthony. Oh don't worry. You would never have been harmed. You know exactly what we want."

"Perhaps I may surmise more than you think. We'll discuss that at a later date. Right now I'm here to give you a warning."

"You're warning me? How amusing Anthony, what are you warning me about?"

"I don't want the accountant hurt. I know you have him."

The phone was suddenly dead in his hand. Anthony looked at it and grimaced. He turned the phone off, opened the back and removed the battery for good measure.

CHAPTER 46

Runway #3 at Daytona Regional Airport is usually reserved for special flights, VIP stuff, and this afternoon was no exception, but no one seemed to know who or what this flight was. A gleaming silver Citation jet waited at the edge until a dark SUV pulled up disgorging a single passenger who moved up the gangway and disappeared into the cabin. Moments later the boarding steps retracted and the jet moved down the runway, accelerating until it vanished in the clear sky.

Valdemar Khan looked out the window as the plane passed through a high cover until it reached its cruising altitude at 35,000 feet. The phone call from Father Anthony disturbed him more than he thought it would. Perhaps that's why he'd disconnected the call. He kept looking out the window, and didn't move until the jet landed at Long Island's Islip McArthur Airport three and a half hour later.

The temperature change from Daytona to Long Island was startling as Khan got off the plane. A limo waited there, midnight blue with darkened windows. The chauffeur waited besides the vehicle and handed Khan a heavy jacket as he reached the door. He put the jacket on and got inside the limo without a word. One hour later the limo double-parked on Metropolitan Avenue in Brooklyn, directly in front of the offices of the William Brogan

Foundation.

Even though it was now just past ten PM, the receptionist waited at her post. "Good evening mister Khan," she said. "Nice flight?"

"Fine, Miss Dolan," he said and passed her without a glance, entered his office, and took a seat behind his desk. Anton Dimitri sat directly in front of him.

"Coffee?" Dimitri asked.

"Yes."

"Miss Dolan, please bring coffee for two," Dimitri said, speaking into the intercom. Moments later the receptionist walked into the office carrying two cups and condiments.

"That will be all for tonight, Miss Dolan, please lock the door when you leave, thank you."

The two men sat across from one another. A mid-December wind picked up and whistled around the closed window blending with muted traffic noises from the avenue.

The men finished their coffee and it was Khan who broke the silence first.

"What happened, Anton? It's all over the news."

"Same as in 1962, some kind of psychic surge. Jimmy's Power has dimensions we can't even fathom, yet. You know how I feel about this."

"If we do as you want, just kill him, the biological secrets will follow him to the grave. Jimmy is our next step on the evolutionary scale, and eventually we will have him alive. But getting back to yesterday's event, can this be traced back to us?"

"Not a chance. We've been able to find out that six of the raiders did not survive. The remaining four are vegetative comatose. They are all mercenaries, former South African Special Forces, two from the French Gendarmerie Nationale, and two from Saudi Commando units. None ever knew for whom they worked. All were paid through cash dead-drops, training took place in the mountains near Baku through so many shell units as to be impenetrable. Nothing will get back to us. What will we do about the priest?"

"He is not to be harmed."

"What is it with you and that priest?"

Khan raised his head and stared at Anton, the full weight of the man's eyes boring into his like nothing he'd felt before. "You are dangerously close to insubordination, Anton."

Dimitri tried to speak but it came out in a stammer.

"...I mean...that is...I apologize. It will not happen again."

Valdemar nodded and resumed as if nothing had occurred. "We have new resources coming on line, one of our very own has now been promoted to a key surveillance position within NSA. Be sure you have several teams ready for immediate action. I expect an intercept soon."

"We'll be ready," Dimitri replied.

uttering the words would tip off those who hunted us.

Anthony drove the car steadily, avoiding major highways (surveillance cameras on big roads) he explained. The women thought it was paranoid.

I didn't think so, not for one second.

We passed through New Jersey, headed west to Pennsylvania through farmland and patches of heavy woods filled with pines, scrub oaks and elms denuded of leaves at this time of year.

Just as darkness fell Anthony stopped in a small town at a house with a B&B sign. Guido had given Anthony an envelope filled with large bills so we paid cash for an overnight stay. A motel would have required a credit card that could be traced while a struggling small town Bed & Breakfast would gladly accept cash.

We left early the next morning after a good old-fashioned Pennsylvania Dutch breakfast. Now we changed directions, heading south toward West Virginia as Father Anthony consulted his maps, and the rest of us napped as he drove.

We crossed into West Virginia, drove the back roads at the foot of the Appalachians. The houses became less frequent, more dilapidated as befit the lower economic status of the region.

We gassed up at a large shack that passed as a service station, still bearing ancient Veedol signs over five decades old. An old man sat on a rocking chair under a porch that looked as if it would collapse under any breeze. He smoked a pipe, drank out of a jar and regarded us with suspicion. A young man with missing front teeth and a vacant expression pumped our gas. We were in the hill country, sparsely populated by clans whose blood feuds ran as deep as Sicilian vendettas.

We continued and the backwoods road became rougher, unkempt. Now Father Anthony stopped consulting his maps. He knew where he was.

Anthony turned off what could be called the main road into a narrow backwoods trail covered by asphalt, cracked and missing huge patches filled in instead with sand and dirt. Soon the asphalt disappeared altogether and the road turned to gravel and more dirt. Strangely enough the road at that point seemed better maintained than the asphalt part. Tall piney woods rose on either side in total desolation. We could have been in a countryside of two centuries ago. It had been several hours since I saw a cell phone tower. Even telephone poles and cables had vanished.

The path twisted and turned with the Chevy sedan gamely negotiating the path, its wheels hugging the edges of the trail, scrub oaks grinding against the side, screeching as if to warn us off.

The path ended at a small clearing. Anthony got out of the car and we all followed. The clearing showed signs of maintenance. The tall grass had been cut, probably with a scythe, overgrowing branches were chopped and stacked on one side, scrub oaks grew everywhere interspaced with taller evergreens. I saw squirrels scampering on branches rising over our heads, heard birds tweeting in the trees and crows cawing in the distance. The air was cold and pure after washing over the Appalachian and laundered by miles of forests. Outside of the scant wildlife, the silence was complete, the desolation absolute.

Father Anthony stretched, drew a deep breath, opened his arms, looked at us with a wide smile and said, "Well, here we are!"

CHAPTER 48

Antonio "Tony the Tuna" Raimondo sat at his seat in the Bernardino Social Club, like so much royalty. "Tony the Tuna" a moniker derived from a truck hijack in the Bronx many years ago, a crime that resulted in Antonio's illicit possession of some twelve thousand cans of tuna fish that he'd managed to fence one miserable case at a time. But that had been many years ago when he was barely a teenage hoodlum. Since then he'd come up in the world— way up. Making his bones two decades ago he'd risen in the organization, became a "made man" soon afterward, and now Caporegime in the old Columbo crew from Brooklyn, second only to the boss himself, Guido "Guy the Rope" Spatafore.

Tony the Tuna's face was a mass of fissures and erosion, dark olive tones from his Sicilian heritage where a dull glass eye floated above the mottled flesh next to the remaining eye that held enough malice for two. The loss of the eye resulted from a grueling war with intruding Columbian drug gangs. But Tony the Tuna had given more than he'd received and if he'd chosen to do so, the handle of his Sicilian switchblade would not be long enough to hold all the notches to be carved. He was the one thing many mobsters bragged about but few actually became: a genuine tough guy, someone to be feared and whose displeasure should be avoided at all costs.

The Bernardino Social Club was a dive, a place of peeling paint on plaster walls whose scant Christmas decorations never came down. Several tables and chairs gathered in a semicircle around a bar devoid of stools but whose shelf held a surprisingly good array of top shelf imported liquors. The entrance was a single narrow door where the name of the place was spelled out in neon lights half of which remained dark. The club didn't advertise and wanted no new customers and yet was incredibly profitable, at least that's what the books and tax returns revealed–a classic money laundering organization where some of the profits of loan sharking, gambling, prostitution and drug sales were washed clean. At the rear of the club a set of double doors opened into a kitchen where the bartender, a skilled Italian chef in his own right, created wonderfully aromatic Italian dishes for the patrons, all of whom were key players in Tony the Tuna's organization. The Tuna himself (as his soldiers called him-but none to his face) held court at the last table, his back to the wall, always, next to the kitchen where a rear exit could be found after opening a trompe-l'oeil wall plaque.

On this night The Tuna sat sipping a tumbler of Remy Martin, perhaps his only affectation. Two of his soldiers sat on either side of the man, and the bartender busied himself cleaning up in the kitchen. The Tuna had a great meal of shrimp scampi, filled with garlic and pungent butter sauce, washed down with primo Chianti and followed by an espresso and that fine French cognac. He felt good, and so was more surprised than annoyed at the three men that walked in the door of the social club.

The first thing he noticed was that the leading guy was missing two fingers on one hand, the second guy looked like a professor, completely out of place, but the third man was the one that concerned him. Black as the ace of spade, a *mouliann* for fuck's sake, in his social club! He seemed too sure of his world, carried himself with a confidence he shouldn't have felt, not in the Bernardino Social Club at any case. He heard one of the other men call the black one by the name "Ergun"—a black guy with a Greek name, now he'd seen it all.

The Tuna figured them for some sort of athletes from a professional sports team, strutting around on a night in town. He'd run into that before and knew how to handle it. Physical strength and martial arts skills developed in genteel suburban gyms could never stand up against knuckles hardened by scar tissues from numerous brawls where broken bottles, brass knuckles, blackjacks and blades were used with no quarters given and none expected.

The Tuna turned to the man on his right and nodded toward the newcomers. The man said, "right, boss" in a voice that held the timbre of a growling bear. He was the Tuna's top enforcer and bodyguard and when he stood, he topped out at four feet six. He wore a white shirt open to the third button where Italian gold gleamed in a row of chains and medals. A sports jacket covered the shirt with the fabric strained by the bulk of anabolic steroid-enhanced heavy muscles. His movements were surprisingly fast for a big man and his rages legendary, fueled by the steroids and the mind of a psychopath.

Tony the Tuna watched as his enforcer approached the three men—this should be interesting.

As the big man approached the trio, he sort of stumbled and shook his head as if dizzy. The Tuna noticed the black man, staring intently at his enforcer, the eyes electric, emitting a magnetism that couldn't be ignored. The enforcer stumbled again, his eyes rolled in his head showing white, and that's when the black man took a step forward and hit him once, a smashing, bare knuckled blow that slammed his head around as the Tuna heard the distinct sound of a neck vertebrae snapping.

The air thickened and time seemed to stand still in the Bernardino Social Club. The Tuna tried to move his hand toward the nine millimeter Glock he carried in a shoulder holster under his vest, but things didn't seem to work right, as if he stumbled through a paralyzing fog that reached to the core of his being. He saw the second man, the one with the missing fingers draw a small handgun, step up to his other man who just sat there like a mouse transfixed by the stare of a cobra. The second man shot him in the forehead, turned to the bartender and did the same. Neither had moved, just waited for what seemed the inevitable.

Now the man walked up to the Tuna, gun still in hand, whiffs of cordite reaching his nostrils. The Tuna tried to stand but the man put a hand on his chest and gently pushed him back in the seat.

"We need some information, Mister Raimondo, it is Raimondo, isn't it?"

The Tuna found he could now move his muscles but a strange lassitude had taken over and he barely found the strength to mutter "go fuck yourself," before he felt the prick of the needle in his shoulder, and at that exact point in time, he knew he was irrevocably lost.

CHAPTER 49

Valdemar Khan heard the thrilling of his cell phone, the encrypted one, pushed a key and heard Anton Dimitri's voice.

"We have progress, Valdemar."

"Tell me."

"We used our contacts in law enforcement, but Spatafore is gone, too well hidden to get him, but we did locate his second in command, a guy named Raimondo. Spatafore doesn't make a move without him. I took Ergun with me, helped with the persuasion."

Khan knew Ergun and his Powers very well as they were nearly a match for his own. Ergun had been a slave for one of the founding members of the Essex Junta and had been given a Greek name by his master. When the Junta was formed the slave Ergun was also treated with the newly discovered serum. The idea was far from benign since all that was wanted was a long-lived slave. But that had been impossible when Ergun's Powers developed and soon surpassed that of his master, thus Ergun was freed nearly a century before the Emancipation Proclamation.

"What'd you find?"

"Apparently Spatafore picked them up right after Jimmy dispatched our team. He drove the four of them to some safe house he shares with Russian mob guys in Brighton

Beach, Brooklyn."

"Birds of a feather gangsters I suppose."

The irony escaped Anton, and he continued, "You might say that, it suits their needs. Anyway they only stayed overnight and Spatafore gave them a car, clean, no history. They took off the next morning."

"Any idea why one of Brooklyn's top mobster is helping the priest and his friend?"

"According to Raimondo, and by that time between the drugs and our, hum…powers of persuasions, we can be sure he doesn't really know, but he thinks Spatafore is in fear of his immortal soul and wants help from the priest, so he's turned to what you might call the light."

"Interesting. Where did they go in this car?"

"Well, that's the difficult part. We have the description and license plates, and as you know we have access to video surveillance on the roads and bridges. They show up on the Belt Parkway, Verazzano Bridge, the outer crossing bridges and we lose them after that."

"Nothing on I95?"

"Negative, wherever they went, they must have taken back roads. But we have constant surveillance and NSA phone watch, even landline calls will be tracked pretty fast. We'll get another crack at Jimmy, you can be sure of that."

"No, leave Jimmy for another day."

"But…"

"Listen to me, Anton. It's like that old redneck saying, when you're ass deep in alligators remember the objective is to drain the swamp. Just get the Waterman girl, Joline, the rest will be for another day."

"All right, I'll take care of it."

"See that you do."

CHAPTER 50

I watched Joline's face, the expressions running to surprise, incredulity and finally settling into seething anger. For a moment I thought she was going to pick up one of the branches lying on the ground and just bash in Father Anthony's face. Sister Anita didn't look much happier.

"Are you fucking kidding me?" Joline said, her breath coming out like plumes of steam in the frigid air. "My brother is prisoner somewhere, maybe tortured or dead, there are goons after us, we've been on the run for two days, you bring us to the middle of Bumfuckville nowhere, and you think this is funny?"

Sister Anita put her hand on her arm but Joline shook it off. She was getting a head of steam like an old fashioned locomotive. "And you too," she told Anita, "How can you put up with this shit? I should strangle him with that stupid Roman collar."

Father Anthony looked positively stricken. I'd never seen the usually unflappable priest appear so contrite. Then Joline turned to me, "And you stay away from me, I don't want any of your psychotic bullshit."

"You mean psychic?" I replied.

"Whatever, stay away from me, you may be cute but you're too fucking weird."

One out of two isn't bad. I'll absorb weird to get cute. I

was beginning to like this girl.

"Was I too weird when I pulled you out of the bay? You have to know you'd be dead if it wasn't for my weirdness," I said to her, using my gentle-hey-I'm-not-so-bad voice.

"Look, I'm sorry for getting carried away, but you need to explain all this shit to me."

"I think she's right, Father," Anita cut in. "We need to know what's going on"

"I didn't mean to set you off, Joline," Father Anthony said. "I should have known the stress you're all under, I thought a little levity might ease the tension."

"Worked like a fart in an elevator, didn't it, Father? Now I'm asking real nice, pretty please with sugar on top, where the fuck are we and where are we going? It can't be in the middle of this little mountain jungle."

For a moment I believe Anthony actually blushed. He turned away, walked toward the thickest edge of the clearing and threw a "Give me hand, please," over his shoulder.

I followed him to the edge where a large pine had fallen in a tangle of thick branches and vegetation. Anthony grasped the end of the pine trunk and pulled. The whole thing moved a bit, I grasped the trunk next to where he held it and pulled.

The whole thing was a cleverly hidden door, fabricated to look like fallen tree limbs and pivoting on a solid tree disguised by ancient, gnarled scrub oaks. As we swung the "door" away, it revealed a shed completely concealed under a canopy of evergreens whose branches joined overhead in perfect concealment. Inside the shed rested a Ford panel truck, a Toyota Tundra and a large All Terrain Vehicle big enough to hold six plus cargo.

"Just give me another half hour and it will all come together, I promise," Anthony said as he climbed in the driver seat of the ATV and turned the key.

Nothing happened.

Anthony got a spare battery from a utility box in a corner of the shed, hooked a set of jumper cables to the ATV and the engine started immediately.

"Sometimes these things don't get used for weeks so they keep a set of fresh batteries hooked up to a solar charger," he explained.

"Who's they?"

"You'll find out, Joline. Trust me for another half hour…Please."

Joline looked away with a shrug, and her eyes settled on mine. "Sorry," she said," You're really not weird at all, and you did save my life." Then she smiled and it felt like the sun peeking out from between clouds. "But I did mean it, about the cute part, that is," she added.

I really like this woman, but where could any of this go? It wasn't the first time I'd been infatuated with a woman but the mind of an old man in the body of a youth present some particular problems that are not the paradise most people thought it would be. The simultaneous burden of age and youth in the same body transforms one's thinking. And just how long could you stay with one person, how long until they notice their own crowfeet, wrinkles, aches and pains while for all practical purposes you remain seventeen? Besides all that, there remains the fact that I am being hunted by the most powerful cabal in the world—have been my entire, long life.

I smiled back at Joline, said, "You're pretty cute yourself." I kept the illusion that the glow in her cheeks was actually more than the chilled air.

Anthony parked the car in the shed where the ATV had been and we closed the gate, concealing the shed as if nothing had passed, then we all piled into the vehicle with Anthony at the wheel.

Father Anthony drove the ATV to the opposite end of the clearing and approaching the wall of evergreens and scrub oak he slowed nearly to a crawl. "Tighten your seat belts and hang on," he said, and we did just that.

CHAPTER 51

The front bumpers and roll cage of the ATV breached the wall of vegetation and slowly pushed through, over bumps, logs and holes, slogging up and down and sideways as we all held on. At one point I thought the contraption would just tip over, but somehow it held on, driven by Father Anthony's experienced hand. It was obvious that he knew what he was doing and exactly where he was going.

Soon the vegetation thinned out, changing to a rocky trail bordered here and there by strategically placed stones. We continued as the trail angled upward, climbing the side of the mountain, tall junipers mixed with a variety of evergreens all around us like trail markers. The air grew colder and we huddled in our seats. Clumps of snow that wouldn't even begin to melt until April or May appeared around us and soon covered the trail as Anthony kept going. We must have traveled at least five or six miles until the land leveled out to a plateau composed of huge pines and ancient oaks whose leaves had fallen months ago.

Anthony picked up the pace a bit, steering around trees, mountain boulders and depressions in the land caused by some prehistoric cataclysm in a frozen wilderness that hadn't changed in eons and seen precious few humans. But as Anthony steered around a stand of thick pines, their needles silvered with snow, I soon realized how wrong I was. There were people around after all.

A wall appeared directly in front of the ATV, heavy stones expertly fitted one to another rising some eight feet above us curving slightly into a circle that disappeared into the surrounding, thick walls.

Anthony followed the wall for about fifty yard until we came to a huge gate that would have looked at home as the drawbridge of a medieval castle. It was made of thick logs whose sides had been sawed flat, fitted together and lashed with chain. It would take heavy artillery to break it down, and probably more than one shell.

Anthony stopped the ATV and shut the engine. The air was frozen and the silence nearly absolute except for our stamping feet as we tried to keep warm, our breath steaming up, hands deep in our pockets since none of us had gloves. Anthony walked to the left of the gate, dislodged a protruding stone and pulled out a chain with links thick as a man's finger. The chain vanished somewhere into the depths of the wall and Anthony gave it three sharp tugs.

Joline and Anita sat back in the ATV and just huddled there, by now too tired for more questions or arguments.

"Are we there yet?" I said to him, softly enough so the women wouldn't hear us.

"I thought the years would have given you patience. You'll find out soon enough."

"Ah, the everlasting mysteries of the church, eh Father?"

Anthony smiled and said nothing.

Ten minutes or so passed until the gate began to swing inward, revealing steel tracks guiding the hidden wheels in the bottom of the logs comprising this giant door. No noise came out of the silent mechanism operating the gate, not a squeak, just a sort of low rumble that could have been a distant and unseen storm. Anthony motioned us into the ATV and slowly drove through the gate into the world of central Europe a thousand years ago.

CHAPTER 52

The first thing that struck me was the utter change from a primitive, empty stillness to a place where a population busied themselves as they would have way back in the middle ages. As the gate slowly closed behind us Father Anthony kept the ATV at walking speed. The wall we had just crossed stretched out on either side to disappear into thick clumps of tall evergreens. A field stretched out to our left that rolled for what seemed several acres as men worked back and forth digging among tilled rows of some winter root vegetables, filling motorized carts with the stuff. We traveled a well tended path, fields on one side, stone sheds on the other interspaced with other buildings created in perhaps centuries past with hand cut stones precision fitted as if they were made of modern poured concrete.

Men walked in and out of the buildings, carrying things, pushing carts, occasionally empty handed. They all wore a variety of heavy clothing ranging from modern track-suits, heavy cottons and parkas to obviously handmade woolen garments. They wore beards, spoke in low tones, they peered at us with faces a bit rough but well fed and all generally appeared to be under no stress whatsoever. We saw no women among them as the ATV made its way down the path that ended at what could only be described as a great hall.

"This looks like a scene from one of the Zombie movies," I heard Joline say to Anita.

"A what movie?" Anita said.

"Zombie movie, haven't you seen any? No I guess not, you've got to get out more, sister."

"I'm out plenty, especially the last couple of days."

The building was as meticulously crafted as all the others, but somehow more…well, majestic is the word that came to my mind. For one thing this building held many windows, each with its own ledge adorned with carvings and representations of horned devils and gargoyles following the ancient European superstition of placing such stone caricatures to ward off evil from those within its walls.

This particular building stood two stories, taller than all the other structures that were ground level only. Two steps marked an entrance at least twelve feet long and I guessed this building must also have a cellar and basement. Twin doors swung inward, each adorned with a large, acquisitively formed, bronze cross above a Latin inscription.

Two men stood on the steps. One was dressed pretty much like those we had seen in the fields except for a large cross, worn around his neck on what looked like ivory beads. The other man wore a robe of dark wool with a thick sash around his waist and the same ornate cross around his neck. There was an air of serenity about these men and a calm reflection to their eyes.

We all stayed behind as Father Anthony climbed the stairs and stood in front of the men. Then a most curious thing happened: Anthony stood in front of the men and held out his hand. Each man in turn fell to one knee and kissed the ring on Anthony's hand. I heard the words "Your Excellency" and "Monsignor." Funny, I never paid much attention to that ring on Anthony's hand.

I turned around and saw Sister Anita cross herself and close her eyes in prayer. Joline simply looked too surprised to say anything, although I would have given much more than a penny for her thoughts. Both women seemed simply stunned by the sudden change of environment, a turn of event that nothing could have led them to expect. I wasn't as surprised, I'd expected something like this from Anthony, although I must say the ring-kissing and Monsignor was not something I'd anticipated.

Anthony said a few words to the two men and they opened the doors. He waived us in and we walked into the large room that I later found they called the great meeting hall.

Stone carvings with religious motifs took up much of the wall space. Chairs, a table and two credenzas were the only furniture in the room. Beautifully hand made with meticulous craftsmanship, they would have brought a fortune in any upscale antique shop. The room was warm from the radiance of a great wood fire absorbed and reflected throughout by hand laid masonry.

We were ushered into an adjoining room, a refectory of some sort with rows of benches and tables fitted out with dishes, bowls and hand carved cups and utensils. Torches lined the walls at three-foot intervals, and each table held five candelabras at equally spaced intervals. None were lit since daylight poured through the large windows. Dust motes danced in the light beams like legions of tiny angels.

Anthony waived us to a table and asked us to sit. Everyone took off their coat in the warm room as the other two men brought in steaming earthen cups of tea and a plate of fresh baked goods.

"We hope you will share our meal with us tonight," said the first man, the one with the robe, "But in the meantime I hope this will suffice. You must be hungry after your journey." We thanked him and he gave a slight bow and left the room. We were now alone with Father Anthony.

I looked at him and said, "Monsignor, eh. When'd you get the promotion?"

Anthony smiled at me, the flesh around his eyes crinkling. He could be charming when he wanted.

"Never mind that," Joline cut in, "Where are we, Disneyland West Virginia? And how the he…heck will this help us, and specifically how will this help me find David?"

"All right, Joline. You deserve an explanation."

"Fine, just be straight, don't bullshit me."

We looked at her and said nothing.

"What?"

"No, it's a fair question after everything that happened," Anthony said. He took a sip, munched the last piece of cake and finished his tea.

"Any time you're ready," Joline said. I could feel the sarcasm drip like congealed honey. Father Anthony smiled again and continued as if nothing had been said.

"It really started in March of 1391 in Seville, Spain…"

"1391?" Joline cut in. "You do know what year this is now, right?"

"To understand how we got here, we must first know how we started, wouldn't you agree?"

Joline said nothing and Father Anthony continued. "During that year of 1391, there were many outspoken people with different religious ideas, ideas that wandered far from traditional Catholic teachings. Archdeacon Ferran Martinez of Seville preached increasingly inflammatory sermons against such people who were called heretics. The sermons resulted in massacres in Seville and Montsegur. Far from horrifying the faithful, it actually enflamed the masses resulting in a pappally authorized Purification of the Faith, what we now call the Spanish Inquisition. Jews, Moors, Protestants and a singular sect called Albigensians were targeted with numerous innocents caught in the middle. Hundreds of thousands were tortured and executed in the most horrific manners including being burned alive. It is a sad chapter in history where religion and the church became a driving force toward acts of unspeakable evil. This period lasted for a little more than a century, and even though it abated somewhat, most people don't realize that the Inquisition lasted for many centuries, right through the Middle Ages, the Renaissance and the so-called Age of

Enlightenment. As a point of historical fact, the Inquisition was not officially disbanded until the year of 1834, just about three decades before the American Civil War."

"I remember studying that period in my theology classes," Sister Anita said.

"I suspect the world will never forget this, but we do not seem to learn very much. The Inquisition was every bit as horrific as another Holocaust perpetrated by a man called Hitler. Fifty years later we allowed another holocaust in Africa in a place called Rwanda. So you see my friends, learning the lessons of history is not a strong point of the human race. But let's get back to our lesson. Even though the Inquisition abated somewhat, it was replaced over the centuries by various forms or religious persecution against anyone or any group different from traditional Catholicism, which brings us to a group called the Disciples of the Benediction."

"The Benedictines," Joline said, "I've heard of them, they make a good liquor."

"Liqueur, a wonderful after dinner drink," Father Anthony said. "But no, they are not the same, the Disciples of the Benediction formed a monastery overlooking the Bay of Arcachon in Southwest France. They also made this wonderful spirit and it is a little known fact that to this day the two orders make the same liqueur. When you buy a bottle of Benedictine you cannot be sure if it is the Benedictine Order or the Disciples of the Benediction who made it. The Disciples were largely ignored until Monsignor Roland DuPres became Archbishop of Bordeaux in 1710. The Archbishop was very influential with the French Court since Bordeaux was a major naval port of great importance in the ongoing war with the greatest maritime power of its day—England. In June of 1712 a mob burned down most of the abbey, killing a dozen monks in the process. Eager to escape religious persecution, two ships left Bordeaux for the new world, secretly financed by the English Crown for reasons that are not clear to this day. One ship was filled with Huguenots,

French Protestants, and landed at Savannah, Georgia. The other ship carrying 214 Disciples of the Benediction lost its way and landed at the estuary that is now Port Elizabeth in New Jersey. Having arrived in late September—that's how long such voyages took in those days, June to September—they began a trek through what was then the frontier, westward through Pennsylvania and into West Virginia until they were stopped by the Appalachians. Fully half died during that winter, but all feared religious persecution far more than harsh winters and the rigors of the frontier. The survivors built this monastery over the course of centuries, and that is what you see today, perhaps one of the best kept secrets of the Catholic Church."

"But I've seen monks of all ages working the grounds. How do they join this order if it's so secret?" Sister Anita asked.

"They don't join, they are recruited among the faithful. I myself am one of their recruiters."

"Well don't look at me, Father. I'd rather join the Marines," Joline said, her words losing their previous edge, eliciting grins and chuckles from the rest of us.

"It's a special calling, a life of complete devotion, spiritualism, hard physical work and total isolation. There are no phones, no electronics, not television or radio, not even electricity. Much of the food is grown right here, the rest secretly traded for the liqueur they make here. It is one of the most isolated places on earth. You won't find it on any maps or survey. You can't Google it or look it up in some encyclopedia. That's why I took you all here, so we can figure out our next moves in complete safety."

"Okay, I get it, I'll even buy it, Father. But some things don't make sense. How can this place be so isolated, what happens if somebody gets sick, or dies suddenly? They have to get to a hospital or be buried if they don't make it, records have to be kept, how can this stay hidden in this day and age? And how do you propose to help find my brother, no electricity, no laptop, no communication, come on."

"Alright, let's take your concerns one at a time: First the easy one. We have a number of generators available even if we don't need to use them regularly and we certainly have laptops, even satellite internet access if needed although both are scarcely used. We also have our own medical facility right here run by a brother who is also a Physician's Assistant, and by the way, I'd put him up favorably against any MD. If anything major is needed, the patient has a choice to leave the monastery for treatment or take their chances here even if it means dying."

Joline stared at Father Anthony, her face stern, eyes blank but holding some hints of disbelief as the priest continued.

"Death doesn't have the same meaning here among the Disciples of the Benediction as it does in the rest of the world. We look at life as a mere preparation for meeting our Lord. There are no recorded instances in over two centuries of a Disciple choosing to leave for medical or any other reasons. We also have a cemetery right on this mountain, a final resting place where their remains face a glorious sunrise each and every morning."

"So they're free to leave this fortress if they choose?"

"It is hardly a fortress. Oh perhaps a couple of hundred years ago there was some thought given to military defense against armies of religious persecutors but such thoughts have long vanished."

"So anyone can leave at anytime?"

"Everything you see is simply meant to keep our existence a secret from the world. Everyone is free to leave at any time, none are held against their will. There are no restrictions or restraints of any kind."

Looking back on the events that followed, I should have known by the conversation what would happen. Normally I would have, but on that day I was perhaps too taken in by the mysteries of this fabulous monastery and its ancient order, or perhaps I was just too bone-weary from the events of the last forty eight hours, whatever the case I was as surprised as anyone the following day.

Joline disappeared during the night.

CHAPTER 53

Joline made up her mind right there and then, during her conversation with Father Anthony that she would leave that night, no if's and's or buts! Her one thought was to find her brother, it burned within her, drove her like a nuclear furnace for she was sure, right down to the last molecule of her body that David was alive and needed her, and she'd be dammed all to hell if she was going to sit on her ass on top of a mountain waiting for something to happen.

Joline firmly believed there were only three kinds of people in the world: Those who made things happen, those who watched things happen, and those who asked what happened? And she knew she was one hundred percent the first kind.

She spent the rest of the evening walking around the main building and grounds. It was just like Father Anthony told her. No locks, no keys, the gates opened with a simple lever, the ATV was left near the gate with keys in it. It was pretty quiet as such vehicles go, but even if it woke the devil himself Joline doubted that anyone would give pursuit.

She ate a hearty dinner in the main dining hall with about a hundred brothers. She'd always thought a monastery would be filled with somber, quiet monks in dark robes and hoods humming weird Gregorian chants, instead she found a lively group, chatting and laughing, passing large plates of rich stew and delicious baked bread back and forth. Jimmy had gone off somewhere with Father Anthony and Sister Anita sat in deep conversation with a couple of older monks.

The brother next to her passed a pitcher of tea and she asked with a grin, "Got any Bud Light?"

He was young with a heavy salt and pepper beard and easy smile. "Not yet," he replied, his English thick with the accents of Eastern Europe. "But some of us wanted to brew some beer for dinners, but the elders, how you say…nixed that idea."

"That's okay, give it time," Joline said. "You'll be an elder someday then you can brew all the beer you want."

The brother laughed and replied, "Maybe by that time we'll have the wisdom to turn it down."

Word passed that Monsignor Anthony would say High Mass in the chapel in a short while. (What the hell is a Monsignor, anyway?) Joline thought, appalled at the inappropriateness of her own thoughts.

One of the monks asked if she would join them. She said no, she was Jewish. He smiled at her and said, "You might make the distinction but God doesn't."

"Yeah, well thanks anyway. I'm just too tired, I'll turn in early."

They had given her a tiny room to herself. The place was about the size of the walk-in closet in her condo. One cot, one night table, one tiny armoire, one window, bathrooms down the hall. She set her watch alarm for four AM, collapsed on the cot and fell asleep almost immediately. Her last conscious thought of the day was, hang on David. I'm on the way.

She awoke to the soft sound of a chugging, whistling train—her alarm. She got up and looked outside. She heard the whistle of the wind at the window, felt the glacial coldness of the glass. She visited the bathroom, the great residence still and quiet as could be. Returning to her room she dressed for the trip.

While everyone was at mass she'd explored the vast halls and rooms of the great house. She found a storage room filled with clothing of all sizes. Evidently everyone helped themselves as needed and she had done just that. She put on a quilted pair of Long johns with a Wal-Mart tag attached, a heavy pair of homespun heavy wool, quilted top and heavy parka with arctic gloves. She left the room, went downstairs and out the large doors into the winter night. The air was cold and burned her lungs but the clothes were suitable and kept her reasonably warm. Thankfully a quarter moon shed enough light for her to find the ATV. She fumbled with the controls, found the keys and started the engine. She turned on the lights, drove the path to the big gate, found the latch and let herself out. She wanted to close the gate but couldn't figure out how to do it from the outside so she left it open. They could take care of it in the morning.

Starting down the path was strange at first. Even though the evergreens were filled with colors the harsh halogen lights of the ATV washed everything in black and white. The wind wasn't too strong but enough to blow snow from the top of the trees onto the path so it seemed as if she drove in a mini blizzard. She veered off the path a couple of times but the heavy undergrowth and surrounding rocks, placed there probably hundreds of years ago by Disciples, steered her back. She knew she should feel some guilt at stealing away like this, but on the contrary, she sensed the ancient spirits of monks passed away so many years ago, felt them as if they were lighting her path, approving of her actions.

Halfway down a giant stag with tremendous horns jumped in her path and she let out a cry as the animal vanished. She'd seen enough National Geographic documentaries to know the only thing that might hurt her in these mountains went on two legs. She continued, doing well for a city girl, she thought.

The sky was lightening as she finally reached the clearing at the base of the hills, and not a moment too soon. The fuel gauge hovered around zero. She briefly wondered how they filled the thing up, but no matter. She parked the vehicle across from the hidden "door" to the shed, engine running, and lights on. She struggled with the door but couldn't budge it. Running out the cable from the winch on the front of the ATV, she looped it around the log that Anthony and Jimmy had opened and winched it until the gate opened. The Chevy sat there, waiting for her and she felt a quick relief. She'd had the fear that somehow the car would have been taken and she'd be left there, to walk down a mountain path into a deserted backwoods road to hitchhike. But all was as they'd left it yesterday afternoon. She turned the key, started the engine, backed the car out and slowly drove down the path toward the road.

Finding the road, she didn't quite know where she was, just drove until the sun came up strong and her watch read nine AM. She came to a blinking light on a blacktop two-lane road marked CR106, went ini-mini-moe and turned left. Five miles later she came into a town called Darby's Junction. One tiny post office, one two-pump gas station, one small diner with a lone telephone booth out front and no Junction. She parked the car at the diner, jumped in the phone booth and called her office collect. She recognized Jonthra's voice as she answered.

"Jonthra, it's me."

"Joline, where the hell you been girl? We're all sick about it, first your brother then you vanish. Where are you?"

"I need help, I'll give you details later, can't tell you about it over the phone. I'm somewhere in West Virginia in a tiny town called Darby's Junction."

"Is anyone following you? Are you in any danger right now? I'll call the State Troopers…"

"No, no, that's the worst you can do. I need some protection."

"I've got Parker and Lee on call. They're the best."

"Who?"

"You know, Parker and Lee, the two ex Delta Force operators you and Fred argued about hiring. I'll bet you one of my oversize bras you'll be happy as a pig in shit that you lost the argument and paid the big bucks for those guys."

"Yeah, no shit. How quick can you get them here?"

"Walter will get a chopper right out of LaGuardia, we'll have them on your ass within an hour, hour and a half, tops."

"Where do I go? I don't have maps or a GPS."

"Okay, hang on a minute." Joline waited and a few minutes later Jonthra got back on the line.

"Alright, you should be on County Road 106, take it for six miles until you get to State Road 209, make a right, stop outside of a town called Chapel Hill. There's a regional airport on the outskirt, we'll have them land there and meet you. Stay by the intersection of SR 209 and a road called Sunny Way. What are you driving?"

"Blue Chevy, don't know the year."

"It's okay, stay there, they'll find you. These guys are the best in the world."

CHAPTER 54

Fort Meade, Maryland–National Security Agency

From two, linked Cray supercomputers called Razzle-Dazzle by their operators, stretched electronic feelers like an immense spider web. Ultra sensitive beyond reason, Razzle-Dazzle held enough room for scores of secretive programs such as the one Supervisor Mayfield operated.

Mayfield was career NSA, a spymaster extraordinaire whose entire working life had been spent in the glass and steel bowels of the massive global surveillance system known as the National Security Agency. Supervisor Mayfield was like thousands of other agents within the giant Fort Meade complex. Endowed with exquisite analytical skills, an engineer's knowledge of computer systems and Top Secret clearances, he was one of the very best. But Mayfield had one thing the others did not have: he was compromised.

Lured decades ago by the cabal calling itself the Essex Junta, he'd satisfied himself that what he was called upon to do had not made him a traitor, he was not a Snowden, not in the least. Everything they'd asked of him had been obscure and minor, never betraying secrets or causing any harm that he could discern, and Lord, what he'd gotten in return!

Diagnosed with Parkinson's disease in his thirties, he'd resigned himself to winding up like that actor, Michael Fox, until Valdemar Khan approached him. After the injections started, the Parkinson's vanished like yesterday's nightmares, and over the last two decades he's enjoyed perfect health, didn't even seem to get older. And now he'd give them what they wanted, so little in return.

He sent the email.

Several hundred miles away Anton Dimitri heard the particular ring that told him email arrived from one of his important sources. He hit the key and read the message:

--Phone call meeting requested profile to Executive Services Corporation from landline town of Darby's Junction West Virginia, ten minutes ago--

Anton quickly replied:

--Send text of conversation--

--Will do, need about an hour--

"Bingo, gotcha again and you're not getting away this time," he whispered to himself, picked up his cell phone, hit the encryption key and a set number.

"Anton here, we've got a location on our fugitives. Vicinity Darby's Junction, West Virginia. How long until we get a couple of teams out there?"

"Wait one," came the terse reply, and moments later, "We have two teams not too far, I can have them there in a couple of hours."

"Quality?"

"First line."

"Do it."

CHAPTER 55

Republic Airfield, Long Island, NY.

The Bell Ranger XB7 waited on the runway, state of the art turbine engines warmed up and idling as a limo pulled out and disgorged two passengers. Both carried huge satchels nearly five feet long. One man was average height and build, clean-shaven, the kind of guy that looked like a retail clerk at Home Depot, but a closer inspection would have revealed a different story: Icy blue eyes brimming with intelligence and cunning, not an ounce of fat over muscles that looked like steel cables that had somehow come to life.

His partner was taller, neatly trimmed beard, same kind of eyes, what those in the know called "cop eyes" watchful, suspicious, not missing any tricks, with muscles honed through countless special operations in all the bad shit holes and against the worst people the planet could vomit.

As the limousines pulled away, the men threw their duffel bags in the compartment of the Bell Ranger and jumped in. The pilot looked at them and said just three words:

"Baker and Lee?"

The bearded one replied, "HooHa."

The engine revved and the helicopter leapt into the sky,

banked toward West Virginia and soon reached its cruising speed of one hundred and ninety knots.

At nearly the same time, in a location by the Pennsylvania-West Virginia border, two men got into a black Lexus and pulled away, followed by three more in a Jeep Wagoneer. All five bore that hardened look of men who'd seen heavy combat, but with an edge of cruelty that most veterans didn't have. From the harsh light in their eyes one could tell they weren't adverse to sadism and murder, that in fact it was part of their repertoire.

Like the Bell Ranger out of Republic Airport in Long Island, they too headed toward Darby's Junction, West Virginia.

CHAPTER 56

Winter mountain light poured through the leaded glass of the main dining room where Father (Monsignor?) Anthony waited for me, plates of scrambled eggs, rolls, and coffee in earthen mugs on the table. Next to it, a laptop rested there, screen lit, filled with columns of figures scrolling down.

"Good morning," he said. "Dig in."

I'd slept late that morning, much later than usual. The activity had sapped my energy and the extra rest was welcomed. It was nine AM and only a few monks remained in the dining room. They were the kitchen and cleanup crew, a duty Anthony told me was rotated among the brothers.

"This is delicious," I told Anthony in between bites of eggs and buttered fresh rolls. "They must have their own chickens."

"And bakery. Whatever else they need is brought in twice a month. They gave up many earthly rewards for this life, but good food wasn't one of them."

"What about this?" I asked, nodding toward the opened laptop.

"I ran a generator this morning while you were in dreamland, recharged the battery and checked out the flash drive Joline left with us. I think she's got a spare by the way or she wouldn't have left it with us so readily."

I reached over and turned the laptop toward me, looking at it for a few minutes. None of it made sense.

"You understand this?"

"Some."

I said nothing, studying Anthony's face. Deep worry lines creased his forehead. He sighed, slowly shaking his head. His eyes held the look of someone peering into a dark abyss, fearing what a sudden light would reveal. Finally he answered my unspoken question.

"This indicates vast sums of money being moved around, but I can't tell from where to where. The word "Jeunessa" appears frequently."

"That's the new food supplement coming out soon, the one they call the Boomer Youth Drug. I heard on the news they had advanced sales totaling over a billion worldwide, two hundred million in the US alone."

"Yes," Anthony replied. "I'm sure that's what they're referring to. I just don't know enough about this to tie it together. What I'm really worried about is the references to Dr. Li Wu at Brookhaven National Lab on Long Island and something called Targeted Vectors."

"You might as well be talking in Latin, Father."

"If it was Latin, I'd understand it. Targeted Vectors must have something to do with genetics. Dr. Wu was instrumental in deciphering the human genome. He's the leading geneticist in the world."

"Don't mean to change the subject," I said. "But do you know that Joline is gone?"

"Yes. Evidently she took the ATV, and probably got the car from the shed."

"I'll be going after her," I said. "She's in danger. Will you come with me?"

"I can't. There's something else I must pursue and I don't think there's a lot of time left."

"What could that be?"

Anthony frowned, stared at the laptop and as I looked in his eyes I realized the priest was downright petrified.

"There are references in there," he said. "References to

something called GKR."

"GKR? What's that spell?"

"I think it means Global Kill Ratios, it's segregated by continents and it totals over three billion."

CHAPTER 57

Over an hour passed until Anton Dimitri received the follow up email from his NSA agent. The message contained the text of the phone call made by Joline and revealed the rendezvous point for her rescue in West Virginia. He smiled, and hit a speed dial on his cell.

Eighty three miles east of Darby's Junction, West Virginia, team leader one received the call, responded with a terse "affirmative" and keyed in the location on his GPS. Moments later the Lexus and Jeep Wagonneer containing both teams headed out.

Cruising at less than six thousand feet and maximum speed, the Bell Ranger crossed into West Virginia from Pennsylvania. Deviating from the flight plan filed earlier, the chopper banked north, rapidly dropping altitude, skimming forests, narrow country roads and farms whose plowed fields ran straight as longitude lines on a map.

Soon the machine landed in a slow hover into a field of wildflowers bordered by a dilapidated fence that ended at a rundown barn with missing doors. Two men jumped out of the helicopter, both carrying heavy duffel bags, and broke into a run as if the weight of the bags didn't exist.

They stormed into the open barn and moments later drove out in a dark green Landrover with heavily tinted windows, all through the resources of Executive Protection Services, Inc.

The Landrover tore through the field, and jumped onto the narrow dirt road heading toward Chapel Hill, trailing a cloud of dust.

CHAPTER 58

Joline paced near the location Jonthra had given her on the outskirt of the town of Chapel Hill. Town was a generous term, she thought. Back on Long Island it wouldn't even make a decent strip mall. One Ace hardware, two feed stores, one supermarket set in a building that must have predated the Civil War, two traffic lights, a Sheriff's office and a few other buildings, and that was it. One good thing about the location was its proximity to State Road 867, not a major highway, but still a two-lane blacktop road moderately traveled, leading to points out of West Virginia.

Several vehicles passed, flatbed trucks loaded with agricultural products, dusty pickup trucks and a few soccer-moms driving suburban cars, all of them slowing down to gaze at the stranger, waiting, obviously not from "around here".

She paused as one vehicle approached, not slowing down at all, a dark Lexus with New Jersey tags, definitely not local. She stepped up to the edge of the sidewalk and that's when it happened….

The Lexus swerved toward her, she jumped back but it was too late. Four wheels suddenly locked, the Lexus almost hit her as a man jumped out. For a big man he moved fast, much faster than her own reflexive actions. In two bounding paces the man caught her and buried a fist in her abdomen. The breath exploded out of her and as she doubled over, the man grabbed her around the waist, effortlessly tossed her in the front seat and jumped in. The driver floored the gas and the Lexus tore out onto the street, Joline held in the front seat between the two men. She struggled to catch her breath, tried struggling all the way, her hand pushing feebly at the man next to her. He pulled out a knife, long and thin, the kind used to fillet fish, and spoke to her, his accent South America, thick moustache dancing, eyes so dead she knew instinctively that gutting her wouldn't bother him at all.

"Tchu move again, I cut you bad, *comprende?*"

Joline froze, knowing for certain the man wouldn't hesitate. She retched once, closed her eyes and tried to be still as a statue.

"There, there…" Parker, passenger of the Landrover said, pointing back where a dark Lexus had passed them. "That's her, they got her."

Lee didn't say a word, whipped the Landrover into a tight U turn, cutting off a pickup and a dusty old station wagon with three teenagers in it. He floored the gas but the Lexus was faster and the distance between the vehicles lengthened.

Now the Lexus approached the edge of town, nearing a Purina feed store. A flatbed farm truck pulled in front of them, driven by a gray haired man in overalls who looked like he'd never gone over the speed limit in his life, and on this stretch of road, it was 35MPH.

The driver flung the Lexus around the truck then braked again, facing yet another pickup. The driver tried to pass again, but this time had to pull back for an eighteen-wheeler in the opposite lane.

That's when Parker and Lee caught up to them.

Lee spun the wheel, passing the farm truck, and instantly saw the tactical situation. He floored the accelerator and the Landrover leaped forward, spinning the wheel he whipped into the opposite lane, passed the first three feet of the Lexus and swung to the right, narrowly missing the eighteen-wheeler in the opposite lane.

The front of the Landrover nailed the left rear quarter of the Lexus, classic police tactics, sending the Lexus into an irrecoverable spin. The car spun once, twice, then came to rest, the nose crashing against a low brick wall, the hood crumpling up, a cloud of steam erupting from a burst radiator.

Lee and Parker exploded out of the Landrover. The man in the passenger side had just gotten out, in the process of leveling a black matte automatic nine-millimeter when Lee triple-tapped him with the modified Uzi machine pistol he carried. Three rounds, center high body, throat, neck and lower head, in case he wore a Kevlar vest, all three shots in a tight grouping, Special Forces style. The man went down, blood spurting in a thin stream onto the windows of the crashed Lexus.

Parker reached the driver's side as the man was pulling out his own automatic weapon. In one incredibly fast movement, Parker crashed the butt of his weapon through the driver's window. The glass shattered along with the driver's jaw, and he followed with two more smashing blows, brutal hits that nailed the driver in the temple and upper jaw. The man's eyes rolled in his head, and he slumped like a puppet whose strings have been suddenly severed. Parker flung open the door, grabbed the man by the collar and waist, hoisted him out of the Lexus and flung his inert body into the rear seat of the Landrover.

Joline saw her captor get out of the car, heard what sounded like three coughs, saw the blood spurt out of the man's neck as he collapsed to the ground. Then her attacker flung open the door and was on her in a heartbeat.

She saw a man with a short beard reach into the car, grab her by the arm and back of her shirt, felt herself yanked out of the car, the man's hands like granite wrapped in leather with paralyzing strength.

The man carried her toward the open rear door of the

Landrover where she could see the inert form of the driver. She screamed a thin screech of terror, a plea for help that would never come. This was the second time in four minutes this was happening to her. She tugged at her captor, screamed again, and he slapped her.

The open-handed blow nearly shut her down, put her in a sort of shock. She wasn't used to this level of violence, had never been hit in her life, and in mere seconds had been turned into a punching bag. She was stunned, dazed as white lights danced in front of her eyes, she gasped, hiccupped and her captor threw her into the rear of the Landrover, right on top of the body of her first captor. Now he jumped in behind her, slammed the door shut and yelled to the driver who'd by now gotten back behind the wheel, "Go go go."

CHAPTER 59

The driver punched the gas and the Landrover tore into the road, passing around a couple of trucks and a stopped car.

She felt her captor raise her from the floor and the still body of the man they'd taken. Now his hands were gentle, his eyes concerned as he carefully helped her sit up.

"Are you okay, Miss Waterman?"

She felt confused. The events had thrown her into a tailspin. "I…uh…" she stammered.

"I'm sorry, Miss Waterman. Please accept my apologies for the slap. It was necessary, our time frame is kind of tight."

She blinked, the clouds in her head just beginning to clear. This man had gone from raging maniac to concerned protector in zero seconds flat. She just couldn't reply.

"I'm Parker, and this is Lee," the man said, nodding toward the driver, a clean-cut man who looked as ordinary as a Wal-Mart employee, yet had gunned down an assailant in under a second. Then she realized what just happened.

"You're the Delta Force guys. Jonthra sent you." She whispered.

"That's right, but we're not out of the woods yet," he said hooking a thumb back. She glanced out the back window. Several vehicles were following, one closing in, a midnight blue Jeep Wagoneer. A quarter mile behind the Wagoneer, two Sheriff's patrol cars approached, blue strobe bar lights on, sirens howling. Far in the distance another patrol car could be seen rushing in.

"Don't have much time to explain, Miss Waterman, but here's the law, there's only one: You may write our checks, but here in the field, we rule. You do everything we tell you, no delays, no questions, no hesitation. That's it, that's all you have to do. Got it?"

"Yes, I got it…but…"

The rest of her question vanished as a burst of bullets shattered the main rear window, ricocheted through the vehicle, blew out the left rear window, thudded into the back of the seat inches from her shoulder. Parker heaved her to the floor and ducked as Lee threw the Landrover into violent back and forth movements as bullets thundered around them, tearing up the asphalt, pinging off the roof and sides.

"Better do something fast, Parker." Lee said from the driver seat, with as much panic as someone ordering chicken from a takeout joint.

"I'm on it." Parker replied as he reached into one of the duffel bags. Joline raised her head an inch or two and peered behind them. The Jeep Wagoneer was closing in and her heart jumped in her throat as she saw a man standing on the front seat, his head and shoulders sticking out of the sunroof, firing an assault rifle at them. Another man leaned out the passenger window, also firing a gun.

"Down, goddamn it." Parker shouted at her. She tried to bury herself on top of the fallen driver. She smelled the blood covering the man's face, the sweat and fear stink of him as he lay under her, his body swaying with the violent movements of the Landrover. Another round of fire burst through the vehicle, the other rear window exploded, one of the rear view mirrors shattered, more rounds pinged and whinnied around them.

She saw Parker duck with a folded two-piece tube he had retrieved, pulled a plastic tie from it, flipped it close on a swivel. She read the letters MOD-LAW and remembered what it meant from her defense courses. Modified Light Antitank Weapon. No…they couldn't…

Parker yelled, "now!" and Lee suddenly held the Landrover rock steady.

Parker gripped the weapon steady and squeezed the trigger.

A tongue of flame shot out of the rear, melting the plastic dash, blackening the right side of the windshield as Lee ducked below the steering wheel.

Joline looked out again and saw the little armor-piercing rocket closing on the Wagoneer. It traveled less than a second, and in that moment she could have sworn she saw the driver's eyes wide open, the face of a man staring into eternity, about to be called to task for a life of darkness.

The rocket hit nearly dead center of the Wagoneer. The initial explosion blew the roof a dozen feet in the air, the body of one gunman cart wheeled, trailing red flames. The vehicle's engine block was blown clean off the frame, spinning into the side of the road. The vehicle leapt several feet in the air, engulfed in a fireball of white heat. It came down on its side in the middle of the road and skidded another six feet in a second bigger fireball as the fuel tank exploded. The entire road surface had turned into an impenetrable blaze, greasy smoke rising in the winter air.

"HooHa" Parker said. "That'll teach them to bring guns to a rocket fight."

Behind the fireball Joline could make out the stopped form of several trucks and a couple of law enforcement cruisers, flashers on, unable to pass the inferno that had suddenly appeared out of nowhere in their peaceful farming town.

She kept looking back as the battered Landrover increased the distance between them and the scene until the only thing visible that remained was the column of smoke.

CHAPTER 60

Lee continued to drive the Landrover but did not take any of the side roads leading to the Interstate. After the altercation with Joline's would-be abductors, the vehicle looked like it had been used as a target in a military firing range. Windows blown out, windshield and right side of the dash burnt to shreds from the rocket's backlash, side mirrors destroyed and nearly every inch of steel punctured by automatic weapons fire, the Landrover was a tribute to its manufacturer's iron quality.

The vehicle came to a culvert on the side of the road, and Lee guided it down an incline to a wide but shallow stream. He navigated the vehicle, slowing it to walking pace as it bounded up and down to the variety of stones composing the riverbed. Dusk was starting to set in and it wouldn't be more than an hour or so until nightfall.

"Where are we going?" Joline asked.

"We're going to hide this thing for the night," Parker answered. "By following the stream we won't leave tracks visible from the air. With the ruckus we caused back there, you'd best believe there'll be a flock of law enforcement aircraft out for us."

"How'd you know this was here? You didn't even look at a map."

"Basic tradecraft, Miss Waterman. We don't go into any

operation unless we have the terrain memorized."

"Oh, okay. I've got to call Jonthra, let her know where we are."

"Not a chance."

"What, what do you mean? I need to touch base with her."

"Miss Waterman," Lee cut in, his tone that of an adult explaining to a child why he can't play with the gas stove. "We start out each operation with the assumption that we are compromised, and it has saved our butts many times. In this case we are certainly compromised from the get-go. Those guys knew exactly where you would be, even had a second team waiting in case somebody like us showed up. Their only error was underestimating the level of competence we brought to the game. So no, Miss Waterman, no communications at all with anyone until we say so."

Now darkness approached fast and it was already difficult to see more than a few yards ahead. The air was cold, although not as cold as it had been on the mountain. She heard the gurgling of the shallow river around stones and gullies, and in the distance the steady whump-whump of searching helicopters.

After a few hundred yards, the Landrover entered a heavily forested bend in the river bordered by a narrow patch of sand. Willows, deciduous trees and tall evergreens intertwined above, shutting out all views from above. Lee stopped the Landrover and for good measure the men threw a camouflage net over the vehicle, making it totally concealed from above.

The prisoner had come to, and he looked pretty bad. His jaw hung at an unnatural angle, one eye was swollen shut and blood coated his mouth with a single tooth embedded in his lower jaw.

"I bet you'd like to know why we took this guy along?" Lee grinned at her.

"Well I didn't think it was a Club Med thing." Joline replied. She felt better, regaining some of her composure.

"Intelligence." Parker said.

"Oh…Oh, I got it, wait, I mean you're not going to waterboard him or something, are you?"

"Nah, pulling fingernails off with pliers should do it."

Joline stared at Baker. Finally he cracked a smile. "That sort of thing never worked too well anyway. We've got better methods, nowadays."

"Well go easy on him, look at the poor guy."

"Sure," Lee said, pulling the prisoner to his feet. The man wobbled, a thin stream of blood leaking out of his mouth. His tongue lolled while the whole face was a swollen mass of black and purple contusions. Lee spoke gently to the man in Spanish and gave him two injections in rapid succession. The man offered no resistance and soon his head lolled on his neck as if all muscles had been severed. Lee questioned him relentlessly while Joline watched, both dreading the violence she believed would follow while anticipating what the prisoner would reveal.

About a half hour passed until the questioning stopped and Baker led the man away into the squid-ink darkness of the forest. She asked Lee where he was taking him, but the man held something out and said, "put these on."

Joline grasped the object. It felt like binoculars with straps secured into plastic bezels. She had no idea what to do with it.

"How do you put it on, what is it?"

"Stay put," Lee said as he slid the object over her forehead and the utter darkness gave way to a visible landscape lit by a garish glow emanating from all sides.

"NVG, Night Vision Goggles. Here, eat this, you'll need the energy, we'll be hiking all night," and he handed her a standard Army MRE, Meal Ready to Eat.

The Delta Force operator showed her how to mix the package and she spooned the contents out with the enclosed plastic implement. It tasted like cardboard with the consistency of toothpaste.

The night seemed alive all around Joline, erupting in a cacophony of chirping, croakings and squeaking under the background of river water rushing over rocks. The difference was that for the first time Joline witnessed the teeming life of the night forest through the NVG's. Squirrels bounding through branches stretching overhead, an owl taking off after some unseen prey, a couple of raccoons cautiously winding their way, looking for scraps from their camp. It fascinated her until Baker emerged from the other side of the vehicle, the side facing the forest. The prisoner wasn't with him, and suddenly it hit her.

"Oh God. Where is he, you didn't…"

"Relax. He's fine. I tied him up, it'll take him all night to get loose and get away."

"But he's hurt, you can't just leave him like that."

"That's exactly what we're going to do. Look, Miss Waterman, these guys are bad apples, came here to do the dirty boogie for cash. They'd just as soon kill you as look at you. He's lucky I didn't gut him with that pigsticker he would have used on you."

The imagery hit her head on: That was the man who'd pulled that wicked knife on her and in the depth of her guts she knew the man would have enjoyed using it on her. She shuddered, shook her head as if to clear it and asked Baker, "So what did you find out?"

"Not a lot because he doesn't know much."

"How do you know he told you everything?"

"Injected him with a souped up version of Sodium Penthatol, the so-called truth serum, robs the will power, makes them pliable so they tell you everything you want to know."

Now Joline saw Lee step forward and caught the glance between the two operators. "The Order, I'd bet." Lee said.

"Got that right." Parker replied.

"What are you talking about? What's the Order? What did the guy tell you? Come on, I'm your boss, remember?" Joline said, hating the pleading tone in her voice. She couldn't help thinking that Jimmy or Father Anthony would have handled things differently, with more confidence.

"The Order," Parker said, "is just a name we gave for

something we really don't have an answer for. Over the years, as the wars on drugs and terrorism heated up, more and more special operations were used, and the more often we ran across strange stuff. Mercenary types hired by untraceable and unknown parties, huge amounts of cash used for hired guns who had no clue as to the origin of their orders, whose goals were hidden and obscure. We ran across these things throughout South America in drug interdiction and cartel wars, Afghanistan, the tribal lands of Pakistan, and other dangerous territories. And it wasn't just Delta, Navy Seals or Army Special Forces. We all encountered it. When we brought it to our superiors nothing happened, as if something higher up squashed it. That's the situation with this guy. He doesn't know who hired him or why. All he's got is his Swiss account and directives to capture or kill you."

"But why, who's behind it?"

"Sorry, Miss Waterman, but that's way beyond our pay grade. Now please, we've got to get ready to roll."

"Roll? Roll where? Let's call my office, they'll send somebody to pick us up."

"No way," Baker said. "I told you before, this operation is compromised. They got there before we did which means they somehow intercepted and understood your message to Jonthra. One phone call from a landline, that's some serious surveillance horsepower there. We're imposing complete operational blackout. As to where, we have a safe location about a twelve mile hike from here, on foot we'll get there before daybreak, so like I said, let's roll."

They each carried heavy duffels with food, weapons and ammo. She was placed between them, carrying nothing, and still she doubted her ability to keep up with those superbly conditioned warriors until Lee's next words caused her spirits to soar.

"Oh, by the way, Miss Waterman, we have a message to tell you from Walter, at your home office. Your brother David Waterman is free, back on Long Island, safe and sound with all charges dropped. Walter said you'd understand."

CHAPTER 61

Losing time is like losing blood. The minutes bleed into hours, into days, into weeks, but unlike blood you can't get a transfusion of time, and David in his confinement just watched it bleed away never to return.

They had moved him to this room, relocated him in such a way as if they dared him to try anything, and he hadn't, thought about it, but didn't try it.

The reason he didn't try to escape when they moved him was because of the black man they'd sent to escort him, just one man—a guy named Ergun. He knew the man's name because he'd only spoken one sentence to David "I am Ergun. I am here to place you in a different room. If you do not comply I will hurt you in ways you cannot imagine."

David believed him. Not because of his size either. Sure the man was big, at least six foot two or three, a couple of hundred pounds and no fat that David could see. But that wouldn't have stopped him. He'd handled much bigger men with his martial arts skill. Ergun had midnight skin-tone and the facial features found in Senegal, or Dahomey. The eyes were the start of a psychic spiral that sent David's mind into a dark well of fear. Tar—brown eyes whose depths were flecked with gold where flashes of silver seemed to dance, the man projected an aura of Power and ruthless strength that nearly paralyzed David. He'd never encountered such waves of energy that pulsed and awakened the fear center of his brain, the lizard part that only seeks to preserve itself through abject submission or flight, and of course for David, flight was impossible.

He'd followed Ergun down a flight of stairs to the end of a narrow hallway into the room he was in right now. Ergun didn't need a weapon to threaten and coerce David. His presence was enough. David had entered the room, heard the door click behind him and that had been that.

His prison had pile carpet, a single bed with the most comfortable mattress he'd ever lay in, covered by a duvet spread offering perfect warmth when the lights dimmed for eight hours and the temperature dropped to a level perfect for sleeping. Soft light came from translucent panels in the ceiling, easy music out of hidden speakers and three times a day a slot would appear in the wall and a tray of food would slide into a recess. One corner of the room held an open shower, a toilet and a sink, all operated with buttons that shut the flow off after a given time. It was a combination of Maximum Security and Club Med.

At first he yelled, shouted, banged on the walls, creating a muffled thud that he knew didn't even penetrate. He'd pulled up the carpet to find a solid steel floor as if they enclosed him in a metal box and threw the furnishings in like an afterthought.

After a while he'd just given up and waited.

A door suddenly opened on the other side of the room. He hadn't even known it was there. Ergun stepped three paces into the room, stopped and stared at David.

He felt his hand begin to shake, he wanted to scream, demand to be released. Instead he grasped the shaking hand with his other one, and now both hands shook. What was the matter with him? Did they put something in his food? He felt nauseous, the room was spinning and Ergun seemed to grow, his mouth opening to a hideous grin, the white teeth elongating to fangs. David shook his head, closed his eyes and reopened them and the illusion vanished.

"Come with me. You have a meeting with Mister Khan."

Ergun said. He turned and stepped out of the room as if no question existed that David would follow.

David followed.

Just a couple of doors down the hall, no more than thirty or forty feet, Ergun opened a door, waved David inside and closed it behind him.

He was in an office not much bigger than the room he'd just left—same carpet, a desk, a couch and two chairs facing the couch. The air smelled clean but laced with chemicals and piano music flowing from somewhere, the volume so low as to just be faintly audible.

Valdemar Khan stood next to the desk. He wore an all white suit that fit so well it had to be handmade, a pink shirt and lavender tie. He looked completely at ease and in control like the chairman of the board of a huge, successful corporation.

A woman sat on the edge of the couch. She was an older woman, prim, wearing a business suit that gave her a serious allure she might not have had otherwise. The woman looked familiar and it took David a few moments to recognize her as the secretary/receptionist of the William Brogan Foundation.

"Thank you for coming, David." Khan said, and nodded toward the chair facing the couch. "Please sit, we have much to discuss."

David felt heat flush to his face as the anger of his confinement rose like bile from a lousy meal.

"Fuck you, Khan. Let me go, right now."

"Oh my," the woman said.

"I do apologize, David. I only need a moment of your time. I brought Miss Dolan to help state our case. I believe you met Miss Dolan? She's been a trusted employee for many years."

David fought the urge to rush the man, just smash his face, then he remembered that Ergun would be close by, probably watching through some hidden camera, and Khan didn't look like a pushover either.

"Please, David, sit, give me a chance to explain."

David sat.

"May I get you coffee, tea, water?"

"No, let's get this over with."

"Very well," Khan replied, and sat on the couch next to the woman, both facing David in his chair.

"Miss Dolan, would you hand me that photo album on the end table, please."

David watched the woman turn slightly and stretch an arm over to grasp the album. In that moment Khan reached behind him and pulled out the largest handgun David had ever seen, leveled it at the woman's head and pulled the trigger.

The bullet that had to be the size of a grown man's thumb, hollow point steel-jacketed copper, left the barrel at supersonic speed and exploded into the right side of Miss Dolan's head between the temple and the point where the lower jaw hinges to the skull.

In the enclosed space the blast was devastating, the results horrendous to a degree that David could never have imagined.

The top three quarters of Miss Dolan's head vaporized, instantly filling the room with a red mist. Droplets of gore splattered the walls, couch, and desk, laying a pattern of splashed blood on Khan's immaculate white suit. David felt the blood hit his face and body, pieces of skull and bloody little chunks of flesh hit him in the face, clinging to his hair, nose, cheeks and clothes. A single eyeball splattered against the wall and slowly began sluicing toward the floor trailing the optic nerve like a demonic snail from some nether region of hell.

The hydrostatic shock of the bullet strike lifted Miss Dolan's entire body two feet off the couch. Her death convulsion flung her sideways, striking the wall, the corpse coming to rest in a tangle, showered bloody from the open wound that was all that remained of her head. The carotid artery stuck grotesquely out of the shattered jaw emitting one final gory pulse. The horrid charnel house scent of the dead woman mixed with the odor of the emptying bowels and gunfire-cordite in a miasma of smells rivaling any battlefield.

The noise and shock overwhelmed David, toppling his chair, flinging him against the wall. He'd never imagined such a level of violence could exist. His mind turned to abject terror, entering into a shock similar to that causing Post-Traumatic Stress Syndrome in combat soldiers. He made a gurgling noise, deep down in his throat, vomited and just lay there, bile drooling from his mouth, gurgling-whimpering noises erupting from the depth of his being.

Khan rose from the couch, the big silver Desert Eagle fifty caliber automatic, the world's biggest handgun, shining in his hand like a venomous snake's fang. He brushed a piece of white cartilage and bloody little chunks of flesh from his face using the delicate, decorative handkerchief from the pocket of his white suit, now polka dotted with gore.

Casually, like a man reaching the end of a satisfying and successful business day, he stepped behind the desk, placed the gun in a drawer, took out a small towel, a bottle of water and a single pill, and walked over to where David crouched against the wall.

Slowly, as if he didn't want to startle him, Khan squatted in front of David until their faces were level.

"There, deep breath, please," Khan said, his voice smooth and hypnotic. David's mind floated in a whirlpool of horror and confusion. He listened to Khan, and tried to steady his breathing.

"Here, take this," Khan said, handing him the pill and bottle of water. "It's a mild sedative, it will calm you so you can think clearly again and we can proceed."

David took the pill and held it in the palm of his hand.

"Go on."

He placed the pill in his mouth, took the bottle of water Khan held out and swallowed.

Khan took the bottle of water, spilled the contents onto the towel and gently cleaned David's face.

His eyes on Khan, he offered no resistance although he

knew Khan's gentle demeanor reached new heights of hypocrisy. Slowly his thoughts steadied, his breathing became normal. Deep within David a fear bloomed like a nascent flower in sunshine. It was something new, born of the terrible murder he'd witnessed. He somehow knew given time this fear would turn into a buried kernel rooted deep in his psyche. Eventually he'd conquer it, but the effects would never vanish.

Khan grasped David under his left arm and helped him up. He guided him back to the chair and gently forced him to sit.

"Now, let's get to our business," Khan said.

"Can…can we, maybe…" David stammered, his eyes fixed on Miss Dolan's bloody corpse.

"Go elsewhere? No, I think not. This is an ideal setting for what we are going to discuss."

"But why? What did this woman do?"

"Do? Why, nothing. She was an excellent employee. But like all our employees, she had a purpose that had to be fulfilled."

"Purpose? I don't understand."

"Her purpose, David, was to impress upon you our resolve and the entirely ruthless methods we are capable of using when something stands in our way. That was her purpose, to demonstrate to you that nothing will prevent us from reaching out goal, to imprint this in the deepest levels of your mind so there will be no mistakes on your part. Do you understand now, David?"

He just nodded at Khan, didn't have the words to respond to the depths of evil he'd been hurled into.

"Good. Now before we begin I want you to see something, David."

Khan stood and stepped toward the end table. A piece of gory flesh squished under his foot and David turned his eyes away. Khan returned with the album from the end table and handed it to David.

"Open it."

David opened it and the shock nearly overwhelmed him,

again. His mind felt as if he'd been tossed to the edge of an abyss, slowly being pushed over while something venomous hissed and slithered in the darkness below.

The page held a photo of his sister Joline. He wanted to close the album but Khan held his hand tight on the glossy surface.

"Open each page, David. Look at each one and understand. Go on…"

David opened the album, page by painful page. Each plastic enclosed sleeve contained a surveillance photo of his sister. Joline getting out of her car, entering her office, her condo, the supermarket, a clothing shop, hardware store, her company's training facility on Long Island, twenty nine pages in all, each time and date stamped.

"Yes, David, that's your sister, Joline. Is there any doubt in your mind we have the ability to snatch her anytime we want, just like we did with you?"

"Please, no…"

"Answer the question."

"No, you have the ability."

"Good, I'm glad you understand. Now here is what you must do. Go back to the Foundation office, complete a favorable audit report and file the Foundation's tax return with your audit report attached. You will also file a copy with the New York State Bureau of Charity as required by law. You will return immediately to Long Island and visit the Police with one of our attorneys. We will by then have settled your legal issue in the death of Bennett Whittier. The guilty party was found with undisputable proof of your innocence and your kidnapping. Unfortunately he was killed in a police shootout upon resisting arrest. What a pity."

Bennett Whitier dead? Police shootout? He'd never known any of this. All he remembered was an altercation in the office and waking up a prisoner.

"It will all be explained to you," Khan said, reading the confusion on David's face. "Now allow me to explain what will happen if you do not comply with our request: Your sister Joline will be kidnapped and taken to one of our secure locations. There will be no ransom demand and no trail will be left for the authority. She will be tortured and die a cruel, painful death. It will take two to three days, and during that time you will be forced to watch. When Joline finally, and mercifully expires, it will be your turn. Do you understand my words, David?"

"Please, yes, yes…I understand."

"Good. On the other hand, once you comply you will never hear from us, ever again. Now, will you do as we asked?"

"Yes, yes. I'll do it."

CHAPTER 62

Jeunessa Rollout–Minus Five

In what would later be described as the biggest public relations sales effort in history, the commercial culminated a month long blitz of print, Television, radio and internet ads:

Five days to your new life! The message flashed on the screen for twelve seconds (an eternity for television ads) interspaced with a variety of subliminal images until the message began with a Robert Redford look-alike announcer: "That's right, five days to your new life, just five short days until you are able to pick up your very own supply of Jeunessa"—the camera pans to a suburban neighborhood, not impoverished, but not too plush either, the kind of houses nearly everyone, especially if they're Baby Boomers, can identify with. It's midday and a big Buick, the kind favored by older folks, pulls into the driveway of one of the houses. A man gets out of the driver's side, followed by a woman, obviously his wife, on the passenger side. She's carrying a small package as she walks around the car and they meet at the front stoop. Her steps are slow, measured, there's a slight stoop to her posture, perhaps the beginning of some spinal curvature. The camera closes in and viewers get a close up shot of the couple. His face is wrinkled, the eyes puffy, and some turkey wattle appears below the chin. He looks tired. His wife is equally wrinkled with the beginning of drooping jowls on either side of her face. She smiles then frowns, "that darn arthritis" she says as she takes a package from her purse and removes a small jar. The camera pans on the jar and the name Jeunessa and its logo on the label. A smile comes to the woman's face as she looks at the man. "Maybe this will be like everyone's talking about," she says, and the picture fades.

Instantly the image returns and the words "Two Weeks Later" flash on the screen and the picture re-appears. Now the man is mowing his lawn under a bright sun. His steps are fast, his back straight as he vigorously pushes the mower. The man stops, and the camera pans on him as he wipes his brow. The wrinkles are much less noticeable, there's an electric look in his eyes and a smile on his lips. He turns toward the door where his wife just stepped out on the porch. She's wearing a clingy pants suit, her hair is done up and she's quite attractive, like an older fashion model. There are no signs of jowls and the wrinkles are reduced to a few laugh lines enhancing her face. She smiles at the man and shouts, "Eddie, don't get too tired, we have dancing lessons tonight."

The man looks at her and says, "Okay, don't worry." He turns to the camera, winks and says, "Since Jeunessa, I can go all night!"

The camera pans back to the original announcer. "Look," he says, his voice perfectly modulated, his face gives him the appearance of a well-maintained fifty. "Jeunessa can't promise that you will live longer, although studies show that an extra dozen vigorous years is certainly possible. Vibrant good health may bring that about and that's exactly what Jeunessa will give you: Vitality and health that you would never have thought possible. So make the best of whatever years you have, take Jeunessa. I have, and after celebrating my seventy ninth birthday last week, I feel better than ever"

Now the announcer holds up a jar with the Jeunessa label and finishes:

"Thanks to Jeunessa. Take it today before supplies run out."

An offscreen voice, brimming with enthusiasm, now cuts in:

Jeunessa–Just five days to a new life!

Outside of Essex, Connecticut

Since it wasn't a full board meeting of the Essex Junta, the high tech displays were not being used as the three men sat around the table in the meeting hall.

The Chairman sat at the head of the table, on his right Valdemar Khan. A technician had just placed a flat screen monitor on the table, inserted a quarter-sized disc in the machine, pressed the "on" button and quietly left the room as the film began.

Interior shots of a factory panned across the screen. The manufacturing facility consisted of a warehouse-size single room with vaulted ceilings where high-tech lamps recessed into hidden panels lit the scene like a noonday sun. The place was filled with steel tables topped with machinery that held rows of moving bars each containing an array of hundreds of thin bars that ended in points. The bars were automated, rotating rapidly so the points dipped into shallow vats of serum, immediately pulled out again, moved upward and paused under heat lamps for about three seconds then flipped into preset plastic packaging. By that time the material on the points had dried to a single point the size of a small aspirin tablet. Each package was left on a tray, open end up, awaiting some final step before being sealed. Thousands of such trays could be seen stacked in piles, each pile set at the mouth of yet another conveyor, except that this particular conveyor, the largest of all, sat dark and silent, the final step not yet ready.

The Chairman reached over and shut off the device and the monitor went dark. He looked at the man to his right, the Botany Science Chair, and said, "What happens next?"

"What you saw Mister Chairman are shots of our production facilities in Delaware, a duplicate of our other one in Virginia. However, Mister Chairman, we are awaiting the compound, without it, this is a meaningless waste of large sums of money."

The Chairman just stared at him with a dry-ice look and said nothing.

"Well, uh, Mister Chairman, when we get the final compound, it will be placed onto special trays at the end of the assembly belt where each pill will be dipped exactly one two hundredth of a second, that is all that is needed for a lethal dose when taken twice daily for just three days. Each package will be immediately sealed, cut into strips and an even dozen strips of the now packaged pills deposited into rows of jars. Soon as the jars are filled, they will instantly be rotated through a machine and emerged on a conveyor belt with sealed tops and the Jeunessa label with logo glued to the front. As the jars reach the end of the conveyor belt they will be placed into plastic boxes for shipping, twenty-four to a box. Assuming we receive the compound in three days as promised, we will ship over six million doses per day, every day. Twelve million doses will be available on the day of the rollout, increasing to eight million doses daily thereafter."

The Chairman nodded, and turned to Khan. "Mister Khan, what is the status of the project on your end?"

"As you know, Mister Chairman, we just solved our most vexing problem. The Foundation tax returns were filed yesterday along with favorable audit results. The accountant was most cooperative so we can be assured funding will continue without IRS interference. I will handle the compound next with Doctor Wu at Brookhaven lab. It will be delivered within forty eight hours as promised."

The Chairman nodded and Khan felt a flood of relief. The Chairman was the only person on earth he truly feared. There was a quality of menace to the man that was almost supernatural and to incur the Chairman's displeasure was unthinkable. Khan recalled those who had opposed the man over the centuries and how they inevitably ended. He controlled any visible emotions, but surreptitiously squeezed the fingers of one hand under the table until he felt the nail penetrate the flesh of his palm. The Chairman had that effect.

"I trust Mister Khan that you will tie up those loose ends that may come back and hurt us?"

"Yes, sir." Khan replied without hesitation. "It has been arranged and will take place shortly."

"The accountant?"

Khan paused for a moment as he thought of his promise to Father Anthony–The accountant, David Waterman, is not to be harmed.

"Problem?"

"Uh, no, Mister Chairman, but this cannot be done quickly. If he were to be terminated so fast after filing the audit report with the IRS, I fear that suspicions would be raised along with unwelcome scrutiny."

"I understand, but his presence is a greater threat. Terminate him in the next couple of days, make it an accident."

Now the Chairman fixed his gaze on Khan. It reminded him of a bird of prey locking onto a living meal. Khan felt a frisson, like the shadow of a ghost dancing across his grave, he thought, as he replied, "Yes, sir. I will take care of it."

CHAPTER 63

Joline watched through the NVG's as Lee and Parker placed vegetation and branches over the shot-up Landrover. Between the large evergreen branches curving into a canopy over the vehicle and the camouflage job by the Delta Force operators, an observer would have to literally stumble into the Landrover to find it, much less locate it by aerial search.

"Ready, Miss Waterman?"

"Call me Joline, and yeah, I'm ready, I was born ready."

Event through the green-coated world of the NVG's Joline could see the grin on Parker's mouth—the top half of his head obscured by a camo do-rag and the NVG's. "Okay, let's do it." he replied, and led the way. Joline followed with Lee directly behind.

Joline was in excellent shape. As CEO and stockholder of Executive Protection Services, a company that depended heavily on the physical conditioning of its employees, she couldn't afford being a couch potato. She ran four miles a day, at least five days a week, coupled with steady weight and martial arts training. But the events of the last couple of days had put a strain on her physical resources. When you added the superb conditioning of the two Delta Operators—training forged through the fire of countless special operations—she found her resources taxed to a whole new level.

Using a hand held GPS, Lee had calculated the necessary pace to reach their next point before dawn, and it was grueling.

The terrain bloomed around her in the transparent world of the NVG's. First a narrow, serpentine deer-run then a series of meadows, some bordered by ancient, rotted wood fences, others enclosed by long stretches of scrub oaks that caught on boots and pant legs, to be relieved by much welcome stretches of piney woods whose carpet of fallen needles felt positively plush under her feet.

She stumbled, almost running to keep up, feeling Parker close behind her. Time stretched, her breath came in ragged pulls, sharp lances of pain riddled her feet, the muscles of her thighs burned and the whole trek began to take the hypnotic quality of a long, measured torture session, the kind you get in a nightmare of epic proportion. How Parker and Lee did it while carrying those heavy satchels without ever a misstep was beyond her understanding. Were these guys even human?

It was nearly one AM when she stumbled, couldn't recover, and fell flat out, her head bruising painfully on a half-rotted log. She came up on one knee, stood and tripped again. This time she felt a steel band grab around her waist. She turned her head to see Parker's face a few inches away.

"Lean on me," he said, placing her arm around his shoulder, just above that heavy bag lashed to his back.

She didn't argue.

Joline couldn't tell at what point she finally gave out, when her legs buckled and the muscles refused to obey. She felt the world spin, the NVG images upside down, and she realized Parker had simply picked her up in a fireman's carry, like some wounded soldier retrieved by his buddy. A little part of her burned with shame, but an even greater part brimmed with gratefulness as she closed her eyes and let the darkness take her.

She awoke a couple of times along the way. In one instance she felt a subtle difference in the man who carried her, and they were now in the lead. It was Lee, sometime during the march they'd switched, took turns carrying her like a sack of laundry, but by that time she just didn't care.

She came to again and said, "Let me down, I can walk." He obliged her.

Joline looked at her watch: A little past five AM. A slight pink tinged the eastern sky as she raised her NVG's. Dawn was approaching.

"You okay, Joline?" She heard Parker say behind her.

"Yeah, uh, I'm sorry, thanks for the help."

"That's why we get the big bucks," she heard him reply. "Just hang tight, we're almost there."

"Where is there?"

"You'll see."

She kept going, didn't have the extra energy to waste on more questions. Like the man said, she would see.

As the sky lightened her NVG's were no longer needed. She peeled them off her forehead and let them hang around her neck by the leather strap.

The air was frigid, she saw her breath in plumes, smelled the thinning forest around her, inhaled the scent of manure and hay from some nearby field.

Another ten minutes or so and they crossed a fence, this one weathered but maintained. Another hundred yards and they came to a dilapidated barn without doors. Planks hung askew among shards of peeling paint and a wooden hex sign that could have dated back to the revolutionary war. Two loft openings and the missing doors gave the huge barn the appearance of a square head with a gaping mouth whose teeth had fallen out long ago.

Lee stepped inside, flicked on a tiny flashlight, located a Coleman lantern, turned it on and hung it from a protruding hook.

Farm implements and machinery occupied one side of the barn, their wood handles cracked and weathered, the metallic parts covered with rust as if they'd just laid there for the better part of a century. It was the other side of the barn that drew Joline's attention: A thirty foot Tioga Class

C motor home was parked there, resting on four hydraulic jacks built into the machine. An exhaust tube stuck out from the side of the RV where a gas heater hummed, a nightlight faintly illuminated the interior.

Both men put down their packs by the door, and Parker turned to Joline.

"We're going to rest here for a while, till about midday then we'll get going again."

Joline leaned against the open doorway of the RV. The interior was warm, inviting. "This is yours?" she asked.

"Yup, part of our domestic operations equipment. Don't worry, it's all on your billing," Lee said. He took an MRE (Meal Ready to Eat) and offered it to Joline. She declined it. He reached into his pack, pulled out a bottle of water and a small pillbox, shook one out and offered the pill and water to Joline.

"What the hell is that?"

"Tylenol PM, works wonders. Take it, we'll be moving out in about five hours and you'll need the rest."

"Move out where?"

"We're hoping you'll be able to help us with that question."

A little later Parker came out of the RV with a couple more MRE's and freshly brewed coffee, handed a meal and cup to Lee and sat next to him.

"How is she," Lee asked, scooping mouthfuls of a pasty greenish substance from the plastic pouch.

"She's fine, out like a light on the main bed in the back. I'll take the couch, you take the bunk above the driver's compartment."

"Fine. I know you couldn't talk about it with Joline, but now tell me, the prisoner, what'd he really say?"

Parker shook his head, "Curiouser and curiouser."

"Don't give me that Doctor Seuss stuff."

"That's Alice in Wonderland."

"Okay Mister Madhatter, what'd he say?"

"His immediate boss was that guy with the two missing

fingers, you know the one we ran into in mexico."

Yeah, Parker remembered. It had been one seriously fucked up operation, lost three of their own along with a couple more DEA guys and some native *Federales*.

An entire team of five Delta Force operators had been put on loan to the DEA at the request of the Chief of Central Intelligence who reported directly to Homeland Security. They had been told of drug cartel activity in the mountains near Puerta Vallerta. Those activities represented a direct threat to the security of the United States, not just for the obvious drug issues, but because some serious intelligence intercept suggested it could become a pipeline for terrorism. The whole operation had been Top-Secret, even the Mexican Federal government had been involved at some level.

Dropped in darkness by three "Nightstalker" Blackhawks, fourteen men arranged themselves in a half-mile semicircle. Four Mexican Special Forces Federales, five DEA agents, and five Delta Force operators. Two nights of observations and finally a key man identified and the trap sprung. It was the kind of operation that Parker and Lee had carried out many times in much more dangerous places, like Afghanistan, the Pakistan Tribal areas and the Hindu Kush mountains. But this one went horribly wrong, and all because of the man with the missing fingers, the one they figured was a leader of what they called The Order.

To this day, neither could say with certainty what exactly happened. It should have gone well, all the elements were in place and all did their job, but they might as well have been laced with some kind of mind-altering gas, a form of LSD in aerosol—at least, it's the only way it could be explained unless you wanted to go into some serious occult or mind control activity.

The man with the missing fingers simply stood and stared as the world spun around them, their will evaporating, some kind of hypnosis taking over the reasoning process. The men had been executed, one at a time, no screams, no protest, as if each welcomed the fate meted out.

Lee and Parker had been the tail end of the trap, the end of the funnel where the prey was to have been driven. Perhaps the greater distance had saved them, because each had felt the influence, struggled against the urge to simply give in, walk toward the man for the welcome relief of a couple of steel jacketed bullets in the brain.

It had been painful, like walking barefoot on coals, the mental aspect of it all no relief. They'd crawled away, every nerve center on fire, and somehow escaped.

Lee and Parker had been the only two who'd made it to the extraction point.

Yeah, he remembered the man with the missing fingers.

"Did he tell you how to find that prick? I'd like to have a chat with him."

"No, but I did get a few more details out of him. It should help us in our next moves, because whoever they are, they want Joline real bad."

"Well, this info should help us. Oh, by the way, the guy was one of the leaders at Bellasposa, you know the little village in Columbia, near the Venezuelan border."

"The massacre, forty women and children, the one they blamed on the Narcotrafficantes?"

"Yeah, he was one of the scumbags."

"I guess you really didn't leave him tied to the tree."

"No, I did, only not breathing, gave him a fatal dose. I figured it was a great combination of justice and operational security."

Lee finished his MRE, stood and said, "Let's get some shuteye, big day tomorrow."

"Yeah, and I think we need to make a detour in New Jersey."

"Nikki?"

"Yeah. I get the feeling we're definitely going to need her."

CHAPTER 64

Brookhaven National Laboratory—Upton, Long Island, New York.

Dr. Li Wu sat very still at his desk, the photo in front of him, a young smiling Chinese girl holding a wide-eyed beaming child of no more than two or three years.

They were all that was left, all he had. He tried not think about the other photos, the ones that haunted every waking moment, turned him into an insomniac, worried at his gut until he was ready to do anything—even the unthinkable, which he'd already done.

The man who called himself Valdemar Khan had reached him about eight months ago. Khan knew all about his work including some things that not even the President of the United States and his Council on Science knew.

And he'd had the photos.

Dr Wu and his wife, Mei Lin had only one child, the beautiful young woman in the photo on his desk. The little boy was their grandson, their only grandchild.

It was less than a year since Mei Lin had died suddenly, the cause of her death as mysterious as the forces of the universe controlling such unfathomable events. Since then he'd often thought that Valdemar Khan and whatever devils he represented caused the death of his wife, in fact, deep down in his soul he believed it, but could never act upon such a thing even if irrefutable proof came to him special delivery from Lucifer himself. Dr Wu remembered when he'd first been "recruited" by Khan….

He'd been working late in the lab, something he'd done every night since the burial of his wife. The familiarity of the lab and his work soothed him while the empty house echoed everything he'd lost.

Khan had walked into the biology building where Dr Wu's lab was located. He wore a temporary lab ID and carried federal credentials.

"Dr Wu, my name is Valdemar Khan and I need a few moments of your time."

Wu had always been a good judge of character, and this man invoked an unpleasant sensation. For a mad moment he believed that's how encountering an evil spirit might feel like.

In the next few moments he discovered it wasn't far from the truth.

"We need your help in creating something for us," Khan said.

In the silent lab, Wu felt a frisson of fear. They were isolated and the menace of this man was something palpable. But his fear wasn't as great as one might believe for he'd already lost what was most precious to him. Not even forfeiting his life could be worse.

He would soon find out it just wasn't so.

"I'm not the one you need to talk to," Dr Wu replied. "You need to see the central office where research grants are dispensed, and…"

Khan had just placed a series of photos on his desk and they froze his blood. He heard the humming rush of air molecules hitting the drums in his inner ears, felt the beating of his heart. The very stillness of the room was a living force mocking him and the twisted turns his destiny had suddenly taken.

"Where…how did you get this? Where are they? Please…"

Khan had placed four photos in front of him. All were pictures of the young woman and the child in various poses, obviously captives, even more obviously terrified.

"Yes, they are captives, Dr Wu, somewhere in the foothills of Mongolia in Mainland China. Their fate is entirely in our hands. They can live or die, it's up to you."

"Please take me instead. I'll give you anything you want."

"Yes you will, Doctor. Here is what we need..."

And the monstrosity of the request had taken his breath away. If it had been just him he would have given his life rather than carry out this grotesque task. But with the life of his only child and grandchild, well there had been no contest.

Now the time had come, the end of the line had been reached as Valdemar Khan walked into his lab, same as he'd done eight months ago. This time he just asked a single question: "Is it ready?"

"Yes. The drums are in the storage room, second door on the left."

"Good, we will load them on the truck immediately."

"No, wait. You promised."

"Yes," Khan replied. "The compound and your life for that of your child and grandchild. We kept our bargain."

Khan produced another set of photos and laid them on the desk. The woman seemed to have aged, the boy obviously so, but the setting was different, a luxury hotel room.

"They are in Taiwan, awaiting a flight as we speak. She has received a special visa and research grant to the University of Southern California. Green card and citizenship will follow. She will prosper and look back on her parents with fond memories."

"How do I know, what proof..."

"There is no proof and you have no choice, yet it is so, my word is the only thing you have, but it is solid. You may also be assured that if you don't keep your end of it, all this can be reversed and great harm will come to them. By now you already know of our Power and abilities."

When he replied, Dr Wu's voice was like fine silk flowing across a glass table. "Yes, I do. Please take the compound and go."

Khan strode to the door and opened it. Four men walked in. They wore white coveralls with insignias of some obscure federal bureaucracy and ID badges around their neck on metal chains. They pushed hand trucks as they followed Khan to the storage room and loaded six fifty-gallon drums into the back of a waiting truck.

When they were done, Khan walked back into the lab and placed a black metal box in front of Dr Wu.

"Have a good evening," he said with the faintest shadow of a smile running across his face, and left the building, closing the door behind him.

Dr Wu remained in the chair, facing the black box on his desk. He closed his eyes and reverted to Zen, the sacred philosophy that had been his strength for this last year of his life.

What is, is. Have the serenity to accept what cannot be changed.

Time passed as Dr Wu sat in the stillness of the office, serenaded by the buzzing of a defective neon light, flickering like the last moments of his life. He slowly reached over, opened the lid on the metal box and peered inside, into a smooth black surface in which two LED's blinked.

The first LED was a simple blinking dot. The second was a digital counter.

4

He closed his eyes, let the serenity flow.

3

His wife's face floated in his memory, a gentle smile on her lips, *Soon my darling*

2

His beautiful daughter and her precious child

1

The serenity

There was no pain. That no longer existed for Dr Wu as he looked down upon the giant fireball and huge column of smoke that contained the vaporized molecules of his body, and in that moment, as his spirit, the essence of his very soul ascended to the next level, he knew for certain that his daughter and grandchild would be fine.

Valdemar Khan led the convoy, the truck containing the barrels of compound behind him and a security vehicle following. He was a few miles away, just entering the Long Island Expressway when he heard the explosion and felt the blast wave rock the car even at this distance.

He smiled and led the convoy toward the Jeunessa production facilities, first the one in Delaware the second in Virginia.

CHAPTER 65

In the end, we decided to stay together, Father Anthony and I. First order of business was to decipher the information on the flash drive, then to locate Joline. What to do afterward seemed murky. I guess it depended on what was on that memory stick and how it related to the events of the last few days. I knew it was all tied together, exactly how, I didn't understand but we sure would find out.

We went to thank the brothers who had hosted us, and say farewell—temporarily we hoped—to Sister Anita.

We found her in the monastery's clinic, in a large room containing six beds, all with patients. The place was as clean as any location could possibly be, and as with all such facilities I'd ever been in, smelled of rubbing alcohol and antiseptic.

Sister Anita wore a white coat with a stethoscope around her neck and a blood pressure cuff hanging out of the coat's pocket. Her coffee-colored broad face focused on a patient to whom she was administering an injection. She finished, swabbed the arm with cotton, smiled at the patient and tucked the blanket up to the brother's chin. She straightened and seemed to notice us for the first time. I was sure she'd seen us before but chose to ignore us—patients first, after all.

"Good morning, Father, Jimmy."

"Good morning, Sister," we both said.

"Going somewhere?"

I let Father Anthony handle that one.

"Uh, yes, we have to…"

"Find Joline? Figure out the mysterious stuff on that memory drive you've all been fussing with?"

"How did you know? About Joline, I mean."

She cocked her head and looked at us both. She reminded me of that movie actress Queen Latifah.

"Wasn't exactly hard to figure out, you know. Both of you go ahead and leave, go on, git. The doc in here is about ninety if he's a day. These people need help, serious help. I'll probably be here a few days, that's for sure. Keep in touch let me know what's happening. Communications here are just great, right?"

"Uh, well, you could…" I finally managed to say.

"That's a joke, college boy." She told me. Then she stepped forward and held me in a warm hug. "Take care of yourself, and the Father, okay, Jimmy."

I nodded, stepped out of the embrace, and we both started to leave when she stopped us. "Wait, Father, you forgot something. I need it very much."

A puzzled look flashed across Anthony's features, then he figured it out. He stepped forward as sister Anita went to one knee. He said a few words in Latin, made the sign of the cross over her and said in a clear voice,

"Dear Father, watch over this woman, your servant. Help her do your work, guide her with your mighty and benevolent hand and bless her with your grace. In the name of the Father, the Son, and the Holy Spirit, Amen."

He bent until his face was level with Sister Anita and kissed her on the forehead. She looked up at him, reached for his hand and kissed his ring.

The sun had traveled midway to noon when we left the monastery. Patchy brown clouds raced across the sky leaving enough blue showing that we knew it probably wouldn't snow that day, even this high in the mountain. The air was as cold as a butcher's frozen meat locker. We wore a hodgepodge of warm clean winter clothing, probably the same sort of thing Joline had on when she left in the middle of the night. We entered a shed next to a wide courtyard containing several big tree stumps upon which a half dozen monks chopped logs into chimney-sized pieces. The air smelled of freshly splintered oak and pine resin, a clean and timeless scent that made you want to inhale the deepest breaths one's lungs could handle. I felt good. In such a setting anything seemed possible.

The shed contained seven ATV's, and we chose the smallest one, a four-passenger contraption with a small carrying compartment.

It took the better part of an hour to reach the clearing where we exchanged the ATV for one of the two remaining pickup trucks, and closed the entrance again. Father Anthony drove, and as I looked back I would never have been able to tell where the barn containing the vehicles was, and certainly not the well-hidden trail leading up the mountain to what I had come to think of as "the lost monastery."

Father Anthony drove as I sat silent in the passenger seat. Following the little mountain dirt road, we soon came upon the county road we had traveled just a fortnight ago. Anthony turned on the road, retracing our previous route.

I let the silence linger a bit more, then decided it was time to ask the question that Anthony had successfully dodged the last few days: "So, Father Anthony, what's your real place in all this?"

"What do you mean?"

I had to smile. He was good. He looked as sincere and honest as Pat O'Brien playing the priest of Boy's Town in an old fifties movie.

"You're going to make this difficult, aren't you?"

He looked as if he was about to finally give me some answers as he negotiated a curve and had to suddenly stop. A State Police roadblock took up the entire road. Two cruisers were parked on either side of the barrier flanked by four unsmiling troopers wearing "smoky" hats. One of them stepped forward and waived us to the shoulder of the road.

CHAPTER 66

Jeunessa Rollout–Minus Three—US Marine & FBI Joint facility–Quantico, Virginia.

Guido "Guy the rope" Spatafore walked back and forth in the room they'd given him. One standard US military issue cot, a cheap metal government desk bolted to the floor as if any self-respecting thief would ever steal such a thing. A chair behind it, a steel locker and wooden footlocker that looked as if it dated back to the Korean war. Guido had been drafted in the early seventies and served his two years, one of the last before the draft had been abolished, so he was familiar with all this stuff.

Guido knew they had put him in the Marine section of the base even though he'd been taken there in the middle of the night. He paced to the window where a platoon was drilling under a leathery "gunny" Gunnery Sergeant calling cadence:

Ain't no use in looking down,
Ain't no discharge on the ground
One two
One two
Three four!

Yeah, he'd been there before, what he couldn't figure out was if all this was really necessary. The door wasn't locked but the agents had told him to stay within the building, food would be brought to him and the latrine was down the hall. He had the entire first floor to himself. Secrecy was of maximum importance and Marines like soldiers everywhere spread gossip like butter on hot toast. A civilian walking around a Marine Corp building for a few days would fire up all kinds of speculation no one wanted.

Guido had a lot to explain and didn't quite know how to do it. He had a wife, two kids, one grandchild and like all Brooklyn mobsters a couple of *comorahs*, girlfriends. He'd just sat down to try and compose some sort of letter, when the man Joline knew as NYPD Detective Barry Anderson walked in the room without knocking. Right behind Anderson another man followed trailing a large suitcase on wheels. Both men wore suits and felt overcoats.

"Good morning, Guido. Everything okay?" Anderson asked.

"Good as expected."

"Fine. Let's get going then. Take off your shirt, please."

Anderson brought two chairs that had been in one corner of the room, placed one in front of the desk and the other on the side. He removed a digital tape recorder from his pocket, placed it on the table and waited.

As Guido removed his shirt, the other man placed the suitcase he'd brought, on the desk. He plugged the power cord in a wall socket and removed a wire harness where a dozen wires ended with round pads. After cleaning his skin with a special jell, the technician fastened the wire leads to a variety of locations on Spatafore's arms and bare chest. When he was done, he sat behind the desk, looked at Anderson and said, "ready".

Anderson reached out, turned the recorder on and began: "This is a record of an interview with Mister Guido Spatafore," and he continued with the date, time, place and name of all attending, then concluded with the following:

"Pursuant to an agreement with the Justice Department, New York District, the Federal Bureau of Investigation and the District Attorney, City of New York, County of

Queens, you have agreed to give full and unrestricted cooperation and testimony in return for immunity and entry into the Federal Witness Protection Program. Is that correct, Mister Spatafore?"

"Yeah."

"You have agreed to have your answers recorded and the veracity thereof verified by means of the polygraph machine, commonly known as a lie detector, that you are currently hooked up to. Is that correct?"

"Yeah."

"In order to calibrate the machine, we will ask you a series of questions and will ask you to give us obvious lies to about one third."

Guido said nothing.

"What is your name?"

"Guido go fuck yourself."

The technician frowned, Anderson smiled and it went on for about twenty minutes until the technician told Anderson he was ready.

"About fuckin' time." Spatafore growled, and Anderson began the interview.

"Why did you decide to cooperate with law enforcement?"

Guido closed his eyes and slowly shook his head as if a dark force tugged at the corners of his skull. That question was the easiest to answer in the private recess of his mind and nearly impossible to articulate to strangers.

Spatafore was second generation Sicilian-American whose family ties to Mafiosos and the code of silence called *omerta* reached through the centuries where disputes were settled by the Lupera, garrote and knife.

Like most members of what remained of New York's five families, and certainly all of its "made men", Spatafore was Catholic. Unlike most of them he'd never quite bridged the incongruity of a life of violence and crime and the Catechism of the Church. As the years mounted and his personal death toll passed the other side of six murders, he felt his sanity slipping away, the fear for his immortal soul and the paralyzing guilt dragging him off the planet as he tried to hang on with hooks planted deep in his psyche. One night, just moments before dawn, he found himself holding his big nine millimeter, safety off, thumb around the trigger as he held the weapon backward, barrel nearly touching the roof of his mouth.

He'd come to one thin hair of pulling that trigger, 2.9 ounces of pressure would have done it and it scared him like nothing else for he knew that it would simply be another murder–albeit self inflicted–held on his celestial ledger.

That's when he decided to see Father Anthony.

So Guido Spatafore ended his self-created pact with the devil and began another one, this time with Father Anthony and the Church. Father Anthony had not been an easy confessor. To obtain true absolution, Guido had to give up the life, cooperate with law enforcement to eradicate as much of his past as possible and begin a new life of service under the WitSec, the Federal Witness protection service.

"Mister Spatafore?" Anderson urged him on.

"You know why, I told you the first time. I'm not repeating it and it ain't that important anyway, so skip that part if you want this fuckin' thing to work."

"All right, Mister Spatafore…"

"Guido."

"Guido. This is the third, and possibly final interview and this one relates to the events that occurred four nights ago at Saint Agnes Church."

Guido started to get up, looked at the wires connecting him to the polygraph and said, "Can you get me a bottle of water, I keep'em in a small cooler in the locker." Anderson got up and gave him the water. Guido downed half of it before speaking.

"You should stick to wise-guy stuff, cause I don't know shit about it."

"I'll be the judge of that. How long have you known Father Anthony?"

"I'd say thirty years at least, maybe more going back to

Bensonhurst, around the early eighties. Strange guy this priest."

"Strange? In what way?"

"Well, its kinda hard to explain, it's like…he don't get older, he's just like he was back in the neighborhood…I dunno, maybe it's me."

Anderson looked at the technician who nodded yes– Spatafore was telling the truth.

"This is important, Guido. It ties in to other, similar events and people I've run into."

"Yeah?"

"Yeah. So is it you or does the priest not age?"

"No, I guess it's not me. It's just that it's so fucking strange when you think about it. He don't seem a day older than when I met him."

Another nod from the technician—true statement.

The session went on for another three hours into the details of how Father Anthony had worried for the safety of some people he was helping, how he'd sent Chuck to protect them but instead wound up being a victim in what the press was calling the "St Agnes Massacre". He told them everything he knew and in the end asked one final question of Anderson: "So tell me what happens now?"

"You're going to stay here for a few more days until federal marshals transfer you to a big city on the west coast. You'll be working for the Salvation Army in one of their missions, running soup kitchens, taking people through detox, that kind of stuff. A life of service, that's what you asked for."

"Yeah, that's what I wanted, but I gotta ask you for one more thing."

"What's that?"

"Take care of Father Anthony and his pal, that young guy Jimmy."

CHAPTER 67

Jeunessa Rollout–Minus Two

Relentless, Joline thought, these Delta Force guys are like no one she'd ever encountered, and she'd run up against the worst and the best.

They woke her at noon. Within the confines of the unlit barn, it might as well have been midnight so dim was the interior of the RV. By the time she got up, drank her coffee, ate some scrambled eggs that Lee had made on the motor home's gas stove, the two men were itching to go, pulling her along like a tidal wave.

Parker took the wheel as they drove out of the barn, down into the hardscrabble road leading to the nearby interstate. The patchy clouds from yesterday had solidified into a heavy cover rendering the sky like gray cottage cheese. Scattered snowflakes began to fall, whirling and dancing around the windshield, driven by a light breeze and the motor home's steady 65MPH. Finally, Joline realized that wherever they were going, it didn't seem to be where she wanted to go.

"Where are you heading?" She asked.

Parker didn't say a word, kept his eyes fixed on the road. Lee just looked out the window.

"Guys? I asked you a question."

Lee turned in the passenger seat, faced Joline who sat on the motor home's couch.

"We're going to pick up Nikki," he said, and faced the road again.

"Well shit, that explains it all. What am I talking to the fucking Sphinx here? I know we're in the field and you're in charge, I understand, I'm also grateful that you saved my ass, but I've got a right to some basic answers."

"Gotta tell her, Lee," Parker said, eyes still on the road. Lee turned again and answered her: "Forgive us for not being loquacious. We're not used to having civilians along on our operations. Right now we're going to pick up someone in New Jersey who may be a big help to us. After that I'm guessing you want to go see your brother on Long Island. We'll provide security because the probability of more trouble with whoever is after you, is rather high."

"You think?…Okay, okay, I'm fine with your program…now that I know. See how easy that was? Stick with me a while and I'll have you positively babbling."

Parker mumbled something, the only word she caught sounded like "female".

"What?"

Parker said nothing, Lee just grinned. Joline decided it was best to ignore it and change the subject.

"So where'd you get the RV?"

"We own it, comes in handy sometimes. We had one of our contact preposition it soon as we had operational details from your office."

"Oh, good thinking, thank you."

"Don't thank us, you're paying for it, renting it from us by the day, it's part of our fee."

"I'm sure, but thanks anyway."

"You're welcome," Parker replied.

"Wow, civilization is setting in."

By that time they were well out of West Virginia, rolling through farmland interspaced with patchy woods, the snow coming in heavier now. They passed through Route 70, cut over to 99, drove for a couple more hours, the

Appalachians rising to their right, peaks vanishing into low clouds, until they reached the town of Bellefonte, then cut left to Route 80. After a fuel stop, another hour found them turning into a well-tended road. Lined with freshly painted white fencing, the crushed gravel path led past manicured fields where thoroughbreds ran between fenced paths laid out in parallel patterns.

Parker stopped the RV in front of a fieldstone house bordered by a manicured lawn. Lee stepped out and whistled twice. A brown four-legged missile flew out of the open door, bounded on his chest nearly knocking him over. The instant Parker stepped out, the big dog immediately jumped on him, squeals of pure joy pouring out of his throat, licking his face as he squatted down, trying its best to knock him down in order to better lick his face. It took a full five minutes for the dog to settle down, and when Joline stepped out, still had enough enthusiasm to nuzzle her as she petted him. Finally the dog calmed down. It was big, at least a hundred pounds of pure Doberman, with pointed ears, cropped tail, jaws that delivered a couple of thousand pounds per square inch pressure through sharp fangs, and eyes brimming with that unique canine characteristic of love, and loyalty as fierce as it was unwavering.

As the dog finally curled up at Joline's feet, Lee said, "Joline, meet Nikki. Her full name is actually Nietsche, named after the German philosopher."

"Is this a joke? You named a dog Nietsche?"

"No, the German breeder did, they're funny that way. We just shortened it to Nikki."

"Okay, I get it, this is way cool, but let me ask you, is this take your pet to work day?"

"Well," Parker said, "she's a bit more than your average pet."

"Yeah, how's that?"

"She's a highly trained war dog."

CHAPTER 68

As previously arranged Valdemar Khan called the Chairman at a pre-set time.

"Mister Chairman."

"Valdemar, I have received important information from my sources. The William Brogan Foundation is under surveillance."

"Are these sources, well, reliable?"

The line remained silent, each second weighing on Khan until he finally spoke.

"I'm sorry, Mister Chairman. I did not mean to imply that your sources are less than unimpeachable. It's just that I'm very surprised."

"As well you should be. Security is your job, along with Dimitri. You should have discovered this. I'm the one who should have been notified."

"I'm sorry, Mister Chairman. Please give me the details, I will respond personally with three teams…"

"No! Enough with these mercenaries, they simply are not up to the job. They've let Jimmy through the net dozens of times, and recently, the priest and those others. Get rid of those teams. I want you and Anton alone to handle this. I will send Ergun, the three of you have greater combined powers than all our mercenaries put together."

As always, when speaking with the chairman, a certain

element of fear hovered around those conversations, for Valdemar knew, indeed as they all did, that the Chairman's Power exceeded all of theirs. That's why he was the Chairman in name and fact. He hadn't arrived at it by corporate vote. Khan said nothing—acquiescence was understood.

"We're just a couple of days from completion of the Jeunessa project, our most important endeavor in our two centuries of existence. Nothing must stand in the way of the Jeunessa rollout. Do you understand?"

"Yes, Mister Chairman."

"For now, just stand by and observe the surveillance. I believe nothing will happen until the accountant's sister arrives along with the priest and possibly Jimmy. From my questioning of the accountant, we know they acquired information that cannot be allowed to go public nor given to any authorities. The accountant is already at the foundation's office in Brooklyn. His sister is on the way as is the priest. When they arrive that is when the surveillance will act. Whoever they are, you must deal with them at that time in any manner you choose as long as they are neutralized. Take the accountant and his sister, if they resist, kill them. By the time the IRS acts on this it will be way too late. Same with the priest, neutralize him, alive if you can, dead if you must."

"And Jimmy?"

"By himself he is no threat. If you can capture him, fine. If not let him go. He cannot harm us and we will catch him sooner or later."

"Very well, Mister Chairman, it will be as you say."

Khan put away the phone and did the best he could to suppress the queasy feeling settling in his gut.

Father Anthony complied with the trooper's instructions, parking the pickup where he was told at the edge of the barricade. He started to open the door when the trooper shouted, "Driver, stay in your vehicle." Anthony stopped, the door half open.

The State trooper walked until he stood a few feet from the door. His face was sharp, as if nature decided to put his facial bones together using only ninety and forty-five degree angles. The skin was suntanned in spite of the winter season and his face held the eyes of the veteran policeman who's seen too much and trusts no one. He glanced at Anthony's Roman collar and his eyes didn't soften one iota. Behind him a younger, heavily muscled Trooper backed him up, one hand easy on the butt of his service revolver.

"What's the problem officer?"

"License and registration please."

"Sure," Anthony replied as he reached into the glove box, pulled out the registration and handed it out the open window—and that's when everything changed.

As the trooper reached for the registration, Father Anthony grasped the policeman's hand. I knew exactly what was going on in the trooper's mind at that moment because I'd figured out that Anthony had the Power.

It began before the touch, a narrow psychic wave so the trooper already felt a sense of other worldly disorientation like distant storms on a late summer night. He would have fought that with his police training but still it had its effect. Then came the touch as Anthony grasped the trooper's hand, it flowed between them like a blending of minds, fierce and electric.

The trooper blinked, shook his head, looked at Anthony and said, "All right, Father. You must go around and take Route 109, we've closed this one, looking for some fugitives. Please drive carefully." All the stern police attitude had left the man's voice.

I concentrated on his partner and the actual touch wasn't needed. He followed the older trooper's direction and we turned around and left.

We drove most of the day until the snow increased and the truck began to skid through the accumulations. We saw the lights of a Motel 6 ahead, pulled in, got some sandwiches from a vending machine and turned in for the night. Silence took up the spaces between us, thick and filled with things yet unspoken.

Tomorrow would see the resolution of many issues between Father Anthony and I.

CHAPTER 69

It feels kinda nice, Joline thought, maybe I should have gotten a dog a long time ago. Nikki sat as close to Joline as she could, long muzzle resting on her lap, brown eyes fixed on her with the adoration unique to the canine species. If she could have, she would have jumped, all muscular one hundred pounds of her, right onto Joline's lap. She stopped petting the dog, looked at Parker and Nikki nuzzled her hand, pushing into her lap, the message clear: Keep petting me—that's your job!

"Oh for heaven's sake," Joline said, and resumed petting. Parker looked at them and grinned, "She's really taken to you," he said.

They were in the RV, parked on the gravel lot fronting the main house of the horse farm. Parker had told her the farm belonged to his uncle and they boarded Nikki there.

Joline didn't reply, petted the huge head with both hands. Now the big dog jumped on the couch next to Joline and placed a front paw and head on her lap. She rolled her eyes and continued petting.

"She allowed on the furniture?"

"Who's going to tell her no?"

Now Joline scratched behind the dog's ear. Nikki turned over for a belly rub, and Joline complied.

"Okay, Miss Waterman…" Lee started to say.

"Joline."

"Sorry, Joline. We need to agree on our next moves. I'm guessing your first order of business will be to see your brother, and that's fine. But obviously there are some dangerous people out there for whom it's not fine at all. In fact it appears they will only be happy if you are captured or dead, and so we must proceed accordingly."

"And what do you suggest?"

"To begin with, we need to know everything that happened, from day one to now, don't hold anything back, keeping us in the dark is worse than holding secrets from your lawyer. That may get you in jail, but keeping things from us will get you dead."

"Yeah, yeah, I understand," Joline said, and softly added under her breath a very quiet "fuck."

"What?" asked Parker.

"Nothing. Okay, here goes…" and she told them everything she knew, starting with her luncheon meeting with David, through his disappearance, the events at Saint Agnes, hiding out in Brighton Beach, fleeing to the monastery, she held nothing back.

Parker took some notes on a legal pad, both asked questions occasionally, and when she finished, looked at both of them and said, "that's it, everything."

Nikki had fallen asleep, both rear legs hanging off the back of the sofa. Joline gently laid the dog's head on the cushion, got up, brought three bottles of water from the refrigerator, and sat down again. Outside the snow began accumulating, darkening the windshield. Lee turned on the interior lights.

"What I want to do is get to our training facility in Manorville, store the RV there, get one of our vehicles, pick up my brother, get his story and take it from there."

"No problem there, Miss Wat…uh, Joline. Now let me tell you what we know and what we may be up against."

Joline nodded, and said nothing.

"There are some operations going on globally that are past the boundaries of the national interests of nations, be they under American, Russian, Iranian or South American influence. These activities are not drug cartels, nor are they terror groups or extremists of any sort. They have a secretive agenda that is simply unknown to us. There are many rumors and urban legends floating around about these groups, they're called by a variety of names, the Illuminatis, the Immortals, and many more that may or may not exist. From the information I gathered out of our prisoners last night, this group exists, the one we call The Order, that's what we're facing."

"How do you know all this, about the Order and these operations, I mean?"

Parker smiled and cut in. "The world of US Special Operations is tighter than most people realized. We all originate from various branches of the service, Army, Navy, Marines, and are funneled down though selection processes, Army Special Forces, Delta Force like Lee and I, Navy Seals, we pretty much know each other. Not all of us stay in it for life. Lee and I had about a dozen years before we went private. Others have also gone on their own many of them work for other branches of government. We have friends in the FBI, Homeland Security and numerous state and local law enforcement. It's a tight community, we know and trust each other, and we talk."

Joline could remember many instances in her business of executive protection where such contacts among her operators had proven invaluable, and she realized the essential truth of Parker's words.

"So what else do you know about those people? I get the feeling this Father Anthony and that strange guy, Jimmy, know enough to write a book, but aren't telling me shit."

"Probably, and no offense, but perhaps it may have been with good reason."

Joline found she couldn't argue with that, and let Lee continue: "There's one individual with a distinctive deformity, he's missing two fingers on his left hand. We've run into his group before. His name is Anton Dimitri. Wherever he pops up in the world, violence follows him and people die, and there's something strange there."

"It's all strange," Joline said.

"Yes it is, but with this guy, it goes beyond the pale. We've heard stories and other documentary evidence that this guy uses some sort of mind control. From some of the stories and results that we know to be true, there aren't many other explanations for Anton Dimitri."

"Wait, you know the guy's name?"

"We compare notes with a former Seal, him and I enlisted in the Crotch together."

"What?"

"The Marine Corp," Parker cut in.

"His name is Barry Anderson. He's with the FBI and he gave us that info when we told him of some of our encounters on a special operation with the DEA in Mexico."

Joline thought for a moment, she recalled that NYPD detective, his name was Anderson also, but it couldn't be the same guy.

Now it was Parker's turn to continue, "And this other guy, Anton Dimitri was involved in both the attempts on your life in Saint Agnes Church and yesterday in West Virginia. I got all that from our prisoner."

"Good thing you took him."

"Not for him," Lee mumbled, and grinned.

"What?"

"Ignore that, Joline. But you see what we're facing. We'll do as you ask, go to Manorville, pick up a vehicle then pick up your brother. But there is one condition."

"What's that?"

"It is a continuation of this operation. We control it from start to finish. You do only what we say without argument. Full operational security applies at all times. Do you agree, yes or no?"

"Yes," said Joline, without a nanosecond's hesitation.

CHAPTER 70

Father Anthony and Jimmy had driven almost non-stop until they reached their destination: Drexel University in Philadelphia, one of America's largest 15 colleges.

Father Anthony drove out of the main road through the stone gates into the large parking lot mostly devoted to the biology department. Since Drexel was considered a prime pre-med school with biology a main component, the lot was about three quarter full. The snow had lightened up but the wind held that face-biting quality.

We sat in the front seat, Anthony in the driver's position. He'd left the engine on and the heater worked well. It was cozy in the truck's cabin, but we both knew that wasn't the reason we didn't jump out to our meeting with Professor Renee Dupont.

Things had to be said. We both understood that.

"So," I started, "anything you want to tell me, Father."

He leaned back against the headrest, looking relaxed, his eyes filled with the quality of someone shouldering a burden that must be relieved.

"Many things, Jimmy. I do believe the time has come after all these years. What do you want to know?"

"What's the relationship between you and the head Junta immortal, Valdemar Khan?"

"He is my brother, literally."

"And he ain't heavy?"

"He's heavy, more than I can bear sometimes. Perhaps I should start at the beginning, as if you knew absolutely nothing. Sounds good?"

I nodded. Yes, it sounded good.

"It began with the creation of the Essex Junta in 1804, after the re-election of Thomas Jefferson. A group of Federalists that included some of the top leaders of the day, there was a Massachusetts Senator, two supreme court judges, former secretary of state Timothy Pickering, members of the Forbes, Cushing, Perkins, Sturgis and Paines families. But the founder, and main driving force was Alexander Grant, one of the architects of the constitution. He was also a doctor and tireless researcher, and good friend of Benjamin Franklin. The original purpose of the Essex Junta (who derived its name from the town of Essex Connecticut where it was founded and secretly resides to this day) wasn't very noble. They wanted to lead the northern states out of the Union by getting Aaron Burr elected as Governor of New York. The new governor would then lead the Northern states in a breakup of the union and the safeguarding of their individual business interests, not the least of which was the continuation of slavery."

"Nice," I said. "Obviously and thankfully, it didn't work."

"No it didn't, but the fact is that two hundred years ago a powerful elite conspired to change the course of a nation in order to further their own business interest. They failed and many people believe to this day that the Essex Junta has turned into a secret cabal that is still trying to maneuver world events in their favor. They're right, but not in the sense of the urban legend it became. You see, Jimmy, around 1804-1809 Alexander Grant discovered the secret serum that has gifted them with such longevity that Grant, now called the Chairman, is alive today. But then, you knew that, didn't you, Jimmy?"

Yes, I knew that. I just nodded, said nothing so he could continue.

"Alexander Grant stumbled upon a combination of chemicals and ingredients from the Abelia-Vie plant grown only in the mountain country of Puerto Vallerta. We'll never know exactly what he was looking for, probably for a cure for one of the many ailments that afflicted humanity in that year, possibly the one called "consumption" for you see he was a widower, his wife having died of that consumption, a catchall name for a variety of fevers they couldn't explain or cure."

"And instead discovered immortality."

"Yes, he did. But it's not really immortality. It's a powerful anti-aging complex. We are growing older, Jimmy, but at such a slow rate we'll probably live for five or six centuries. No one really knows. Alexander Grant had two sons, Valdemar, and me. Of course we changed our last names since. He administered the serum to both of us, and we continue to take it to this day."

Now I was in a dark loop. Everything I had assumed was turned upside down, raising far more questions.

"And as you know there is a dark side to all this."

"Greed, thirst for power?"

"Much worse. You see, Jimmy, when Mother Nature takes something away she compensates. The blind develop sharper hearing and acute sense of directions, a small vulnerable creature like a certain small Australian octopus has such a deadly toxin that a shark is easier to deal with. There are countless such examples. In our case, the serum gives us longevity and nature takes away something else."

"Something, like what?"

"Our humanity and sanity."

"What?"

"Why do you think there are only a few of us immortals? A handful, maybe six or seven that's it, many that would have been useful have simply gone insane, committed suicide or been killed through mad bouts of violence. The rest of us are also mentally afflicted."

I tossed that around in my mind. I'd never seen any of them with the problems Anthony described, nor had I experienced such things. Of course when I thought about it, I'd seen precious few of them, Khan, Dimitri, the one they called The Chairman, now Father Anthony, and of course those rumors of a vicious killer ex-slave called Ergun, probably a couple more, but that was it.

"I know what you're thinking. You're not afflicted, and the others like Khan, while their intents are obviously evil to us, their mental states appear sane—but they're not. They become Sociopaths, unable to empathize with the suffering of others, unable to identify, feel pity, love or compassion. That is their affliction, perhaps the most cruel of all because of the pain they cause."

"But what about you? You're a Catholic priest, or Monsignor, you care."

Anthony sighed, closed his eyes and in the dim light I saw the top of his knuckles turn white as he gripped the steering wheel with enough force to be painful.

"I struggle with it every minute of every day," He said, his voice holding the shaky quality of someone in great pain. "I take confession, and sometimes hear stories of cruelty and pain, yet I feel nothing. Every single thing I do must be analyzed so I don't hurt anyone. I examine everything as one who cannot feel or understand the hurt of others, like a person who has lost the capacity to feel pain and must watch that they don't put their hands in the fire. Sometimes…it's almost more than I can bear…you see, Jimmy, I believe in my faith and the contradictions are tearing me apart."

I said nothing just let him be as I reached for his hand on the steering wheel. He didn't resist and when our hands touched, I felt a great wave of pain, the touch of a deeply troubled soul.

"Now you know," he said. "And you probably understand by now that while you have the longevity of the Immortals, you received something much greater when your father injected you with a combination of the serum and something he took out of a Nazi laboratory. You have Powers none of them have, you don't need continuing serum treatments, and your mind isn't hampered."

Now the pieces all came together, everything fit. They had to be stopped because whatever they planned would not be tampered by any sort of mercy or empathy—just whatever it was their twisted minds wanted without regard of the suffering of others.

"Come on," Anthony said. "Let's go talk to the professor."

CHAPTER 71

━━━◆━━━

Jeunessa rollout–Minus two days

David Waterman could not think of any time in his life that he'd been this tired. He felt caught in a steel web of lassitude that robbed his will and sapped his energy like some enormous vampire as he sat behind a desk.

He was in the office of the William Brogan Foundation on Metropolitan Avenue in Brooklyn, New York, the same office where he'd performed the audit about two or three weeks ago—was he losing track of time? Had it only been two or three weeks?

He wasn't sure what he was doing there. He'd accomplished everything they had asked; completed a favorable audit report, finished the Foundation's tax return with the required audit report attached. Everything they wanted, he had done, right down to personally filing the documents at the IRS's district office in Hauppauge, Long Island. What else could they want from him?

Ever since Khan had murdered that poor secretary, David had found himself in a sort of alternate non-reality. His spirit floated in a morass of confusion and languor like a dying bug in a specimen jar.

They had asked him to stay at the Foundation's office for a few days in case some "questions" came in that only he would be able to answer. That was bullshit, he knew that, yet didn't have the courage to argue since they held the ultimate trump—his sister Joline's life.

His eyes closed as he stopped trying to stay awake. He didn't even make it to the comfortable cot they had provided for him in the office, just laid his head down on the desk and that was it.

Upstairs, on the second floor of the office, a place containing only one room accessible exclusively through a hidden stairwell, Anton Dimitri sensed David Waterman's loss of consciousness and smiled.

It had been so easy. David's traumatic experience in witnessing the brutal killing of the secretary and the ensuing visualization of a similar fate for his sister had made his mental state suitably compliant. Then came the valiums and oxycons, in his food and coffee, but perhaps the most effective tactic of all: the power of Anton's mind as he reached through pathways little understood, into the very essence of David's brain, infusing it with a potent combination of dread, apathy and torpor.

Bait, that's what he was, dangled right out, drawing Joline, the priest and Jimmy into their trap. Once the steel of that trap snapped shut on them, the secret of Jeunessa would be safeguarded until it was too late.

Outside, diagonally across from the entrance to the William Brogan Foundation, standing almost on the corner of Metropolitan Avenue and 89th street, a van was parked. It was kind of battered, the words "Harvey Plumbing Contractors" in faded red letters on its side, ladder secured to the rear of a roof rack and a battered steel toolbox on the front. The windows were dark and covered with stringy black cloth and a parking permit lay on the dash with a partition hiding anything that was in the large rear compartment.

What no observer could tell was that the ladder held a powerful   antenna   connected   to   sophisticated communication and listening devices and the toolbox held equally advanced surveillance equipment, all of it controlled by a two-men surveillance team inside the van.

Ergun was far from being an average observer, and didn't need any electronics or detection devices, for next to the Chairman, he was the most powerful of the Essex Junta group that also called themselves The Immortals. He simply closed his eyes in the second floor walk-up they had rented for the purpose, and sent the psychic Power of his mind, cataloguing every action of the observers in the van. The watchers were themselves watched, and not just by Ergun either, for in another rented apartment less than fifty yards away, Valdemar Khan also watched and stood ready.

CHAPTER 72

It was late afternoon by the time we walked across the campus of Drexel University to the biology department. Groups of students passed, holding books, riding bicycles in spite of the falling snow, couples holding each other, and I couldn't help feeling a pang of envy at what they had. I may look like them, but I inhabited a different universe.

We entered the biology building and followed the signs. Professor Renee Dupont's office door proclaimed him Biology Chair and underneath the sign a student had scrawled in magic marker "And not every ass will fit." Or perhaps the professor himself had written it.

We knocked on the door and a voice beckoned us inside. The professor was on the phone, behind a most unique desk. Taking up at least a third of the desk space was the mounted head of a boar with long, pointy tusks and fiery eyes placed by a skilled taxidermist. Next to the head a pile of papers lay in disarray, the pile having reached critical mass allowing documents to fall and accumulate on the floor. Various odds and ends covered the rest of the desk including a laptop, two tablets, a variety of pens, nuts and bolts, wires that apparently went nowhere, an empty Dunkin Donut cup, a half eaten cruller and an ashtray filled with butts that spilled onto the surface, crusting that part of the desk with a patina of burnt and dried tobacco flakes.

The room smelled of nicotine and old sweatshirts grimy with sweat and allowed to fester.

The professor waved us to a little couch without looking up. He finished his conversation, put down the phone and focused on Father Anthony.

"Oh my God," He whispered, "You look…"

"Just like my dad, I know, everybody says that."

"It's uncanny, I know it's been more than forty years, but I remember…How is your dad anyway?"

"Passed away a couple of years ago, heart attack."

"I'm so sorry. But when I knew him, he was going to the seminary. How did you…"

Anthony laughed, "Everybody who knew him asks that. He met my mother, gave up the seminary, had me, and when I came of age I took up where he left off."

"Amazing, I don't know what to say."

"First I want to thank you for agreeing to help us. Let me introduce you to my associate, Jimmy."

I leaned forward and we shook hands. The moment our flesh made contact, I tweaked him, and the deal was sealed.

Anthony handed him the memory drive and in the following couple of hours, we were led into a maelstrom of approaching horror and twisted ideals.

CHAPTER 73

The one thing Valdemar Khan had always been able to do was secure his doubts against the prying mental Powers of the likes of the Chairman, Anton Dimitri and Ergun. But now, alone in this tiny room, just waiting for Joline, Jimmy, and Anthony to enter the trap, he let his thoughts run free.

It started with the coming convergence of the aging Baby Boomers and what they called in the Western World, "The Longevity Revolution." What Khan and the others of the Essex Junta saw was a disaster coming in, under the radar, like a great tidal wave that would surely sweep the world and prevent the takeover of humanity they had been planning for two centuries.

The Baby Boomers were the biggest current domestic problem. Over seventy-four million strong, thousands of them turned age 65 every day, and nearly as many retired. The results were slowly turning demographic. As they worked, the Boomers contributed resources in the form of taxes. When they retired, the cycle was reversed and they now began to absorb resources through social security and medicare payouts and other government programs—resources the Junta of Immortals wanted to use. Compounding the problem was a growing political and social agenda. With more time on their hands during retirement, Boomers became more politically active, helping to promote social programs that were in direct conflict with the goals of the Immortals.

Khan ran through the problems again as they had done many times. Every day 220,000 new humans were added to the population, *one billion* every twelve years that would create problems and suck up resources in an ever-accelerating spiral they would be powerless to control. Food would be a major problem with 25,000 people dying of malnutrition throughout the world each and every day. Water shortages were building with about one billion people on the planet lacking access to sufficient water for consumption. Air quality, oil and gas shortages, depletion of natural resources, massive overcrowding, conflicts and wars. The coming chaos would be massive and there was only one way to prevent it.

The herd had to be thinned, starting with the Baby Boomers. That was the way of nature. Once the population was suddenly and massively reduced, Khan and his fellow Immortals would be the only ones with the power and common sense to bring about a true human renaissance.

That was why Jeunessa was so important. The rollout had to be a success at all costs.

He tried to visualize millions, billions dying in untold agonies, medical systems overwhelmed by such unimaginable massive illnesses. Intellectually he knew he should feel some kind of remorse, and as he tried to reach into the depths of his soul, discovered…nothing. His feelings were as bare as the farthest reaches of the Antarctic.

Khan stopped thinking about it, and focused his mind on the approaching people about to walk into his trap.

---◆---

CHAPTER 74

The professor took the memory drive, looked it over carefully as if that alone would reveal its secrets. He reached over the desk, laying his forearm flat on the surface and swept it over a couple of square feet of space, clearing out assorted debris to the side and placing the laptop on the empty surface.

After plugging the flashdrive in one of the USB ports, he fiddled with the machine a bit and the screen lit up with the contents. He scrolled down, shook his head, turned and saw us looking at him.

"This is going to take a while," he said to us. "There's a cafeteria in the building next door, why don't you guys get some coffee, give me about a half hour or so."

Father Anthony and I found the place; mostly vending machines and a counter filled with donuts, bagels, day old pizza slices, and wrapped sandwiches, the kind of stuff students would eat. The place was nearly empty except for a couple texting and a tired looking clerk behind the counter. We got two coffees, split a bagel and sat down.

"So tell me about your dad, the divinity student," I said, grinning at Anthony.

"You know that was me he met, back in the sixties. Not many ways to explain that he's now seventy and I still look like I did back then. They always buy the you-knew-my-dad story."

Longevity required lots of fiddling with the truth because the reality brought up impossible issues.

Forty-five minutes later we returned to Professor Dupont's office and knocked on the door. Nothing—I knocked again and heard a terse "come in."

Still sitting behind his desk, the professor looked like he'd aged a dozen years more. His face was tight, the features pinched and the sides of his hair tousled as if he'd run his hands through it for a while. As he looked at us with eyes that were now haunted, I reached out with my mind and felt the fear in his psyche.

"Where did you get this?" he said.

"That's something you shouldn't know, perhaps for your own safety," Anthony replied.

"Something has to be done. This must be stopped, its…" At that point he just shook his head, words had run out on the professor. I reached over and touched his arm. "Tell us. Soon as we know, that's the first step to stopping it."

A jolt of Power from our touch steadied the professor, I felt his fear recede, the anxiety now manageable as he spoke. "These records indicate huge sums of money shunted across the globe, funneled into organizations through a foundation, I don't really understand all that. It would take a skilled accountant to ferret all that out, but that's not the important thing. It's what the funds are buying—Targeted Vectors research and production."

That was the second time I heard that term, the same words that had shaken up Anthony.

"I don't know what that is, please tell me," I said.

He didn't reply, just looked at Anthony and said, "Surely you've heard of this, I remember you worked with Doctor Wu for a while."

"Yes, I did. But it's important that Jimmy here also understand the details before we contact Dr. Wu."

"My Lord, haven't you been watching the news for the last few days? It's all over television, the newspapers and the internet. Dr. Wu was killed in some sort of terrorist attack, destroyed the entire biology lab at Brookhaven National Lab, killed the professor and obliterated all the Targeted Vector research."

His fear and anxiety ramped up again. I grasped his arm and held it for a couple of seconds, soothing him back to earth. "Tell me," I said softly. A thin ghost of a smile ran across his features. He reached over to the edge of his desk, picked up a thick, rolled joint from under a No Smoking sign, and lit it with a long lighter used to light Benson burners in laboratories. In spite of the calming effect of the Power, his hands shook.

Professor Dupont sucked in a lungful of smoke that must have reached down to his toes. He closed his eyes, held it in for a few seconds, and let out a cloud so pungent it could have drawn cops from a mile away.

He opened his eyes and I felt his mind, soothed by a combination of the Power and Marijuana, the good kind that he probably got from his students, no weakened medical stuff for the good professor.

"Ready now?" I asked.

He blinked and looked at me. "Yeah, sure, where do we start?"

"Targeted Vectors."

He began speaking, his voice was now different, it was the lecturer's tone, as if he was teaching a class of advanced students—a defense mechanism to handle the horrors that he found so difficult to even voice.

"Targeted Vectors," he began, " is missing one word for an apt description. That word is virus. We're talking about Targeted Vector Viruses, something the US Department of Defense funded under the Bush and Clinton administrations. When details began to develop, they frightened the generals so much that the President ordered the project stopped, because you see, another name for this is Doomsday Virus."

"That bad, eh?"

"Worse, it simply can't be exaggerated. The top researcher, Dr Li Wu, the world's foremost expert on genetics, was so horrified he threatened to sabotage the project until it was finally halted. The unusual thing about this virus is that it only acts on human DNA, specifically three diseases: Fanconi Anemia, Ataxia Telangiectasia, and Li-Fraumeni Syndrome. All three illnesses are the results of genetic defects inside the DNA strands and the repair of inter-strand cross-links within the DNA systems. All three illnesses result in abnormalities of skeleton, heart and kidneys and predisposition to leukemia and many forms of cancer in different tissues. This virus would go directly to the DNA Vectors, and target them, hence the name Targeted Vectors."

"That's what would happen to anyone taking this, all these cancers?"

"Worse. The person would at first experience a surge of energy and what would appear to be improved health. When the first symptoms appear, within four to six weeks, depending upon the individual, they will begin to notice lumps, aches and pain, the onset of virulent and multiple cancers. There will be no cure. These cancers will be created end stage from the beginning, and there's something even worse."

"Worse? What can possibly be worse?"

"It's undetectable until the DNA damage is done and the cancers begin, then it becomes contagious. Anyone coming into contact with an infected person gets it. Now you understand the term Doomsday Virus."

CHAPTER 75

Jeunessa rollout–Minus one day

Joline and the Delta operators reached Executive Protection's Manorville training facility on Long Island early the next morning. Even though the guard recognized her, he only let them through after an electronic security device recognized Joline's thumbprint.

As Parker drove, Joline led them to a large Quonset-type hangar where they parked the RV next to one of the side doors. Joline went in, drove out with an armored Lexus SUV and parked it next to the RV.

As they were transferring their bags of equipment from the RV, the guard approached them on a golf cart, holding out a cell phone, and handed it to Joline. "Somebody wants to talk to you, Miss Waterman."

It was Fred Walters, her vice-president.

"Joline, what the hell's going on? The guard notified me you were here."

"Stay out of this, Fred. It doesn't involve the business and there's nothing you can do."

"Everything you do involves the business. Look, whatever's going on, I can send half a dozen armed people to you, that sure as hell can't hurt."

"Wait," she replied and turned to Lee.

"I can get some people, trained and armed agents. How about it, Lee? We can use the help."

Lee said nothing, just shook his head.

"What, are you being macho or is there a valid reason for refusing help?"

Parker stepped behind her. He'd overheard the conversation, and now quietly asked, "Are they Seals, Delta, Army Special Forces or Marine Recon?"

"Come on, you know that you guys are the only ones we've got."

"Then the answer is no, and machismo has nothing to do with it. We're going up against the most dangerous people we've ever faced and anyone without our level of training will get us killed. It's that simple."

She put the phone back to her ear. "Forget it, Fred." She said and disconnected the call.

They left the facility and headed toward Mineola and David's office. Parker drove, Joline sat in the front, Lee in the back, left side, while Nikki perched on the right side. Wind howled through the SUV as the big dog held her head out the open window, ears drooping back, saliva drooling out into the 65 MPH slipstream as they drove on the Long Island Expressway.

They passed the Nassau County line and continued to Willis Avenue. Lee pulled Nikki back and closed the window.

Joline guided them to a spot in front of David's office where they double-parked. Joline ran out and climbed the stairs to David's second floor office. Outside, Parker stood just outside the driver's door, a special operations M-4 automatic rifle with cut down barrel hidden in a quick release sling under his coat. In the back seat, Lee sat with a blanket over his lap concealing another M-4 modified with a grenade launcher tube. He'd opened the window and said a few words to Nikki.

The big dog's entire demeanor had changed instantly. The playfulness had vanished, leaving only a state of alert and a powerful body coiled and ready to spring. As for Lee and Parker, both men constantly scanned their surroundings as if in a distant battlefield instead of suburban Long Island.

Joline bounded up the steps and burst into David's office causing Martha, David's CPA partner, to nearly jump out of her chair.

"Oh my God, Joline, you scared me. Where have you been, everybody's looking for you, especially me."

"Never mind that, where's David?"

"That's why I'm trying to reach you. David's not right."

"What do you mean, not right?"

"It's that goddamned Brogan Foundation thing. Everything's been screwed up since he got involved with that audit. After he got back from wherever he was when he disappeared, he's been out of it, like he's half drugged or something, you can't even talk to him."

"Where is he? Is he at home?"

"No, he's over at that Brogan Foundation office in Brooklyn. He even sleeps there."

"What's the address?"

Martha gave it to her. Joline turned and started out the door. "Where you going?" Martha called out to her.

"I'm going to kick their fucking ass and get my brother back."

CHAPTER 76

Anthony and I must have had the same thought at the same time as we both stood, and our eyes met.

"My God, the Jeunessa, they're putting it into the Jeunessa. All those millions of people will be taking it," I said, my thoughts roiling with the impossibility of it all. How do you visualize the deaths and suffering of so many millions? Even more important, how do you prevent it at this stage? Father Anthony answered that question. At that point, for the first time since I was a child, I was glad not to be alone, to have an ally at my side, helping to prevent the unthinkable.

"We've got to get to the Foundation's headquarters in Brooklyn. I know someone who can help us to stop the Jeunessa rollout. We must stop it or die trying."

He turned to the Professor, his own fears reflected in his eyes. "We're going to fly to New York immediately, Professor Dupont, in the meantime, make a duplicate of this memory stick and get the authorities involved. They're loading the virus into the Jeunessa."

The professor looked bewildered. I didn't think he would have much luck doing all that. I'm sure he'd tried, but it was really up to Anthony and I. We were the only chance that millions, perhaps billions of people had.

We left the professor's office into a deepening

snowstorm. Anthony stopped in the doorway and pulled two small devices from the pocket of his jacket. I watched as he linked them with a short cable. One of the devices had a small screen and keyboard no larger than a pack of cigarettes. Anthony typed on them for a while with his thumbs like a kid texting under a desk so the teacher doesn't see. He did this for about five minutes then disconnected the devices and put them back in his pocket.

"What's that about?"

"I called the cavalry, that FBI Agent I know."

"Really? Aren't you afraid they'll pick up the transmission? They've been able to do that every time."

"Not with this special toy. He gave it to me for just such an emergency. It's called Ironlock. It's programmed to send all communications through a variety of routers making it nearly impossible to track. It also encrypts all messages, military encryption, 265 bits."

"You kind of lost me, but I hope it works."

CHAPTER 77

As we stood in the doorway of the university's biology department office, one thing was clear. We had to get to the offices of the William Brogan Foundation, that's where all this originated and where it had to be pursued. "We need to get to New York fast," I said. "And it won't be easy."

"Normally it wouldn't, Jimmy, might not even be possible with the weather and all, but not if we use, let's say…powers of persuasion."

I grinned at him, knowing exactly what he was talking about. I glanced down the street at a vehicle whose headlights were barely visible through the swirling snow. As it approached I recognized the vehicle as a Campus Police four Wheel Drive SUV.

I stepped out into the street and waved at the vehicle.

Thomas took his job as a campus policeman seriously, and this evening patrol in a snowstorm was no exception. On the other hand he preferred getting off-shift on time tonight, this was not the kind of weather to get into situations that would drag him far past his off-duty time, that's why he felt some apprehension when the young man stepped out of the biology building and flagged him down.

As the young policeman stopped the vehicle, a curious thing happened. His sense of alarm vanished. He felt good about seeing the young man, probably a student who needed help getting to his campus apartment.

The officer stopped the vehicle and rolled down the window, letting out a blast of interior warm air.

"Can I help you?" he said, as he noticed another man approaching behind the first one.

"So glad you're here, officer," The student said as he reached into the police car and placed his hand on the officer's shoulder.

Normally, the young policeman's training would have kicked in and prevented such action from someone approaching his patrol vehicle.

But things seemed askew tonight, not in a bad way, mind you, but in a warm, friendly kind of atmosphere, a sort of dreamlike state that the officer would remember for many years.

The other man reached the patrol vehicle. This one wore a Roman collar and the officer thought it was the most natural thing in world.

"Please," the priest said, "We need to get to the airport fast. It's urgent, help us."

There could be no question that the officer would do everything to help. In fact, even though he'd be at a loss to explain, it was the most natural thing in the world.

He opened the back doors and both men got in. Turning on all his emergency lights, the police SUV headed toward the airport.

James Dooley buttoned the collar of his coat as he closed the hangar door that contained a private Lear jet. The flight had been cancelled and he was going home.

As he closed the hangar door, a police SUV pulled right up to him, and two men emerged from the rear. One of them, a young kid, said a few words to the officer driving the car and the policeman pulled away. The second man walked right up to him.

"What's going on?" Dooley asked.

"Father Anthony," the man said, holding out his hand.

Dooley instinctively took it and his world changed immediately.

"We need to get to LaGuardia, fast," the priest said.

Makes perfect sense, Dooley thought, as an overwhelming urge to help these two strangers took over his mind.

"Well, I can certainly do that," Dooley replied. "The owners of the Lear cancelled the flight because of weather so the plane is ready and free, and so am I."

"You're not scared of flying in this?" the younger man asked him.

"Are you kidding?" Dooley replied. "I've only been out of the Navy a few months. Last year I landed a Super Hornet on a carrier deck during a typhoon. This stuff is nothing, believe you me. I'll file a quick flight plan via fax, and we're on our way."

Minutes later the Lear accelerated down the runway, and clawed its way to a cruising altitude of 32,000 feet. Half an hour later he announced to his two passengers that he was beginning a descent to New York's LaGuardia Airport.

"Now there's a clusterfuck about to happen," the NYPD officer said to his partner.

"What're you talking about?" His partner, a young black man barely out of the academy, replied.

"Well look. It's cold as a witch's tit and these two bozos are heading right for us. Just got out of the airport, no luggage, and they look like a couple of rubes out of Minn-fucking-sotta or something. A priest and his young asshole buddy, heading right for us. Like I said, a clusterfuck."

The two officers sat in their patrol car, parked at the curb of the airport's exit, right past the taxi line. As the pair approached, a sudden mist of confusion swirled in their minds, to be just as quickly replaced by an understanding of the situation.

The driver opened the window and everything crystallized in a sudden rush when the young man reached inside and grasped the officer's shoulder.

Patrick Astre

It all made sense, even when the priest and his young friend got in the back of the patrol car, and the driver lit up the emergency lights, turned on the siren and tore out onto the parkway, heading toward Metropolitan Avenue in the heart of Brooklyn.

CHAPTER 78

Even though Joline was not normally a field operator, still as head of Executive Protection, she knew her basic tradecraft. She'd chosen the Lexus SUV well. The vehicle was armored but it wasn't very apparent. What showed was a high-end automobile that was not out of place in this upscale section of Metropolitan Avenue in Brooklyn where the William Brogan Foundation had its world headquarters. Lexus, Mercedes, Cadillacs, Jaguars and Beemers abounded in the area like Chevies at a NASCAR rally.

Joline drove while Parker took the front passenger seat. Lee remained in the back with Nikki. Joline was amazed at the big dog's new demeanor. She'd immediately ceased being a cute and cuddly pet the moment Parker put her on alert, no rolling over for belly rubs, no sucking up for treats–the vigilance switch had been turned on.

Metropolitan Avenue is a four-lane avenue and Joline drove in the left lane as she passed the Brogan Foundation as if they had no interest whatsoever.

It was early evening, the air smelled like snow about to arrive, as it had further west. The interior of the foundation was lit, and the place appeared to be open yet no one could be seen inside.

Joline turned left at the following light, went one block and turned left again, traveled two blocks, turned again until she regained Metropolitan Avenue. This time she turned right and parked the vehicle. Her side of the street contained apartment houses, a bagel shop and a camera shop, both of whom were closed and dark. Half a block away, diagonally across the avenue, the Brogan Foundation remained lit, apparently open for whatever business transpired within its walls.

Parker opened his coat, locked a round in the chamber of the Sig-Sauer he'd taken in place of the M-4. In the back seat, Lee armed his weapon, a compact Belgian Fabrique Nationale, FN-11, a commando automatic weapon capable of an appalling rate of firepower. Perfectly hidden under his coat, Parker could put his hands in the cutout of his pockets, readying the weapon for immediate action.

"Let's go over this one more time," Parker said. "Lee will stay across the street, walking past the foundation, making a loop by turning at the light. I will go directly inside and find your brother. I'll have no more than five minutes inside by the time Lee arrives at the front door. Hopefully by that time I will be walking out with David. You, Joline, will drive the Lexus to us soon as you see me coming out with David. Six minutes from start to finish. Got it?"

"Yeah, I got that part. But what if you don't come out on time?"

"Give us another five minutes exactly, then get out of Dodge, call the number I gave you, tell them everything. They'll have contacts with a local SWAT team. In no event are you to try to come after us. We're leaving the dog for your protection. Got it?"

Joline said nothing.

"Joline, did you hear me?"

"Yeah, yeah, I got it."

Of course it didn't work out that way at all, it never does.

CHAPTER 79

Joline watched from inside the SUV as Lee and Parker left. They blended in with the skill of experienced operators, what the parlance called "tradecraft". Walking on the opposite side of Metropolitan Avenue, bundled in his long jacket, Lee resembled a retail worker going home after a tough day at the store.

Crossing the street immediately after exiting the SUV, Parker walked briskly to the front door of the Brogan Foundation. He stopped and turned the handle—locked. The interior of the lobby was well lit, as if a crew should be working there, but it was empty. Parker shook his head. An observer would have just seen a frustrated worker locked out of his place of business. He reached in his pocket and pulled out a big key ring, seemed to search through it until he found a suitable key and applied it to the lock.

The key ring was camouflage. What Parker applied to the lock was an electronic lock pick powered by a microchip. A rod studded with small metal rungs pushed into the lock activating the microchip that ran the tiny lock picks. The device whirred and beeped and the door opened. Parker stepped inside and closed the door behind him, leaving it unlocked for a quick exit. He stepped into the room, turned right at the corridor and the door and exterior view was no longer visible.

Parker stopped and just listened. He heard the whirr of the forced-air heating system, the buzzing of a defective, recessed ceiling light, a low hum of street noises from outside and that was it. Yet he felt something, and would have been hard pressed to explain what it was. Those experienced in black ops in the most dangerous corners of the globe would have known what he felt. They called it, the Edge, the Sixth Sense, Premonition, Intuition, whatever it was, it screamed into Parker's psyche. Something waited, observed, biding its time.

Parker flattened his body against the wall, unbuttoned his jacket and let it fall to the floor. He removed the Sig-Sauer from its holster and held it ready in a combat stance. No need to click off the safety. He'd removed it a long time ago. His combat philosophy didn't allow for fiddling with a safety switch. You just kept your finger away from the trigger until you were ready to fire. The fraction of a second needed to click off a safety could be the difference between walking away or a bullet in the head.

Parker slid along the wall, each step a ballet of quiet, efficient movement with the weapon leveled ahead. He made not a sound, his shoes were expensive super-quiet soft rubber soles and crepe. Even his clothing was designed for easy movement without rustling fabric or static electricity.

Stopping at the first office to his right, he kept the weapon leveled, flung open the door with his left hand, and crouched in the entrance, low and shielded by the wall: nothing—just a desk, a computer station and file cabinet illuminated by a small night light.

After making sure the office was empty and held no other means of entry or exit, he moved back into the hallway to the next room.

Same routine, fling the door open, cover the interior for any hostiles while staying sheltered. Again nothing. This was a storage room containing a shelf of office supplies, boxes of printing paper and janitorial supplies. He checked every inch of the storage room and again found no hidden doors.

Parker paused outside the hallway. An otherworld feeling

infused his mind, threatening to infect his body. He felt his hand shake, first time that had ever happened. Pressing the left side of his collar with his chin he activated the tiny sub-vocal transmitter sewn into his shirt, and sent a message to Lee.

"I'm in, first two rooms empty. Some kind of strange shit, I can feel it, but don't know what it is. Are you in place?"

"Roger that," Lee replied. "I'm right outside. Want me to come in?"

"No, standby, proceeding to next office."

In the next office he found David, and it was not at all what he expected.

Anton Dimitri had followed Parker's every movement. He didn't need video cameras or any artificial devices. He had the Power built into his mind from a couple of centuries of taking the immortality serum. He sensed the actions of the man below, felt his anxiety, rummaged in his mind, preparing for the soon-to-come moment when he would take control of the operator. But now he had to focus on the goal: Draw the accountant's sister, Joline, into the web, take her prisoner or kill her along with the accountant and anyone else involved.

Now Dimitri felt a shifting of emotions within his prey, a curious mix of triumph—he had found the accountant—mingled with anxiety, curiosity with a stream of fear running through it all.

Now it was time to act.

CHAPTER 80

Parker pushed open the door to the third office, covering the open space with his weapon, and found another bland office, nearly empty and devoid of any distinction. The place could have been a repository for the five simple pieces of furniture within. One desk, two file cabinets, a chair and incongruously enough, a cot. The surface of the desk held nothing, except for the head and torso of the man sleeping there.

Parker stepped farther into the room, weapon trained on the sleeping man. He approached, faced the desk and squatted so his head was level with the other man's. He'd scanned photos of David that Joline had given him, memorized the accountant's features. It sort of looked like him but it was hard to tell from the position of the sleeping man's head.

Holding the gun in one hand he reached over and shook the man's shoulder. Nothing—he shook him again and this time the man stirred. He lifted his head, barely managed to open his eyes and just looked at Parker as if he'd just come out of some vivid dream. His lips moved but no sound came out.

"You're David Waterman," Parker said. It wasn't a question.

David managed to croak out a yes, then, "Who are you?"

"My name is Parker. I work for your sister, and we're here to get you out. Can you stand and walk?"

David blinked, stared at Parker. He looked like a man emerging from the bottom of a deep well.

"Walk…where?" His voice was blurred, choppy, as if he had spoken through the spinning blades of a fan.

Parker walked around the desk, grasped David by the arm and helped him up. The accountant stood, offered no resistance. His moves were slow, measured as if he'd collapse at any moment. Parker gently pushed him forward and out the office door into the hallway. He keyed the mike in his collar and sent a message to Lee: "Got him. We're coming out."

"Roger that."

The otherworld feeling increased, reaching a crescendo like an orchestra on a grand finale. Parker sensed it, an alien intrusion into his very mind. He staggered under the psychic assault, and tried to hold up David as he felt the shaking of the accountant's body. What the hell was going on? Then a well-hidden door opened in front of them, revealing a narrow stairwell and Anton Dimitri stepped in front of them.

Outside, Lee sensed something was about to go down. Still, Parker had called in, he should be coming out with David any moment. He got closer to the entrance and peered inside. Nothing. Holding the automatic weapon ready under his coat, he decided to wait a few more minutes until they emerged.

Parker understood instantly. The man in front of him was from the group they called The Order. He saw the two missing fingers on his left hand, took in the gun in the man's right hand—Glock nine, his mind catalogued, the way a brain takes in details in a moment of stress.

Parker tried to raise his own weapon, but something was happening. He felt as if he worked in a vat of molasses, every movement dragging, what had become an ingrained battle reflex now subjugated to a viscous lassitude. He barely managed to open his mouth but not a sound came out.

Anton Dimitri stepped closer, raised his mangled left hand a few inches, and turned his gaze to David. The accountant's eyes rolled, the lids closed and his body slowly collapsed into a tangle. Then Dimitri turned back to the immobile Parker and shot him twice in the chest. He watched with a smile as the operator's body was flung against the wall and slid down in a tangle to the floor.

Outside, Lee felt that weird sense of unease, an intrusion directly into his brain, and he remembered the one and only time he'd ever experienced anything like it. Back in Mexico, during that operation that he and Parker had barely managed to escape alive. Some kind of mind control, Lee was convinced that's what it was, the only thing that could explain such events. But not this time, he'd prepared for it, so when he heard the two gunshots from inside the Brogan Foundation, he was ready, and reacted instantly.

Lee burst through the door, holding the compact automatic assault weapon pointed in front of him, he exploded into the hallway and instantly took in the scene. He understood in a nano-second: Parker crumpled against the wall, David laying in a heap on the floor and the man with the missing fingers turning toward him.

Lee felt the tendrils encroaching in the most private recess of his psyche and knew he had precious little time. But he was ready, and hoped his simple plan would work.

He felt the vestiges of his will slipping away, the room spinning and blinking out in a kaleidoscope of psychic energy. The arm holding his weapon froze to his side, but his left arm retained enough freedom. Lee held the hand out and drove the extended fingers into his own leg.

While some may look at a Delta operator of Lee's caliber with some disdain for their intellectual capacity, they would be very wrong. Lee had an IQ that could have qualified him for the Menses Society. He'd been gnawing over the problem they'd encountered back in Mexico, a problem he was convinced they'd run into once again, somewhere down the line, and he'd put together a simple solution.

In the middle three fingers of his left hand, he'd inserted a dime-sized piece of thin cedar taped under each nail. When he drove the tip of his fingers into his leg, the sharpened points penetrated deep into the sensitive flesh under each nail.

The pain was sudden and excruciating. A thin groan escaped from his lips as the agony flashed though his body, white hot and mind numbing.

The psychic band of iron from Anton Dimitri was immediately severed by the sudden pain, the bond of control shattered.

Lee dropped to his knees, brought up his weapon and put a tight group of three rounds into the base of Dimitri's neck, shattering the C3 and C4 vertebras, severing the carotid artery and wind pipe.

Dimitri's body convulsed, taking thee jerky steps backward, blood pulsing from his destroyed neck, then fell heavily on his back, legs twitching as a viscous crimson pool spread beneath the man's dying body.

Like a bloodhound sniffing out the barest scent of prey in honeycomb thickets, Ergun felt the thinnest extrasensory whiff of Joline and the Delta operators, and knew it was time to join in. He left the second-floor hideout across the avenue from the Brogan Foundation building, went down the stairs and stepped onto the sidewalk.

Right at that moment, when the big man's foot touched the sidewalk, that's when he felt the supernova explosion of pain from Anton Dimitri, followed by the extinguishing of the man's life force.

Ergun felt a sudden fear. He'd never experienced such a thing. Of course he'd run into many deaths over the course of his long life, but all had been foreseen and explained. Never had he seen the killing of an Immortal with the

Power by an ordinary person.

Anger now drove his footsteps as he rushed across the street and entered the Foundation.

Like any combat soldier, Lee followed his first instinct: help your fallen buddy. He rushed over to Parker, placed his weapon on the ground and turned over the wounded man. He didn't get much farther than that.

A stab of pain enveloped him. It felt like molten iron poured into his ears, gripping his brain in a steel band. He turned away, held his hands to his temples and tried to stand. Nothing worked, he couldn't feel his legs, his arms didn't respond, and what he saw when he managed to turn his head chilled his blood.

Ergun stepped into the Foundation's lobby, and turned into the corridor. His rage a living white hot coil, displacing any fear or doubts he might have held a few seconds ago. The Power of his mind reached the consciousness of the man who had killed Dimitri, scathing hot, paralyzing, he held Lee as completely as a predator with tooth and claw.

Walking into the hallway, Ergun took the scene in an instant. The crumpled form of one of the Delta operators, Anton Dimitri's corpse bleeding out the remains of his life force, the accountant, legs folded under him, unconscious, and he understood what happened even if he couldn't figure out how it was at all possible. He stepped forward until he stood over Lee, his mind locking the Delta operator into a psychic straightjacket, and slowly squatted down in front of the man.

Lee had followed the approach of Ergun. Helpless for the first time in his long career, he could only watch as the dark man approached like an ancient demon rising out of a subterranean hell. The man's face remained blurred to Lee, as if shrouded in deep fog, but the eyes glittered and the invisible bonds radiating from him, reaching into Lee's very brain held him locked. He saw the big man approach, squat down until his face was level with his own, heard and understood the words Ergun spoke. They were even more terrifying for their soft, caressing quality that emphasized the palpable evil within.

"You vermin. How did you manage to bring him down? Well no matter. Vermin must be exterminated."

Lee saw the big man's hand reach out, run across his chest and envelop his neck. He felt the unbearable power of the man as he lifted him up by the throat, felt his airway close as the finger encircled his neck, squeezing inexorably, bruising, shutting off air to the lungs and blood to the brain.

In that single moment, Lee knew he was going to die.

CHAPTER 81

Since the two Delta operators had left, staying in the car with Nikki had been nearly unbearable. The big dog jumped from back to front seat, even trying to squeeze her one hundred pounds body into the cargo compartment as if to find a hidden exit. She whined, growled, barked in loud explosions of sound that hurt Joline's ears in the enclosed space. She tried to hold the dog still, but Nikki would have none of it, breaking out of Joline's grip repeatedly, displaying such raw animal power that she knew she'd never control the dog in this condition.

Joline saw Parker enter the Foundation, waited as nothing happened for some moments then heard shots, muffled and dimmed through the walls and distance.

She saw Lee rush in, heard more shots, then a big man crossed the avenue, and stood for a moment right outside the Foundation's door.

The instant Joline saw the big man, she felt a flush of fear, a tremor from the depths of her subconscious, primeval yet intuitive. Something was dangerous about this dark man.

Now Joline saw the man enter the building, the door closing behind him.

She hadn't focused on Nikki when the big man appeared, but now she saw the transformation in the big dog. Ears pulled back, lips curled in a posture of threat, she looked like a feral wolf about to attack as she let out a series of barks so loud Joline thought the windows might shatter.

Nikki hurled herself against the glass, growling, barking, leaving wet marks all over the window, finally turning to Joline with an accusing glare and let out another bark.

"All right, okay, just shut up, we're going," Joline said. Nikki stopped, looked at the building across the avenue that had swallowed up Lee and Parker, turned her head back to Joline and let out another series of barks that exploded in her ears like cannon shots.

"Jesus, knock it off." Joline yelled at the dog. She reached in the glove box, took out the .38 Police Special she'd placed there earlier, and tucked it in her waistband. "Fuck you and your macho rules, Parker. You guys need the help," she mumbled as she took the decorative belt from her coat and looped it around Nikki's collar. It looked fragile but she figured it should hold.

She opened the car door and stepped out with Nikki on the makeshift leash. The dog gave a tremendous tug, knocking Joline off her feet. The leash broke and the dog bounded cross Metropolitan Avenue.

"Goddamn it, stop," Joline screamed as a car and a van nearly collided trying to avoid the dog.

Joline followed, running across the avenue, nearly getting hit herself. When she got to the foundation's door, Nikki was jumping up, pacing and barking. Joline pulled the gun from her waistband, took off the safety, opened the door and rushed in the building right behind the dog.

Lee sensed the last moments of his life ebbing away like the tide. Bright spots danced in front of his eyes under the inexorable pressure of Ergun's hands around his neck. His feet were off the floor, his body dying while his mind remained locked in the dark man's psychic grip. Then it happened.

Lee's vision had dimmed to a fading triangle, but in that remaining space, he saw a brown and white rocket, bursting from the ground like a giant projectile, wrap it's fang-studded snout around Ergun's arm with 1,600 pounds per square inch jaw pressure.

Lee heard the crunch as Ergun's arm broke, heard another crack as the impact threw the man to the floor, breaking his arm again. Ergun screamed, Nikki kept attacking, biting, relentless, her feral growls and snapping jaws evoking primitive ancient fears of predators, awakening the primeval horror of being consumed, eaten alive.

The psychic chain was severed and Lee slid to the ground, choking, barely conscious. He saw the dog savaging the dark man as he screamed, but Ergun managed to pull a knife from somewhere, He stabbed the dog once, lifted his arm for another stab.

That's when Joline shot him in the face.

CHAPTER 82

By the time Joline shot Ergun, Valdemar Khan had left his own hiding place, also heading for the Foundation. Like Ergun, he had been a short distance from the Foundation. He sensed the turmoil within but now realized he couldn't approach. Three men had emerged from the surveillance van, joining what looked like an entire SWAT team that had just pulled in front of the foundation. Right behind them an NYPD cruiser pulled up with sirens howling, and lights flashing. Father Anthony and Jimmy emerged.

When Father Anthony came out of the NYPD cruiser he felt like he'd just stepped into a swamp. The ground pulled at his feet like thick mud trying to root him in place. Red mist swirled about him and he felt a living force pushing him, hammering at his consciousness with gossamer tendrils, invisible yet tough as steel. He recognized the force, the psychic Power of his own brother: Valdemar Khan.

Then something else came and wrapped itself around him, cocooning his mind, and he recognized that also: The Power projected from Jimmy overshadowed his brother's, drove Khan's mental assault back with such power that Anthony saw Khan flinch, take a step back and sink to one knee.

Anthony saw his brother, Khan, now just a few yards away begin to crumble under the relentless assault. He placed his hand on Jimmy's shoulder.

"No, don't." Anthony said.

Jimmy relented and the Power suddenly vanished. Khan fell to the ground, got up and began walking away.

A block away the Chairman sensed the struggle between Khan, the priest and Jimmy. He felt the Power of Jimmy's mind and knew that the man was at least his equal in strength.

At this point in time, the Chairman realized that all was lost, at least for this round. Khan was neutralized and would run, Ergun and Dimitri were both dead and the authorities now swarming over the Brogan Foundation would shut everything down.

The Chairman turned his back and walked away. He rounded the corner, hailed a passing cab and vanished.

CHAPTER 83

Chaos reigned in the Brogan Foundation. Joline felt like her entire world had been dumped in a box and shaken until everything broke. Parker and Lee remained crumpled on the floor, next to the corpses of Dimitri and the big man she'd shot to death. (Had it really been her doing that?) She held Nikki, trying to stem the bleeding from the stab wound as dozens of black clad SWAT officers roamed around, shouting and barking orders. Through the confusion she recognized one person.

"Anderson, Detective Barry Anderson?"

Anderson's face broke into a smile and Joline felt her face flush.

"Well, yeah," he replied. "I'm Barry Anderson, but I'm not with NYPD."

Joline didn't reply, too much was going on and she had trouble processing it.

"I'm an FBI SAC, Special Agent in Charge."

"Oh."

"I'll explain everything later, but right now…"

Father Anthony and Jimmy had just walked in, and everything changed in that single moment.

For someone like me, with the Power, walking into a situation such as the eruption of violence in the Brogan

Foundation is like being locked into a washing machine going through the spin cycle. Clouds of emotions, anxiety, fright and sometimes downright panic crashed around us like never ending storm-driven waves. The effort to drown out so much emotion was nearly impossible so I concentrated on safeguarding Joline.

Grasping a passing SWAT officer's arm, I connected. Getting Joline's gun, wiping her prints from the weapon and putting it out of reach in his belt was the most natural thing in the world for him. It made sense, although he'd never be able to explain it—fortunately he'd never have to.

Joline was more difficult. The horror of killing Ergun with a pistol shot in the face was nearly impossible to completely erase. She wouldn't remember the details, the horror would eventually vanish, but a corner of her mind would always hold a dim sense of wrongdoing, an indelible feel of having caused harm.

I watched as medics worked on the one called Parker. They tore away his shirt, revealing a gray and silver Kevlar and titanium body armor, lightweight for special operations. The three bullets in the chest Parker had taken were absorbed into the vest, resembling metallic splatters. While the vest saved his life, the kinetic energy of the rounds traveling nearly at the speed of sound was like getting kicked by an enraged mule. He must have had at least three or four ribs broken and bruises that would last for months. He was just starting to regain consciousness as they were administering oxygen to his partner Lee. The Delta operator had been seconds away from being strangled to death by Ergun. The flesh around his throat was turning purple, huge handprints stood out livid around his Adam's apple. He coughed and choked, but settled down by the time paramedics took him and Parker away on stretchers.

After Joline realized Parker and Lee would survive, and her brother David was all right, she turned her attention to Nikki. She alternated between begging and screaming until Anderson directed one of the SWAT officers to help Joline with the dog and find a vet.

As the evening passed, more law enforcement and officials arrived, but it was clear that the leading authority on this event was FBI SAC Barry Anderson, for that's what he was in charge of, the Essex Junta case, domestic terrorism in progress for over a decade, and now he'd come to the end, ready to wrap up the case.

CHAPTER 84

CVS Pharmacy, Wading River, New York.

The young Suffolk Police officer had never encountered anything like this before. Sure they studied how to quell riots at the academy, but who'd ever think they'd run into something like this, so close to home.

Three squad cars were parked directly in front of the CVS' entrance, six officers blocking the doors best as they could against a screaming, enraged mob composed mostly of Baby Boomers and senior citizens.

They pushed against the officers, threw objects at the glass door until it shattered and the police tried to arrest the perpetrator with no success. The manager finally stepped out and tried to calm the angry mob.

"Please, folks, we do not have the Jeunessa. All shipments have been seized by Homeland Security and the FBI. Ours was due to arrive last night and was grabbed at the airport. We don't have it. All prepaid orders will be refunded..."

The scene was replicated across the nation as every shipment of Jeunessa was seized under a combined task force led by Agent Barry Anderson. Manufacturing facilities were seized and shut down, Bonner Pharmaceuticals, the producer of the drugs was disbanded,

Remko Genetics was also seized, and the story would continue unabated well into the next year.

As all the details came out of what would have been the deadliest event in history, two items were successfully kept from the media and the public.

The true nature of the Immortals and the Essex Junta remained shrouded in secrecy. Hints, shreds of evidence and stories became urban legends, believed by conspiracy theorists, disdained by most people.

The second item kept secret was the covert nature of the most massive manhunt in US history. The ties between Valdemar Khan and the man they called The Chairman, were deliberately obscured.

It was just as well, for neither man was ever found.

EPILOGUE

It was their fifth date, and Joline thought the relationship was going very nicely. In fact she thought with a mixed tingle of anticipation, she might even be in love.

She had a corner table at Casa Bella Vista in Hicksville, the premier Italian restaurant in town. A single candle lit the table set for two, and decorated with one red rose. A waiter had just brought a bottle of wine in a silver bucket when Barry Anderson walked in.

The FBI agent went straight to her table with that easy smile she'd grown to love. He bent down, kissed her full on the lips and she felt something warm grow inside her. Anderson broke the kiss, sat across from her, looked at the table setting, and grinned.

"I'm not late, am I?" he said.

"No, I'm early," Joline replied as she poured him a glass of Chardonnay, the kind she knew he liked.

"How's David?" he asked.

"Much better, still in therapy, but recovering. He's going back to work next week."

"How about your new buddy?"

"Nikki, she's such a sweetheart. She'll pout for a while when I get back cause I didn't take her." The dog had recovered from the stab wound. Parker and Lee thought it was time to retire the war dog, and had given her to Joline.

Best present she'd ever received.

"By the way, any luck on finding that guy, Jimmy?"

Anderson shook his head, "I don't know, the guy is like a wisp of steam. We get scraps and bits of info and nothing leads to anything. He's got to know we just want to talk to him."

"Are you covering Father Anthony? He's bound to get in touch with him soon enough."

"Yeah, we've got surveillance on him, but nothing yet."

"Well, don't worry about it," Joline said, reaching over and pouring another glass of wine for Anderson.

"Hey, you trying to get me tipsy, take advantage of an FBI agent?"

"That's the whole idea" she replied, smiling. She hadn't felt this good in years.

I caught a ride and got dropped off four blocks from St Agnes Church. I wanted to walk the rest to be sure I wouldn't miss the surveillance Father Anthony had warned me about.

I spotted him parked almost directly in front of the church in a totally bland Toyota Corolla. He saw me, and for a moment recognized me, as I knew he would.

I tweaked him.

For a moment the young FBI agent's spirit soared. He'd found that guy, Jimmy that they wanted so badly. Bringing him in would be a major feather in his cap, a real career booster.

He felt something deep in his head, perhaps the beginning of a migraine. He looked at the man, and shook his head. It wasn't a man at all. He saw an old lady, a widow dressed in black, like his grandmother used to dress, probably going to a Novena or something. He sighed and went back to reading his paper.

I walked into St Agnes and took a seat in one of the pews

close to the confessional, behind several people waiting to give up their sins to Father Anthony.

I waited. I don't mind, I like being in St Agnes. There's a peacefulness to the place, a kindness of spirit that's palpable at every turn. I listened to the whispering of prayers, watched the flicker of the votive candles and the light pouring through the stained glass windows, a tribute to the higher power we hailed. I took in the scent of incense, breathed deeply and waited.

Soon the last penitent left the confessional. I waited a bit more then went in.

"Bless me Father for I have sinned. It's been seventy years since my last confession."

I heard the clear laughter of Father Anthony. His voice seemed free, unburdened.

"Jimmy, you came."

"Don't I always?"

"Yes, you do. You're the one thing I can count on. But I didn't summon you. What brings the pleasure of your visit?"

"Just wanted to be sure you're okay, Father. Have you set in a reserve of the serum? It's going to be a long time, if ever until that's manufactured again."

Father Anthony hesitated, yet I sensed a certain freedom, a relief emanating from the priest as he replied.

"I stopped taking the serum weeks ago, destroyed the supply I had. It's not…natural. There is the mental side to it, the way it grabs you and you have to struggle with every moral imperative, because your mind has had all feelings and love stripped away. I've recovered all those things. I know what it's like to be a priest again, a pastor of mankind. But you never had that problem, did you, Jimmy?"

That was a rhetorical question I didn't need to answer. Anthony knew all about it. Whatever Dad had given me so many years ago, had brought me ultra-longevity, perhaps, dare I say it…Immortality. But unlike Father Anthony and the members of the now defunct Essex Junta, I wasn't turned into a sociopath, nor did I need continuing shots of serum.

"Now you'll grow old, like everyone else," I said.

"That's not such a bad thing. I already have immortality through my faith and our Lord Jesus Christ."

I smiled, happy for Father Anthony and his newly found contentment. I took his blessings, gave him a special cell phone to contact me with should he ever need to then left the church.

Outside the wind had picked up and I raised the collar of my jacket. I walked past the vigilant FBI agent who would never see me, and kept going.

Somewhere the remains of the Immortals are free, Valdemar Khan, The Chairman, perhaps one or two more. All the combined law enforcement agencies in America will never find any of them.

That's up to me. I'm the only one who can. Perhaps that's why I'm here, like a macrophage clearing out foreign objects in a human's blood stream.

I turned the corner and walked away.

THE
APOCALYPSE SERIES

Turn the page for an

excerpt from

COLD

FUSION

The Apocalypse Series
Book Two

Patrick Astre

Katamay asked for a tool set and someone ran out to get it. The old man climbed the stage to where the generator stood on a stainless steel table. He disconnected a heavy cable from the outlet built into the side of the device. The generator itself was a twin of the one I had found under the hood of the Hummer, two days ago. We surrounded the trunk-size machine.

Ford looked pretty calm considering the risk he was taking. In front of the entire nation and the world, he had stopped this demonstration and evacuated the auditorium. If this turned out to be a bust, he would be made permanent gopher at the Dunghole, North Dakota FBI office—for life.

"They tampered with it. There's no doubt," Katamay said.

"How do you know?" Ford asked.

"An end cap has been added to give it more room. They put something in there."

Now a lab technician appeared wheeling a Craftsman toolbox, the kind auto mechanics use, but so clean it was probably sterilized. Katamay opened a drawer, took out a small ratchet kit and began removing small fasteners recessed in the surface. Ford took another tool and helped him. Moments later Katamay jiggled the metal and the end section of the generator came off. We all leaned forward to get a look at the insides.

The generator looked like nothing I had ever seen. It was so strange, it seemed unreal. It reminded me of some sort of Science Fiction movie set depicting a graphic artist's view of what alien machinery would look like. At the end where

Katamay had removed the cover, a thick cylinder the size and shape of a large fire extinguisher, occupied the space. It was the only thing that had even a vague resemblance to anything I was familiar with. Solid state circuitry connected it to the rest of the generator. Three digital readout gauges were imbedded in the center of the cylinder. One gauge read 44, the one next to it was 03 and dropped one number each second and the last one must be timing tenths of a second because the numbers blurred incomprehensibly as they changed. The middle gauge hit 0 and restarted at 60. The gauge on the left dropped to 43. Whatever this thing was it counted down toward zero.

Katamay reached over and ran his hand over the cylinder. A mixture of shock and anger ran across his face. He said something in Russian that sounded like a nasty curse.

"These vicious, vicious fools," he continued in English. "They deserve to burn in hell for this."

"What is that Doctor?" Ford asked. "It's an explosive device of some kind isn't it?"

"Oh yes, it most certainly is an explosive device, the most dangerous kind in the world. What you would commonly call an atomic bomb."

Katamay's words hung in the air, grabbing us like a malignancy. We looked at him and no one said anything. Some things are so outrageous they stunt your reactions as if dealing with the most banal of affairs. It was Anthony who broke the silence first.

"You gotta be kidding me, doc. Aren't nuclear bombs supposed to be big?"

"That's what they work on in that building in Brookhaven Lab, out on Long Island. Miniaturization of nuclear weapons. You've heard of suitcase bombs?"

We nodded yes. No one spoke and Katamay continued.

"This thing is the next generation of weapons, probably somewhere between twenty and forty kilotons. A bit larger than the Hiroshima bomb."

"Wait a minute," Ford said. "Aren't you supposed to have a certain amount of Plutonium to reach critical mass? That thing is too small to hold all that plutonium plus the triggering devices, right?"

"Wrong. It's a common misconception. Gathering a critical mass of plutonium is not necessary to make an atom bomb. You can take a much smaller piece and subject it to a neutron density equivalent to that found at the temperatures and pressure inside plutonium at critical mass. When I worked there, they were very close to making a condensed type of plutonium called PL-9. With the advent of supercomputers to do calculations that were previously impossible and metallurgical and chemical advances, we can reach critical mass with small amounts of PL-9 using new alloys and explosives."

Now I understood what went on, what all this had been about. I didn't know exactly who, but I understood the why of it.

'Don't you see?" I said. "First they tried to suppress it, but too many people got involved and it was all going to come out. Now they're going to discredit it. That's the Tinian Protocol they're talking about in those dispatches we intercepted. Look, Chernobyl was a pretty deadly incident. It scared the American public, but they attributed it to Russian incompetence. Sorry Doctor."

"You're quite right."

"Then Three Mile Island came along, and although only a couple of technicians lost their lives, it scared the hell out of the American public and killed the nuclear industry. There hasn't been a new nuclear plant built in over thirty years. Now picture this: Right in the middle of a cold fusion demonstration, with the whole world watching, the generator goes up in a mushroom cloud and vaporizes a million people. That's the end of cold fusion research forever."

No one said anything. As we watched, the minutes gauge dropped to 42.

"We'll get a bomb squad here fast. You can help us, doctor."

"No."

"No?"

"I will help you, but you cannot disarm it. This is not some movie where a bomb squad person comes in and cuts a wire and everything is good. This is cutting-edge, solid state circuitry. If you tamper with it, it goes off. There's a seismic sensor attached to it. If you jar it too heavily it goes off. When that timer reaches zero, it will detonate. That is its purpose and nothing can stop it."

Agent Ford pulled out his cell phone. His hand shook, almost imperceptibly, but it shook. Shirley's complexion had paled a few degrees and I was as scared as I'd ever been in my life.

Ford hit a button on his cell phone, identified himself and spoke.

"Red Zone One Alert. Imminent nuclear detonation within the continental United States." Some squawking came through the phone and he severed the connection.

"I have a Blackhawk on standby at the Milton office. They'll be here in twenty minutes. We'll load it on there and…"

"And do what?" Anthony cut in. "I know the Blackhawk: top speed 165 miles per hour. The bomb will go off twenty miles from here. It might as well go off right here. Population density in either direction is the same."

"We'll fly it to Dover Air Force base."

"You'll get there just when it's about to go off. If you have a few minutes to spare, you'll have to find a suicide jockey with a ready jet, and you got to do it in under forty two minutes. It'll never happen."

Ford looked sick, until Anthony spoke again.

"But I have a way to do it."

The digital read out dropped another number. 41 minutes to detonation.

———◆———

COLD FUSION
available in print and ebook

Award-winning author Patrick Astre served in the US Army Infantry, stationed in Germany during the height of the Cold War. Rising to the rank of Sergeant E-5, Astre finished his last year of service as a Drill Instructor at Fort Benning, Georgia.

Now, Patrick Astre, CFP, EA, RFC is a recognized tax and financial expert specializing on the economic issues of longevity. Patrick is independent and has been advising individuals and corporations since 1969.

Patrick's second financial book was released in mid-August 2007 by Entrepreneur Media Publishing. It is Entrepreneur's "cornerstone" retirement book. *This is Not Your Parents' Retirement* is one of the top sellers in its field, addressing the convergence of the longevity revolution and the aging baby-boomers, woefully unprepared for retirement.

In addition to his financial books, Patrick is the author of numerous articles as well as fiction thrillers. His novel *The Artifact* won the Salvo Press Mystery Thriller of the year Award in 2005.

Patrick is a professional public speaker and member of the National Speakers Association. His seminars, speeches and keynotes are a lively, enthusiastic mix of entertainment, motivation, humor and unique insights.

Some of his clients include Celebrity Cruises, John Hancock, Princess Cruises, LIBOR (Long Island Board of Realtors) Passaic Board of Realtors, and many others.

Patrick lives in Long Island, New York with his wife Lynn. The couple has two children and two grandchildren and enjoy traveling throughout the country in their motor home.